CRUEL DESIRE

CRUEL DESIRE

K.A LINDE

ALSO BY K. A. LINDE

One Cruel Night (#.5)

Cruel Money (#1)

Cruel Fortune (#2)

Cruel Legacy (#3)

One Cruel Letter (#3.1)

Cruel Promise (#3.5)

Cruel Truth (#4)

Cruel Desire (#5)

One Cruel Wedding Night (#5.5)

Cruel Marriage (#6)

Cruel Kiss (#6.5)

Cruel King (#7)

Cruel Desire

Visit my website at
www.kalinde.com

Cover Designer: Devin McCain, Studio 5 TwentyFive.,
www.studio5twentyfive.com
Editor: Unforeseen Editing
www.unforeseenediting.com

ISBN-13: 978-1948427630

PROLOGUE

ENGLISH

"And action," the director called on set.

The entire set went silent. I held my breath as my husband, Josh Hutch, stalked forward with all the command he had in his body. His costar Celeste followed behind him, clad in some torn, skimpy outfit, holding a gun. His suit coat was barely draped over her shoulders.

My husband was the newest Jason Bourne, and I couldn't have been prouder. When I'd taken the job in New York City to work for Court Kensington—the train wreck bad boy whose image I'd been working to clean up—my biggest regret was that I wouldn't get to see Josh act in this movie while on set in London. He was a natural. Born for this moment. I had a film degree from UCLA, but anyone could see it.

Thankfully, we'd figured a weekend that would work after Court's mother won her primary bid for reelection for the mayor of New York. So, here I was, in London. A city I adored with the man I'd been with for the last five years.

"Cut!"

And the breath went out of the room.

Noise came back. Everyone moved again.

The director hopped up from her seat and stepped onto the set. "The chemistry is all wrong here. What is going on?" she demanded in frustration. Whatever she said next was spoken soft and urgent with Josh and Celeste.

This was going to be a minute. When directors got going, nothing ever stopped them.

I turned away from the display and fought back a yawn. Josh and I hadn't slept much last night. We hadn't seen each other in months. So, it had been expected. But it made it hard to stand around and do nothing. Not to mention, I hadn't yet adjusted to the time difference.

With a sigh, I headed toward the snack table. I plucked out a bag of almonds and poured myself a coffee. It wasn't half as good as the stuff in New York that I had gotten used to, but it would keep me awake. That was all that mattered. I leaned back against the table and waited for everything to get going again. There were clusters of crew standing together all over the place, waiting just like I was. It was part of my job as a publicist to be able to read a room, and even through my sleep deprivation, something felt off.

I continued sipping my coffee, wondering what was going on when I caught the beginning of a conversation nearby. Someone who clearly did not want to be eavesdropped on. My ears perked up.

"Yeah, that's his wife," the first person said.

"No wonder they suck today," said the second voice.

"Yep," the first one continued. "We were doing just fine on set until she showed up."

I clenched my jaw. How was *I* doing anything? I'd only been on set for a few hours. Josh hadn't even looked at me. I wasn't a distraction.

"It'll be better when she's gone."

"Yeah, so he and Celeste can start banging again," the second voice said with a laugh.

My body turned to stone. My heart stopped beating. I clenched the coffee so hard in my hand, some of it spilled over the lip and onto the floor.

"I kind of feel bad for her," the first voice said.

"Yeah, I mean, they're not even good at hiding it."

I couldn't have heard them right. Josh and Celeste were... not together. There... there was no way he would do that. Not to me. We'd been together for five years. Three of those years, we'd been married. He had never even *looked* at another woman. Let alone fucked one! Why would he have even made time for me to come out here if that were the case?

No. No, I didn't believe it. I didn't want to believe it.

Suddenly, the room went silent again. The director was in her chair. Josh and Celeste moved back into place. I watched their body language like a hawk. Celeste laughed at something he'd said. She reached out and touched the collar of his shirt, straightening it. She was clearly familiar with him. But Josh stepped out of her touch just as quickly.

Had he done that because I was here? Or was this some fabrication by the crew to explain their on-screen chemistry?

I watched the next take and tried to see for myself that it was there. That they'd slept together. But... it just wasn't.

As soon as the director yelled, "Cut," and called for a lunch break, Josh immediately darted away from Celeste and ran right for me.

Still, the accusation lay there like a brick in my stomach.

I had to address this. I had to know.

"Hey, babe!" he said, leaning down to give me a kiss.

I turned my face at the last moment, and he kissed my cheek.

Fire burned in my veins. Fear. This was fear. I knew what cheaters were like. My dad was a prime example. Josh knew all about that. He wouldn't do this to me.

I searched his eyes. Those kind and caring baby blues I'd fallen in love with. The man of my dreams.

"Can we talk?" I asked, trying to keep the hitch out of my voice.

His brow furrowed. "Sure. We have an hour for lunch. Let's get out of here."

He tried to sling his arm over my shoulders, but I stepped out of his embrace. "We should talk before lunch."

"Babe?"

I took his arm and drew him away from the filmmaker and crew and stagehands. I needed to be alone with him. I needed to know.

We walked back to his trailer, and it wasn't until we were in the small room full of recycled air that I spoke, "Are you sleeping with Celeste?"

"What?" he gasped.

"Tell me the truth."

"English, how could you even ask me that?" He reached out and took my hands in his. He looked bereft without his wedding ring on. I knew it was for the film, but it didn't make me feel any better. "I love you, honey."

"You haven't answered me," I told him, pulling my hands back.

"No," he said automatically. "Of course not. No. Celeste and I work together. What you saw back there was just on-screen chemistry." He gestured to the stage. "It's not real. You know that."

"I do. But the crew said..."

"What did they say?" he asked.

"They said that you two were off today because I was here. That you and Celeste were sleeping together. Fuck, they said they felt bad for me."

Fresh tears rose to my eyes, and I choked on the final words. I wanted to be the strong celebrity publicist who could take on the world with one fierce glare. But this was my life. My life falling apart.

"Oh, baby," he said, pulling me against him. "I'm so sorry you heard that. It's not true. It's just gossip."

I hiccuped once, desperately wanting to believe him. But something felt wrong. It still felt so wrong. I pulled back and swiped at my eyes, angry with myself for crying. "You promise?"

"Yes, of course. Nothing is going on."

"Can I ask Celeste?"

He froze in place. Trapped. Caught.

"Oh god," I whispered. "You really did it, didn't you?"

"No, no, no," he said, denying it again.

"Then, I'll ask Celeste and see what she says," I said, angling for the trailer door.

Josh blocked my way. "You don't trust me? English, come on. You know me."

I narrowed my eyes. "Josh, think about who I am. I deal with cheating spouses every damn day of my life. I know the signs. And I know that if you won't let me talk to Celeste, then that's proof enough."

He sighed heavily and slumped forward in defeat. "Okay. Okay."

I waited, crossing my arms over my chest.

"We did." He cleared his throat. "We did sleep together."

I wrenched back in shock at the words. "How could you? Are you in love with her?"

"No, English. No. It's not like that. I don't care for her. I love you."

"You liked her enough to fuck her!" I screamed back at him.

"No, it's not that. It's just… it's a publicity stunt."

"You dare say that to me?" I asked dangerously.

"It is. I swear. We did it to help the movie. It worked for *Mr. & Mrs. Smith*, and we wanted that for this movie, too."

"You didn't even tell me the movie needed help. I'm a

fucking publicist, Josh. This is my job. And anyway, you could have come to me. You could have told me the problem. We could have fixed it together. In fact, you could have just *told* the press that you were sleeping together. What the fuck do I care about stupid rumors? You didn't have to actually fuck her!"

"You're right. You're so right, English. I'm sorry." He reached for me, but I swatted him away.

"Don't fucking touch me, Josh."

Josh sank to his knees in front of me. "I love you, English. Tell me how to make this right."

I shook my head. There was no making this right. There never would be. "If this is how you treat people you love, then you can go fuck yourself."

I pushed past him and headed for the door.

He was on his feet again, following me out of the trailer. "English, please, stop. We can talk about this. We can figure it out. You know that I'd do anything for you."

"Leave me alone. I've heard enough."

I was trying to hold the tears at bay. I was furious, and I wanted to die inside. I couldn't believe this was happening. I couldn't believe that my life was falling into shambles right now. I'd had the perfect husband, the perfect relationship, the perfect life. And now, it was gone.

"Where are you going?" he asked frantically.

"Home. Back to New York."

"You can't just jump on a plane. That won't fix this."

I glared at him as I flagged down a cab. "Nothing will fix this. Go back to your movie, your fuckable costar, and all the money you're going to get from this film. I hope that it makes you happy, Josh." I laughed sardonically. "Actually… I don't."

The cab pulled up in front of me, and I ripped the door open.

Josh grabbed the door from me. "Don't do this."

"I didn't do anything. You made this decision for us."

Then, I slammed the door in his face, and the cab pulled away from the movie set. I didn't cry until I was back in our hotel suite. Tears streamed down my cheeks and my chin as I packed up the suitcase I'd flown in with. I didn't want to still be here when Josh got back tonight. I wasn't going to stay in London another minute for him to try to win me back. There was no *winning* here. He'd ruined it all.

My face was red and puffy, but the tears dried up by the time I arrived at Heathrow. At the ticket counter, I slid over Josh's black card and asked for the earliest first-class ticket to New York City. Two hours later, the flight was boarding, and I took my seat in the pod.

"Something to drink?"

"Gin and tonic," I told the woman. "And keep them coming."

She nodded and returned with two drinks for me with a wink. I downed the first without blinking and savored the second one as we started to taxi the runway. My phone buzzed in my purse, and I fished it out. A dozen missed calls from Josh. Fuck that. And one from my best friend, Lark.

I should probably call her back.

"Ma'am, you're going to need to put your phone on Airplane mode," the flight attendant told me with a smile.

I sighed and powered the entire thing down. Lark and New York would have to wait until I made it back to the States. Right now, I just needed another drink and to sleep off the heartbreak.

PART I

RULES TO LIVE BY

1

ENGLISH

It had only taken forty-eight hours for my entire life to go to shit.

A trip across the pond, my cheating bastard of a husband, and a near-arrest by my current pain-in-the-ass client. I hadn't slept. I'd barely eaten. The only thing in my bloodstream other than coffee as black as my heart was bitter, righteous rage.

And I needed somewhere to direct it.

I probably should have gotten something to eat and slept off my jet lag. Instead, I jammed my finger into the button for the elevator that would take me up to Court Kensington's penthouse. Because he had royally fucked up, and I wanted to give him a piece of my mind.

The door slid open soundlessly. I slipped inside and impatiently tapped my foot as it whisked me upstairs, opening directly into his apartment. I'd been impressed the first time I walked into his place. All clean, modern lines; open, airy floor plan; and Central Park views. I was used to Hollywood, and this was *so* New York. But I was over it now.

Everything about it just reminded me that Court Kensington had grown up with a silver spoon in his mouth. He might be the hottest, most eligible bachelor on the Upper East Side, but to me, he was just another client for me to clean up his messes.

"Court!" I snapped as my heels clicked onto the polished hardwood floor.

No response came from the confines of his apartment.

I should have known. The man drank like a fish and partied like a rock star. There was no way he would be awake at this early of an hour.

It wasn't stopping me. Not today.

"Court!" I called again.

I strode across the living room and down a hallway that led to his bedroom. The door stood already partially open. I toed it the rest of the way and breezed inside, flicking the lights on.

And what I saw stopped me in my tracks.

Court Kensington's naked body laid out facedown like Adonis on his pure white sheets. His bare ass visible for the world to see.

I swallowed.

I'd seen some gorgeous bodies before. I worked as a celebrity publicist, for Christ's sake. It was part of the job description. We dealt with asshole rock stars, entitled actors, and everything in between. I'd paid off prostitutes and thrown away condoms so they couldn't be used as evidence and seen more dick and pussy that I wasn't fucking than I needed to see in a lifetime. And still, Court made me come to a screeching halt.

Fuck, he was hot.

I hated that he was hot.

That he was the kind of grade A asshole I'd been all over before I met Josh. Before Josh ...

I ground my teeth. Just the thought of what he'd done to me brought me straight back to reality. Nothing like finding out your movie-star husband was fucking his costar to ruin your morning.

"Court, get your ass out of bed."

He tilted his head to the side, squinting up at me through a vision of long lashes. "English?" he groaned.

"That'd be me," I said. "We need to talk."

He blinked a few times and then propped himself up on his elbow. "What time is it?"

"Almost eight."

"In the morning?" he asked blearily.

"Yes. Now put on some fucking clothes. I've had a really long night, and I would like to get this over with."

"Can we do this some other time?" he asked as he pulled the pillow back over his head.

"Does it look like I'm fucking around?"

He peered back up at me. I didn't know what he saw, what degree of not-taking-your-shit was on my face, but he nodded. "Fine."

I hustled back out of his bedroom, trying to clear the vision of that muscular ass from my mind. I knew he'd take his sweet time. So, I brewed a pot of coffee. Because what I really needed was more caffeine in my system.

He came out fifteen minutes later in a pair of black joggers. He pulled a white T-shirt on over his head as he walked into the living room. His six-pack still visible for the few seconds before the material fell over his stomach.

He tousled his dark hair and quirked a smile at me. "That for me?"

"Here," I said, handing him a mug of coffee.

"So, what's this all about?" he asked around a yawn.

I set my empty mug on the counter. "What in the actual fuck were you thinking last night?"

"What do you mean?"

I narrowed my eyes. "You went to an underground

gambling ring. The party was raided by the police. You barely made it out in time."

"Oh ... yeah. I mean, I hadn't *expected* the party to get raided," he said with a shrug.

"You went to an underground gambling ring!" I cried. "Need I remind you that you were recently arrested with your girlfriend for fraud and grand larceny? That the only reason I was hired was to keep you out of trouble, to show the world a softer side of Court Kensington? So that you don't ruin your mother's reelection campaign for mayor of New York?"

"First of all, there were no charges against me. And second, Jane isn't my girlfriend."

"She was at the time, and literally no one else cares that you weren't charged. They see you as the train wreck who doesn't care about *crime*. While your mother is tough on crime. If you'd been arrested last night, can you even imagine the consequences?"

Court shrugged. "It would have been fine. You're blowing the whole thing out of proportion."

"Am I?" I asked. "I would have lost my job. Lark likely would have lost her job. Your mother would lose the primary run. And you, you'd be right back where you started before you had me. We'd lose all ground."

"Fine. Whatever. I messed up." He set the mug down on the coffee table. His blue eyes had shuttered, gone cold. "Can I go back to sleep now?"

"No. You didn't just fuck up. You royally fucked up. You took the one weekend I was out of town and fucking did this on purpose, Court!"

"I didn't know..."

"But you didn't leave either!" I snapped back. "You saw it was illegal and played poker all night. Lark had to drag you out of there, and you didn't even want to leave."

"Okay. I get it. Fuck, English. I fucked up. Get off my case."

"Oh, excuse me for being the first person in your life to hold you accountable for your actions," I ground out.

I knew I was being harsh on him. But he didn't even fucking care about what it would have done. The problems he could have caused. He was so nonchalant. And I just couldn't accept his response. It wasn't enough. There was no change coming from acknowledging he had done something wrong. It didn't *fix* his behavior.

Court stepped forward. His teeth ground together. "What the fuck has gotten into you?"

"I'm doing my job."

"Yeah, well, I don't need you to lay into me at eight o'clock in the morning for something that didn't even happen." His eyes assessed me as if he could see right through the jet lag and coffee buzz and anger to what was lurking below. "What are you even doing in New York? Aren't you supposed to be in London with Josh?"

"I came back early."

"Why?" he demanded. "You were raving about your trip."

He glanced up and down, judging what was in front of him. Seeing me like I didn't like *anyone* to see me.

"Doesn't fucking matter," I said, losing some of my edge.

"Why aren't you wearing your wedding ring?"

"That is none of your business."

A spark of pity flashed through his cerulean-blue irises. "English..."

"Don't," I ground out. "We're here to talk about you. And the fucking shit that you pulled while I was gone."

Anger flared in him. He took another step closer. So close that we nearly shared breath.

"This has nothing to do with me," he growled. "You're putting your own fucking personal problems on me. I don't have to deal with this shit, English."

My own anger was ignited by his. "I'm not doing anything

of the sort. I'm here to whip your ass into shape. I'm not here to coddle you like everyone else in your life. If you don't like it, take it up with your mother. She's the one who hired me to fix your bullshit before you lose her the election."

"I'm not an idiot," Court snarled. "You can put me down and treat me like an ass if you want. But I see what the fuck you're doing, English."

"Good. Then you'll stop acting like someone who needs his hand held every time he walks out into public?"

"Berate me all you want. This is about you and Josh. Not me."

"Go fuck yourself."

His eyes widened a fraction at the words that left my mouth. The fury that had nothing to do with him. But that I was using against him.

I'd thought that I had it all under control. I'd had such a picture-perfect life. I was married to *the* Josh Hutch. He was the biggest up-and-coming movie star on the scene. He'd been handpicked to remake the Bourne trilogy. I was the top celebrity publicist at my agency in LA. Everyone wanted to work with me. We went to premieres and sipped champagne and lived the life.

Except that hadn't been right, had it?

I'd wanted more. That was why I was here. To use this as my next step to achieve my dreams: to open my own agency, a place to work with fewer clients, ones who actually cared and didn't just need someone to secure cocaine and make sure their sex tapes didn't end up on the internet. Or *did*, depending on the person. So, when I'd gotten offered to work for the Kensingtons, step into New York high society, work for a political candidate, I'd thought it was my chance.

And now, all of those pieces were crumbling into ash.

I was left staring into Court Kensington's impossible baby

blues. Wondering where it had all gone wrong. And how I could fucking fix my life like I fixed everyone else's.

"You're a real piece of work, you know that?" Court asked after a tense, silent minute.

He'd moved a step closer. Our breaths mingled. I could feel the heat rising from his skin. The fury that pulled us together like magnets. A sense that we were both so beyond fucked up that, impossibly, we were attracted to each other. We hated each other so supremely that, somehow, at any second, it could tip the other direction.

His eyes darted to my lips. I drew a line across the bottom one with my tongue. A reflex. Or was it?

My breaths came out irrationally loud. I could hear my own heartbeat in my ears. His Adam's apple bobbed as he swallowed. Time slowed until seconds felt like hours. And we just stared, edged, hedged, waited, wondered, wanted.

And then the moment the scales tipped and he moved forward—as if he was actually going to do it, actually going to cross that divide—I jolted out of that awareness. I shoved him back away from me.

"Fuck, Court," I cried.

His eyes rounded as if he couldn't believe for a second that the playboy prince had misread the signs. Then he returned to careful neutrality. Born out of boredom and masks and societal pressure.

"Are you done?" he asked.

"Yes. I'm fucking done. I'm going back to LA."

"What?" His eyebrows rose.

"Don't get too excited. Just for a few days to handle some business. I don't want you to fucking leave this apartment until I get back. Are we clear?"

"I am not on lockdown again."

"Yes, you are. Because I can't trust you not to do something that will land you in the papers."

He glared at me. Any warmth we'd been mustering evaporated. "Whatever."

"Be a good boy," I said, patting his cheek twice.

He looked like he might bite me for the insult, but I was already storming toward the elevator to leave this hellhole. He muttered something under his breath, but I didn't catch it. I assumed he'd called me a bitch.

But as soon as the elevator doors closed, I leaned back heavily. God, maybe I should get some sleep. What the fuck had I been thinking?

I had only one rule: *don't get involved with clients.*

I'd never broken it.

And I had just almost kissed Court Kensington.

2

ENGLISH

I couldn't get what had almost happened out of my mind.

Court Kensington was objectively the worst client I'd ever had. Not because he was particularly difficult to work with or because he was a drug addict or a sex fiend or any number of other impossible things I'd dealt with. It was because he didn't want me. He didn't feel like he needed a publicist. That I just got in his way.

And even though, over the last couple weeks, he had started to listen to my advice, he still didn't want my help. Everyone else came to me. They needed someone to cover up a sex scandal. They needed me to hide an affair from their wife. They wanted someone who could get their career back on track after the stint in rehab. On and on and on.

Court wanted nothing to do with it.

He was the worst, and he made my job hell.

Still, I'd been an inch away from kissing him.

And I didn't even like him. Or want to kiss him.

I sighed as I parked my Mercedes in front of my dad's house in the Valley. I knew why I was obsessed over this. It was easier to think about a stupid almost-kiss with Court than it was to deal with Josh. Or the fact that he was still in London, shooting the final Bourne movie with his costar Celeste. Or that I'd just cleared out my belongings from his house and had them shipped back to New York. Or that I was going to have to file divorce papers.

End the perfect marriage.

I closed my eyes and choked back that thought. I didn't want to divorce Josh. I'd thought we were forever. But I wasn't a pushover. I wouldn't be used. And there was no fucking way that I would ever forgive what he'd done to me.

I still didn't want to do it.

Nor did I want to walk inside and face my dad, stepmom, and half-sister, Taylor. But I couldn't come back to the city and not see them. So...here I was.

Swallowing my frustration, I pushed my shoulders back and stepped out of the car. It looked so out of place out here. I looked out of place.

My dad worked a camera for a local news network. He made okay money, but Ashley didn't work, except to sell some direct sales products. It changed every time I was here. Last time, it had been something to do with her nails; the time before that, she'd had a collection of super-soft clothes. And I was pretty sure she'd done a bender on essential oils. She meant well, but I didn't think she'd had any real success with it.

I stepped up to the front door and knocked. I impatiently checked my phone, tapping my high-heeled foot like a bad habit, and brushed a speck of dust off of my white jeans. Why the hell had I worn them here?

When I'd gone to the house I'd shared with Josh the last three years, I'd torn everything else out of my closet, except this outfit. I'd hired a company to pack up and ship everything that remotely belonged to me. Every scrap of *me* would be gone from Josh's house by the time he returned from London.

Now that I was here, I should have just gone with shorts

and sneakers. I was used to dressing up for my job, and I planned to head to the agency after this. But it still felt wrong.

The door opened. Ashley stood there with her platinum hair in a messy bun on her head and a wide smile on her face. "Anna!"

"Hey, Ash," I said to my stepmom.

I knew that she liked me to call her mom, but I'd never been comfortable with that.

She stepped back to let me in. "Joe! Anna's here."

I followed her inside. My insides squirmed as I looked around the house I had spent high school in. The same couch and picture frames and shaggy beige carpet. No one in Hollywood would guess that I was a girl from the Valley.

"Don't you look beautiful," Ashley said. "Look at those shoes! I'd break my neck in those."

I laughed. "You get used to them."

"If you say so."

Ashley was really great, except that she was my stepmom.

My dad appeared then in a ratty Dodgers baseball shirt and the same shorts he'd had since I was a kid. He half-smiled at me. As much enthusiasm as I ever got from him.

"Hey, Bug," he said. "What brings you all the way out here?"

I reminded myself not to grit my teeth. He didn't mean to sound accusatory every time I came to visit. "I was in town. Thought that I'd come see you all before I headed back to New York."

"Oh, right. Don't know how you can survive that city."

"You've never even been," I said with a small laugh.

He shrugged. "Don't have to go to know LA is the only place I ever want to live."

"Can I get you a drink?" Ashley asked, breaking up the conversation.

"Sure. Whatever you have is fine."

"Margaritas it is!"

My dad sighed. "She's driving. Just get her a Coke."

"A Coke is fine," I confirmed with a defeated Ashley.

She slipped out of the living room, leaving us alone. We stood in silence for a few minutes. Things had never been the same between us. Not since the divorce. Even before that. I never forgot the person he'd been. And then he'd gone and married someone else. It didn't matter that I liked Ashley. He'd replaced my mom and then gone and replaced me.

"Taylor's at the beach with some friends," he said as if reading my thoughts.

"Sounds fun," I mused.

"She's not having the kind of fun you did."

I swallowed back my rising anger that said I didn't need this shit after the week I'd had. "Can't all be that lucky, I guess."

"We're moving her out to New York in a few weeks," he said on a sigh. "Can't believe she got into that fancy art school up there. Nothing I said could convince her to stay in LA and be smart about it."

I'd almost forgotten that Taylor had gotten into The New School. That she was actually going was even more shocking. That my dad, who had ridiculed me for going to UCLA and getting what he considered a useless film degree, would let her go. I had no idea how they were going to afford it. The school alone had to be fifty thousand dollars a year. Not to mention paying to live in New York City.

"That's...wow," I stammered out.

"Will you look out for her?"

My eyes rounded. "What?"

"You know...you have that job. Where you do...whatever you do," he said evasively, not meeting my eye.

"I'm a publicist."

"Yeah, that. You keep people out of trouble. Taylor isn't used to the big city."

"She grew up in LA, Dad. She's going to be fine."

"LA and New York are different."

"I'm sure she'll be fine. The last thing she'll want is me interfering in her life."

Because Taylor didn't *get* me. She didn't want to.

"Just promise to check in on her every once in a while. I'll feel better about her being out there."

I shrugged. "Fine."

"Here you go," Ashley said, appearing then with a Coke for me and my dad. "I heard you talking about Taylor. It'll be so good, knowing that you're close by."

"Yeah," I said softly.

"When do you move back?" Ashley asked.

"Um...actually, I'm not sure. That was...part of why I was here," I said, taking a sip to clear the cotton in my throat. "Josh and I are getting a divorce."

Ashley's jaw dropped open. "What? Why?"

My dad just stared at me. As if...he'd guessed all along that it would come to this.

I stared right back at him. "I found out that he was sleeping with someone else. And I don't suffer cheaters."

He had the decency to wince slightly at the words.

"How awful!" Ashley said. She pulled me into a hug and dragged me over to the couch. "I am so sorry. Tell me everything. You must be a mess."

The last thing I wanted to do was powwow with anyone about the demise of my relationship. But Ashley was sincere, and she wouldn't tell anyone. So, I divested myself of the information. Let her coo over me like the mom I'd always wanted. Then after I drained my Coke, I made my excuses and got the hell out of there.

My breaths came out unevenly when I was behind the wheel. This time had been worse. So much worse. My dad was exactly the same, and no one saw it but me. Worse yet, Taylor would be in New York. I was not looking forward to having my recently graduated baby sister in the city. Or the promise I'd made to look after her.

An hour and a half later, after driving through fucking horrendous traffic, I parked in front of Poise PR. I'd signed up with Poise the minute I graduated from law school at Columbia. When I'd gotten my film degree, I'd thought that I wanted to be a director. But then quickly realized that held no sway with me and decided I'd get a JD and become a film agent. After interning with a very well-known agency the two summers of law school, I realized that wasn't what I was interested in either.

Then one of my friends from film school, Lanie, landed a lead role in a small movie. She came to me, sobbing, because they were pushing her around. I went in with all the overconfidence and bluster I could muster and got everything she wanted and more. Lanie was my first client. And I'd brought her with me to Poise when I decided being a publicist was as natural as breathing.

She was probably going to kill me if she found out I was in LA and didn't see her.

But the City of Angels felt like it was stocked full of demons tonight. And I wanted out as soon as possible.

I beelined for my office. I wanted to grab a few things before I saw my boss, Margery. She had started as a receptionist at another well-known agency, worked her way up to partner, and then left to start her own agency. She had been working in the industry for thirty years and was a bit terrifying.

"Knock, knock," a voice said, stepping into my office.

"Winnie," I crooned. "You look as amazing as ever."

And she did.

Winnie was my closest friend in the agency. She was taller

than me with perfect black locks and light-brown skin. She'd grown up in London; she was of Indian descent and had the most incredible accent. She was also a total basket case, cutthroat, and did whatever it took to get ahead.

She reached forward and grasped my hands. "Fuck yes. Look at you, English. Please tell me you're back. Already, that city has sucked the life right out of you."

"I'm just pale," I said with a laugh. "Life has not been sucked out of me. I have a meeting with Margery."

"About coming back?"

"No. I still intend to stay through November."

"Aren't you bored with just one client?"

"If you met Court Kensington, you'd know that boy can keep you busy."

Winnie winked. "Tell me all about it."

I frowned. "Not like that."

"Oh right, the rules," Winnie said with an eye roll. "I think everyone should bone at least one client. Knocks your superiority down a peg."

"I'll take that into consideration," I said, playfully nudging her.

This wasn't the first time we'd had this conversation. It likely wouldn't be the last either.

Because I wasn't interested in Court. We'd just almost kissed. But we hadn't. And it wasn't ever going to happen. Never, ever.

"Okay, on to Margery I go."

"Is this about the pictures?" Winnie asked.

I narrowed my eyes in confusion. "What pictures?"

Winnie frowned. "Oh god. Tell me you've checked your phone today. That you saw TMZ."

"I...I haven't. I've been a bit preoccupied."

TMZ was publicist gold. The goal, of course, was to make sure nothing showed up there that you hadn't sold to them on purpose. But sometimes, things slipped through the cracks.

I pulled up the tabloid, and Winnie leaned forward to look over my shoulder.

A gasp escaped my lips. “No.”

It was Josh and Celeste. Naked. In bed.

“Fuck!”

3

COURT

Camden laughed so hard that I thought he was going to fall over. "She actually put you on lockdown? That woman has got some balls."

"Shut the fuck up."

He just laughed harder. "Come on. It's hilarious. You're a grown-ass man, and your publicist thinks you're so fucked up that she won't let you leave the house."

"I didn't even fucking do anything."

I snatched up a bottle of his best whiskey and poured myself a double. English had told me not to leave, but I wasn't taking her shit. It wasn't like Camden's penthouse in Percy Tower was a den of debauchery. Or at least, not one that was going to make it into any papers.

"You did get arrested," Camden said with a shrug, taking a hit off a joint.

"Fuck that, man. I didn't know what the fuck Jane was doing."

"Maybe you should have paid attention."

"To what?" I asked. "Jane seemed like every other girl on the Upper East Side, except that she was unique and interesting.

She had money. She had ambitions. She didn't care how obnoxious I was or about any of my bad habits. She didn't even ask me to fund her stupid club. I fucking offered."

"Maybe you should care less," Camden suggested with a straight face.

"Like you?" I asked. "If we're bringing up Jane and the arrest, should we discuss your wife?"

His eyes narrowed. "No."

Camden and Katherine had entered an arranged marriage about a year ago. Half the time, I thought he hated her, and half the time, I thought he was insanely in love with her. With Camden, it was hard to tell where his head was. His life was business, business, business. Running one of the most successful and lucrative hotel chains in the country sure helped that.

"I didn't think so." I plopped into a seat adjacent to him and sipped on my whiskey. "She just drives me up the wall."

"Then fire her," Camden said with a shrug.

"In case you've forgotten, I didn't hire her."

"So? You're the one allowing yourself to be subjected to this."

I sighed. "She's just doing her job."

"It sounds like she stepped over a line."

God, how I wished she had.

How had I fucking misinterpreted her reaction so completely? I'd almost kissed her. Almost reached across that divide between publicist and client. I hadn't even wanted to. It had just been instinct. Which was fucking insane because I hadn't touched another girl since the night Jane was arrested. The first person shouldn't be fucking Anna English. That made no sense.

"This whole thing is just...stupid." I held my hand out for the joint.

He passed it to me, and I took a hit.

"What's stupid is not letting her do her job if it's working. Is it working?"

I shrugged and made another pull. "I guess."

"Then stop fucking complaining. And don't fucking take the whole thing. That's the good shit."

I laughed and passed it back to him, feeling a little more relaxed. "I'm only complaining because this lockdown is bullshit."

Camden stretched his legs and stepped up to the pool table. He racked the balls and set the cue down. He picked up his lucky stick, rolled chalk across the top, and then aimed.

"Solids or stripes?" he asked.

I swallowed the last of my drink and stepped over. "Stripes."

"Strippers it is," he said with a chuckle as he hit the cue ball with perfect accuracy.

The balls cracked together and then exploded around the green felt table. Three went in, and Camden smiled his typical competitive smile. The one that said *I'd better fucking win, or I'll end you*. I knew it well.

"You know what you need, Court?" Camden asked, stepping up to the cue again.

"I think you're going to tell me."

"You need to get laid."

"I am shocked to hear you say that," I drawled, laying the sarcasm on thick.

He pocketed the ball and then smirked at me. "I know you. You haven't fucked anyone since Jane."

"So?"

"And you were actually faithful to her."

"Some people see that as a good thing," I reminded him.

"How many people would even believe that you were faithful to her?" Camden asked as he pocketed another ball.

I was beginning to wonder if I'd even get a chance to play the game.

"Likely no one."

I'd carefully cultivated that appearance. I didn't want anyone to think I cared about anything too much. I'd learned that caring usually ended up backfiring in my face. And look, it had happened with Jane, too.

"So, you haven't had any other pussy in what...two years?"

Camden missed the next ball, and I sighed. Thank fuck.

"Two-ish years. Sure," I said.

Even though I could give him the exact date Jane and I'd first fucked and everything else went out the window. I might be known as a Manhattan playboy, a giant train wreck, and the Kensington fuckup. In fact, I was all of those things. Or at least, I had been for most of my life.

But I'd thought Jane was endgame. You treated endgame differently than the other girls.

Turned out, I had been wrong. And her endgame was just prison.

"It's time."

I dropped the first ball into the pocket with ease. "Maybe."

"You're letting your publicist get to you. Weed and good whiskey aren't even calming your bitching," Camden said with a raised eyebrow. "You're Court Kensington. How hard is it to find a willing supplicant?"

Too easy.

Always had been.

The Kensington charm that won my mother elections and had made my dipshit father so good at business got me whatever woman I wanted. All it took was a deep look into their eyes and a pointed smile.

It was how everything had ever been in my life. My name opened doors. I got everything I ever wanted, including the economics degree from Harvard. Who cared if I only went there for lacrosse when the Kensington name was on the building and I charmed my way through the classes?

I was that asshole. The rich, entitled fuck. And I'd never cared a day in my life.

Until the day I'd been arrested.

The day I found out that Jane had just been using me. That her smiles and charm had used and hurt me the way I'd used and hurt so many others.

"Ah, I know that look. You don't want just anyone," Camden said.

I whiffed the next ball. "Fuck."

Camden chuckled as I slammed the stick back into place and waited for him to clean the table. I dragged my phone out of my pocket to check my messages. Maybe Camden had a point. Maybe it was time to move on. I knew a few people who might take the edge off. None that I wanted long-term, but...still...

A text waited for me from my buddy, Gavin King, our friend from college who ran the New York division of an oil empire, Dorset & King.

Holy fuck! Bro, did you see the pictures posted on TMZ? Isn't that English's guy? <link attached>

I furrowed my brow and clicked on the link he'd provided. "Oh fuck!"

Camden glanced up from the pool table. "What?"

I slid the phone across the table to him. "Look at what Gavin just sent me."

He picked up the phone and scrolled through the photos. "She's hot. Why are we looking at porn?"

"That's not porn. That's Josh Hutch and Celeste Gammon on the set of the latest Bourne movie."

"So?"

"That's English's husband."

"Oh," Camden said. His gaze swept the photos another

time. “Not for long, I’d guess.”

“Yeah. Fuck.” I clenched my hands into fists. “Fuck! I was such a dick to her. And she was dealing with this shit.”

Camden handed me back the phone. “So? Why do you care?”

“I don’t.”

Camden smirked. “Okay.”

Fuck, why did I care?

4

ENGLISH

"No. No. Put that over there," I said, directing the movers.

"English, where do you want this box labeled *Miscellaneous Closet*?" my best friend, Lark, asked from the other room.

"Uh, I have no idea. Just my bedroom is fine. I'll go through it."

Lark wiped her hands on her pants and came back into the living room. "You know, this really isn't that much stuff."

"I know. I didn't take everything. I figured I would buy all-new furniture and decorations. I didn't want to take anything that reminded me of him."

"Makes sense," she said. "Glad we could get the moving done early so that I could be here for you before work."

"Me too."

Lark and I had met in law school at Columbia. She worked on the reelection campaign for Court's mom, Mayor Leslie Kensington. She was the one to recommend me to be Court's publicist after his arrest this summer. It had been great, living with her, but it was time to get my own place.

"Thank fuck the movers finally showed up," I told her. "I thought I would be living in your apartment forever."

"Hey! You love my apartment."

I laughed. "I do. But I felt like a third wheel since Sam moved in."

"Ugh! I never want you to feel like that."

"It's fine. I'm happy for you and Sam. That you two worked things out. It was time for me to move out anyway." I shot her a sad smile. "I just wish that it wasn't this apartment."

"Yeah," Lark said softly. "At least you and Josh never lived here together."

"No, instead, he just bought me this apartment out of guilt. I'm living in my husband's multimillion-dollar guilt gift. I don't know if it's better or worse."

"Ugh. I hate this for you. Why did Josh have to be such a dick?"

"If I knew the answer to that, then I would probably be out of a job."

Lark laughed. "True. I mean, we could sell the place."

"I thought about that. But I don't even know how that would work. It would be complicated."

I ran a hand back through my blonde hair and stared around at the mostly bare apartment. I'd fallen in love with it the moment Josh suggested it. All the natural light and the perfect floor plan. The New York City life I'd always wanted to live. And he'd known that.

"We could get you another place. You don't have to live here," Lark said.

"I know, but I want to. It's like I'm in *Friends* with this giant, unrealistic New York apartment."

"This is a lot bigger than the apartment in *Friends*."

"Yeah," I said with a laugh, "but it's a dream come true. Asshole knew that."

"Damn boys. Can't they be thoughtful when it's just for good?"

"Right?" I cracked a smile. "Anyway, I like that I'm only a few floors up from you. I don't want to move."

"I don't want you to move either. Selfishly."

I stared around at the bright apartment, wondering if staying meant that I was giving in. Giving Josh just another outlet to me. If I would be stronger if I decided to get my own place, somewhere he'd never touched before. But everything was so fucked right now. The last thing I wanted was to move again. To have to go through the process of locating a place that I liked when everything else was in upheaval.

"Maybe we should go out tonight. Get your mind off of it," Lark suggested.

"You can't do that," I said. "The campaign..."

Lark cringed. "I know. We're so close to the primary, and I'm working crazy hours, but I'd do it for you."

"Let's just do it after," I said even though going out with my girls sounded nicer than staying in or going to see Court.

I still didn't know what to make of what had happened last time I saw him. I kept meaning to bring it up to Lark, but it got stuck on my tongue like peanut butter.

"No. You need it now. I can sacrifice sleep for one night," she said around a yawn.

I shook my head at her. "You have a complex."

"God, I know," Lark said with a laugh. "I have to get in to the office. Just text Whitley and Katherine, and we'll meet at Sparks. I'm sure Katherine can get us a booth."

"I bet she can."

"I'll see you later!"

"Bye, Lark."

She exited the penthouse, and I gazed around at the collection of boxes. I knew that I should text Court. I'd put him on lockdown. It was... unnecessary, but my head had been in the wrong place. I wasn't going to apologize. I just needed to figure out where we should go from here. What we should do to help his reputation leading to the primary next week.

But if I were being honest, I didn't want to see him. Or have that conversation. I'd rather spend the day unpacking all of these boxes than face Court Kensington.

I canceled on my girls three times that day.

I alternated between determination to get over what Josh had done and staring blankly out my window for an hour at a time. I hadn't cried since I came back from London and sobbed in Lark's arms. I didn't want to cry either. But that didn't mean that I was okay. I felt… submerged. As if I were underwater and any moment Josh would pull me up and laugh and say that it had all been a dream. That my perfect life wasn't over and things were back to how they'd been.

Finally, Whitley crashed into my apartment and forced me to get ready. She all but threw me into the shower. I wasn't happy with the situation, but I loved her to death. We'd met at UCLA in the same sorority and reunited when she went to medical school in the city. Now she was one of the best up-and-coming plastic surgeons in Manhattan. Even Katherine was going to see her. Not that I had any idea what kind of treatments Katherine could need when she was already one of the most beautiful women I'd ever met in my life.

"Are you done?" Whitley groaned from my bare living room. "You don't even have Netflix set up. What kind of animal are you?"

I stepped out of the bedroom and held my hands out. I wore a skintight hot-pink dress that buttoned around my neck and had a deep slit all the way to my navel. The dress flared to my knees, and I wore white pumps with them. "Acceptable?"

"Hot as fuck," Whitley said. "Damn, girl, you look like an A-list celeb."

"A little too Hollywood then?" I said with a fake laugh. "Should I go put on something black?"

"It's the color of the city. But no, you should never fit in when you can stand out in that."

"Thanks, Whit."

I grabbed my purse and followed Whitley downstairs. We walked outside, and Whitley barely had time to hold her hand out for a cab when a man rushed forward with an enormous camera and took my picture.

I blinked stars out of my eyes as shock overtook me.

"Anna Hutch! What are your thoughts on the pictures of Josh and Celeste in bed?" the man asked.

"Get out of her face," Whitley said, trying to get between me and the photographer.

"Anna, did you know that Josh was cheating on you?"

"No...no comment," I said. Then I found my publicist voice. I straightened and shot him a cool look. "I have nothing to say to you. Except that my name isn't Anna Hutch."

Then I strode away from the paparazzo who had somehow found me and into the awaiting vehicle with Whitley close behind.

I'd kept it together for the photographer, but my hands trembled as we sped away. I'd dealt with the paparazzi for years. In LA, I knew half of the people who stalked my clients for pictures and information. We worked together, rotating favors and exclusives. But here in New York, I wasn't that well acquainted with them. Court wasn't being hounded by the press anymore, which left me time to plan other things rather than dealing with the bloodsucking leeches.

I certainly hadn't been prepared to deal with them personally rather than professionally. Of course, when I had gone out with Josh, paparazzi had followed us and taken our picture. But

I was used to that. They hadn't infiltrated my life in New York yet. Not until today.

"Fuck, what a douche bag," Whitley spat. "I can't believe he just got up in your space like that. You should have used some of your jiu-jitsu skills to put him in his place."

"He was just doing his job," I said, trying to cover my unease.

"Yeah, well, he can go do his job elsewhere."

"I know a lot of them back in LA. They're just normal people, trying to make a living. I had to work with them for Poise, and of course, they followed Josh around."

"The whole thing disturbs me. Like...how rude to ask about your relationship with Josh."

I laughed softly, relaxing as the shock wore off. "I've never seen you worked up like that, Whit. I didn't think anything ruffled your feathers."

"I don't like invasions of privacy. I have lines. That's one of them." She grinned at me. "I know I'm a ball of ridiculous behavior and riotous energy most of the time, but no one messes with my friends."

I squeezed her hand. "Thanks."

We made it to Sparks without incident and found Katherine and Lark already waiting for us at a VIP booth.

Katherine Van Pelt was a force to be reckoned with. She was one of those people who always got precisely what she wanted. At first, I'd thought she was aloof and disingenuous, and then I realized that was the front she put on. She cared deeply for the people who were important to her... and no one else. Which made her come off as callous and frigid to outsiders.

But she had a smile on her red-painted lips when she saw me. "English, you made it." She kissed my cheek.

"Hi, Katherine."

And then she arched an eyebrow at Whitley. "And what tornado are you bringing us today?"

She laughed and pressed an uninvited kiss straight onto Katherine's lips. "I'm the tornado, of course. But I'm sure you want to hear the latest."

"Your dating endeavors entertain me greatly."

"Oh, another Whitley exclusive," Lark said with a laugh. "Should be interesting."

She offered me a drink, which I took gratefully as we all waited for the wild ride that was Whitley's dating life.

"Okay, so I met this girl on an online dating app," Whitley said.

"You were on a dating app?" Katherine asked incredulously. "You don't seem the type."

"Yeah, well, one of my nurses suggested it. Anyway, she was hot, and we had similar interests. I figured I'd give it a try."

"Let me guess," Katherine said. "She catfished you?"

"Nope!" Whitley said. "I screen that shit. I'm no amateur."

We all laughed. I felt the weight of the last week melting off of my shoulders with the familiarity of Whitley's stories and the help of vodka.

"I showed up at the bar to meet her. We hit it off, and she asked if I wanted to go home with her. Which, like... great intro. I was game. Then, we got there. I was thinking I was going to get laid, and suddenly, her *husband* appeared."

"What?" I spat.

"Whitley," Lark said with concern.

She held up her hand. "Not what you think. The dude was into it! She'd picked me up and wanted him to watch or some shit. I'd told her I was bi earlier in the conversation, but I hadn't thought that I'd be ambushed with, like, some sex kink or a threesome."

"Good god," Katherine said. "This only happens to you."

"What'd you do?" Lark asked.

"You stayed," I intuited.

Whitley grinned. "Yeah, I stayed. I had the threesome. But I bounced right after the sex and blocked her number. I'm not here to play party all the time."

"Your life is so..." Katherine said, lost for the word.

"Awesome?" Whitley asked.

"Unique."

Whitley laughed and winked at her. "Pour me some tequila, and we'll see where the night leads, Katherine."

Katherine just shook her head with an amused look on her face. I knew Katherine was simply humoring Whitley's crazier tendencies. That she'd likely go home to Camden and do whatever those two did when they were alone. I still wasn't sure how their arranged marriage functioned. But I didn't ask questions either. What did I know about a functioning marriage anyway?

I forced the thoughts aside and dived headfirst into drinks and dancing. Sweat clung to my back, and my feet already killed me, but it was worth it. Lark had been right. Getting out of the apartment and trying not to think was doing the trick.

I plopped down to give my aching feet a break and checked my phone for any emergencies. I was especially paranoid after what had happened with Court while I was gone. I'd have to go see him tomorrow and fix the damage we'd done to our professional relationship. Another thing I didn't want to think of.

And then, as I scrolled through social media, an incoming call lit up the phone. I cursed when I saw it was Josh.

I was drunk. I definitely shouldn't answer that. I couldn't even math what time it must be in London for him to be calling me right now. Really early.

Still, I stumbled away from the girls and pressed the phone to my ear. "Josh?"

"English," he said with relief in his voice. "I didn't know if you'd still be awake."

"I am."

"Where are you? It's loud on your end."

"That's really none of your business."

He sighed heavily. "Don't be that way."

"What way is that, Josh?" I demanded. "Upset that you cheated on me? Because I am. I'm furious."

"I just found out that you moved out of the house in LA."

"Yep," I snapped. "Sure did."

"Please, English, can we just talk about this? Slow down and figure out what we can do? How we can salvage this? We've been together for five years. Do you really just want to throw that all away?"

"No, I don't. But I don't want to be married to a cheater either. So, I'm not going to be married to a cheater."

"What are you saying?"

I swallowed. "I want a divorce."

It was the first time I'd said the words out loud. Even though I'd been thinking them since the minute I found out what had happened with him and Celeste and rushed out of his flat in London. To me, it had ended that day. Five years together, down the drain. Three years of marriage, just poof! Gone! It was a travesty.

"English," he gasped, the pain in his voice evident. "Please... don't say that. Let's talk this out and make a decision together."

"You already made your decision, Josh."

"Please..."

"Good-bye, Josh," I whispered and then hung up the phone.

I felt like I was going to throw up. And also, I was resolute. It was officially over.

5

COURT

"If you're on lockdown, then why are we going out again?" Sam asked as we exited my apartment together.

"Because I'm fucking tired of being in the house. I don't even know when English is coming back. I'm not going to sit around and wait any longer."

Sam shot me an incredulous look. I knew what that meant. Sam, unlike Camden, was a rule-follower. He was probably the least likely person to hang out with me and Camden, who tore up the town and never gave two fucks about anything. But Sam was also a great guy. Someone who didn't judge my actions. He just gradually steered me in the right direction. Like he was right now.

"We could always just do something less...problematic," he suggested.

"Like what?"

"I don't know...video games?"

I snorted and held my hand out for a cab. "I was thinking lots of alcohol and getting laid. Maybe something recreational."

Sam shook his head. "I don't care if you get drunk and sleep with someone, but if it gets out that you're smoking pot or worse...English will kill you."

"Or worse?" I said with a laugh, getting into the cab. Sam followed, and then we were driving into Midtown. "You say 'or worse' like you've never snorted cocaine before."

"I haven't."

"Well, look at you, growing up in a stable household."

Sam shrugged indifferently. "Not apologizing for that."

"Fair." Sam had gone all stiff, and I nudged him with my easy smile. "All right, relax. No cocaine tonight. We'll just get drunk."

"Good."

"And wait...what's wrong with smoking pot?" I asked.

"Besides it being illegal?"

"Yeah, but it shouldn't be."

"That's true. But isn't English trying to make you look like the golden boy? All straightlaced?"

"Whatever. I don't care."

"Yes, you do," Sam said with a knowing smile as the cab pulled up in front of Sparks.

I threw cash over the seat and stepped out in front of the club. Sam wasn't wrong. I did care. But the cabin fever had set in, and I needed to get away. Plus, Camden wasn't wrong. Getting laid might help take the edge off. It'd be better than sitting around in my house, jerking off again.

I stepped into the pulsing nightclub and immediately felt in my element. I was ready to get rid of the pussy-whipped asshole who had done whatever Jane wanted. Ready to shuck off the constraints I'd put on myself the last couple months. It'd be easier to just move on already.

"Let's find Camden and Gavin," I called out to Sam. "Then drinks."

Sam pointed straight ahead. "Found them."

I followed his attention and saw that Camden stood next to

Katherine. Gavin was dancing zealously with Whitley and Lark.

"I didn't know the girls would be out tonight," I said.

Sam shrugged. "I didn't either."

"Lark didn't say anything?"

"Nope. I'm surprised myself, considering she's burning the candle at both ends right now, coming up to the primary."

"Well, let's go find out," I said.

Unease settled in the pit of my stomach. Going out with the guys was different than meeting the girls out. It was more difficult to pick someone up this way. Though still... probably not difficult.

We pushed through the throng of people on the dance floor and into the VIP section. Gavin saw us first and pointed his finger in our direction.

"Court Kensington has arrived, ladies and gentlemen!" Gavin cried.

We clapped our hands together in an aggressive handshake.

"Gavin, my man."

Lark furrowed her brow when she saw me. "I thought you weren't supposed to be out."

"What are you, my mom now?"

She straightened at the bite in my voice. "Don't be a dick."

"Comes with the territory."

"Only when you want it to."

"Must be confusing me with another Kensington," I said with a sweeping bow.

Lark was close friends with my brother, Penn. And sometimes, when she looked at me, I swore she saw him and not me. I wasn't the cookie-cutter Columbia professor who had defied his family's interests and fallen in love with philosophy, of all things. I wasn't on some moral high ground. Penn and I had a fraught past, and though we were working toward the right direction, it was times like this that made me remember why I wasn't him.

"Why do you always deflect like that?" Lark asked.

I shrugged. "Just tired of people telling me what to do. If I want to be out, then I'll be out. I don't care who tells me that."

"You sure?" She arched an eyebrow and nodded her head behind me.

I whipped around and found none other than Anna English.

Busted.

Fuck.

"English," I said, wide-eyed. "I didn't know that you were back from LA."

"Clearly," she said. Her jaw was set. Her eyes narrowed in my direction. "What the fuck are you doing here, Court?"

"What the fuck am *I* doing here? What the fuck are *you* doing here? I thought you were still in LA. Why didn't you text me or anything?"

English crossed her arms over her ample chest. Something solidified in her eyes. Something lethal. "I just got back."

"I saw what happened with Josh."

She flinched. Yeah, that was the wrong thing to say.

"Which is why I'm out. But it makes *no sense* why you're out."

"Because your lockdown was bullshit," I snapped right back.

"It was for a reason."

"Yeah, because you were pissed your husband cheated on you."

The girls all sucked in breaths at my words. Even Gavin looked wounded. Camden's face was blank, but I could see the questions in his eyes. But it was English who hadn't moved at the words. At the cruel things I'd said to get a reaction out of her.

She just took a step forward. "We're leaving."

"I'm not going anywhere."

Her hand circled my wrist. Her nails dug into my skin. "Now."

"No."

She stared back at me, resolute. "What was your plan tonight? Just going to get wasted and take a girl home? Not care about who sees you or how it looks for the campaign a week before your mother needs to get nominated for the primary? You can be a fuckup all you want when it only affects you. But you're jeopardizing other people's livelihoods, and you're so flippant about it. Do you only care about yourself?"

Her words cut like a razor blade across my jugular. Hadn't people been saying that to me my entire life? I knew she was pissed. That she was just throwing more of her own mess at me. But she'd gone for the jugular.

I wrenched out of her grip. "Fine."

"Fine," she spat back.

She turned back to our friends and grabbed her purse. She and Lark exchanged a glance, and then she forced her way out of the booth. I gritted my teeth and followed her. I'd come out, wanting a fun night, and instead, I ended up with this shit. I'd thought I'd finally be getting laid tonight. Nope. Just fucking dealing with English. I couldn't think of a worse torture that my mother could have devised than getting me a publicist.

I pressed back through the throng of bodies. My anger simmered right at the surface. It was one thing for her to scream at me in my apartment because I'd fucked up when we were trying so hard to change my image. It was another thing entirely to drag me out of a club when I was doing nothing wrong. Nothing that was going to end up in the papers. *Page Six* didn't even care about a Kensington going to a club. That wasn't news.

I'd leave this time. And then we'd have words. Because this wasn't fucking continuing.

I stepped out of the club on her heels. She had her head down, staring at her phone. She looked worried as she bit down on her bottom lip. Then her eyes found mine, and she released her lip and put her phone away.

"Let's get a cab to your place. I want to see that you get home," she told me.

"Fine. And then we'll talk."

She rolled her eyes and said nothing.

I turned my head away from her as she flagged down a waiting cab. That was when I saw a man appear from around the building. He was a lanky, disheveled fucker with a giant camera around his neck.

"English," I muttered in confusion.

She whipped around, trying to figure out why I'd spoken. Her eyes narrowed, and she reached for me in that moment. As if she were going to stuff me in the cab before the man could get any closer.

But the instant her fingers wrapped around my bicep to try to steer me clear, the man yanked up the camera, and the flash went off.

"Fuck," English groaned.

"Anna, do you have a comment about Josh?" the man asked.

And then I put it together. Paparazzi. Us Upper East Siders weren't hounded by the paps like movie stars and rock stars were, but I'd seen my fair share around Fashion Week and in the Hamptons. The press had tried to get a statement out of me after Jane and I were arrested. This guy was different though. He clearly worked for a tabloid and cared less about crimes and more about the scandalous lives of the people he photographed.

"I told you earlier, no comment," English said.

"He already bothered you?" I asked. For some reason, that made all my anger boil over.

I stepped forward, getting right in the guy's face. "You need to stop harassing her."

"What is this, the new boyfriend?" the guy asked her.

"She's going through enough without you hounding her, you piece of shit!"

"Court," English muttered. She pushed me away from the photographer. "God, I'm sorry about that. Ignore him. He's just a client. You do know that I'm a publicist, right? This is what we deal with."

"Sure, sure," he said, sounding disbelieving.

"Could you just delete the photograph you took? It's not what it seems. I can get you an exclusive or probably a favor with Poise PR."

She dug in her bag and removed a business card. The man swiped the card, stuffing it in his pocket without looking at it.

"I'd take an exclusive. With you or Josh."

She sighed. "Not happening. I can get you something else. Or owe you a favor."

He shrugged. "Fine. I'll call you, and we'll set something up."

"Sounds good. Thanks. What's your name?"

"Jeremiah," he said, shaking her hand.

"Nice to meet you, Jeremiah. I'm English. I hope to work with you more regularly in the future. You can discontinue stalking me for more valuable prey."

He laughed and nodded. "Have a good night."

English grabbed another cab since ours had sped off and shoved me inside. She whipped around on me as soon as the door closed. "What the hell were you thinking? Do you want to add assault to your rap sheet?"

"How was I to know that you wanted to befriend the dick who was harassing you?"

She sighed and pressed on her temples. "He was just doing his job. I don't *like* his job, but then again, most people don't like my job either."

"In that, we're in agreement," I grumbled.

She just ignored my comment and pulled her phone back out.

I'd about fucking had it with Anna English. Something was going to have to give, or we weren't going to survive each other.

6

ENGLISH

"I cannot believe that you're following me up," Court said.

"Well, I don't trust that you'll stay put."

"What are you going to do, spend the night to make sure I don't leave?"

I shoved my phone back into my purse and ignored him. Like I'd been ignoring the dozens of texts that I'd gotten from Josh ever since I hung up on him. He clearly didn't think that I was going to divorce him. And I had every intention of doing so.

The elevator dinged open into his apartment. I thought I'd feel relief that I'd gotten Court back to his house where he couldn't accidentally fuck up the entire election, but no such luck. It was clear that he had no clue how closely his actions were still being watched. It wasn't the media circus that it had been right after he was arrested, but people were waiting for him to fuck up again. The opposition was desperate for a reason to come down hard on his mom. Any reason.

Court strode into the living room, and I followed him inside. He held his arms aloft. "See? I made it. Just like a good boy."

"Why do you insist on acting like this?" I demanded.

"Maybe because you're ruining my life."

I snorted. "What life? All you do is fuck around like an idiot."

He narrowed his eyes, and his nostrils flared. "Just because I don't work a hundred-hour weeks like you or Camden or Lark doesn't mean that I have no life."

"If you say so."

"I want to fire you."

I shouldn't laugh at that, but I did. I couldn't stop it from exploding out of me. But all it did was piss him off more. And maybe I wanted that. I wanted someone else to be as mad as I was. Ready to throw down.

"You think that's funny?" he demanded. "I'm going to go to my mother tomorrow and tell her you're not fit for the job."

I took a step toward him. "Do it. See what she says."

Something sparked in those impossibly blue eyes. "I'll tell her that you're not subjective after what Josh did."

"Fine," I said, taking another step. "How do you think that will go for you? Do you think she'll fire me, or do you think she'll call you a petulant child who can't deal with his own problems?"

Court bridged that last bit of distance. He looked like he was ready to put his fist through a wall. It was hot as fuck... and it shouldn't have been. I'd never seen him look like that before. Primal.

"You ask me those questions as if you aren't off your game. You put me on lockdown for basically no reason. You let that photographer take our picture. You went out drinking instead of coming back here."

"I put you on lockdown because you'd almost gotten arrested," I snapped. "And yeah, maybe I wanted to go out drinking to forget about Josh and to forget about you."

"Oh, yeah?" he asked. "And why exactly do you need to forget about me?"

The space between us sizzled with energy. Had I said forget about him? Had I meant to say that?

"Because... you're a fucking train wreck, Court."

His gaze shifted in that second. "I don't think that's the reason at all."

I sucked in a breath at the implication in his words. At his heated gaze. The way he seemed to see straight through me. All the rage that built between us. And suddenly, the scales tipped over. Straight into disaster.

Court didn't hesitate. His hands came up into my hair. His grip possessive and controlling. No question in that hold. Then he bent down, bringing his lips hard against mine. He tasted like whiskey, and it burned all the way down.

He moved against me then, flicking his tongue against the seam of my lips and opening me to him. I groaned deep in the back of my throat as he acquainted himself with my mouth. Our tongues meeting and falling back and meeting again like a courting ritual.

He tilted my face up just a little bit more perfectly to his taking. And then I came crashing back into my body.

This... this couldn't happen. I had... I had rules. Rules that I shouldn't break. He was a client.

I yanked back away from him, trying to force him backward. I reared back and slapped him hard across the face. His head tipped sideways, and a muscle flickered in his jaw. He stared off, away from me, for a matter of seconds. His chest rising and falling with the anger within him.

Then he slowly turned back to face me. A smirk spread across his face. "That's what you wanted, wasn't it, English?"

"Fuck you, Court." The venom in my voice was palpable.

I couldn't do this. I couldn't... even if I wanted to.

He nodded once, as if making a decision. He took another step back into my personal space. I didn't move. I just glared up at him.

"Tell me to stop," he teased, his mouth mere inches from mine.

The word was on the tip of my tongue. And I couldn't say it. Because it was the wrong word. As much as it was utterly wrong... I couldn't deny that, this moment, I wanted it. Fuck the consequences.

"Didn't hear you, English."

I glared at him harder. But I didn't say a word.

His hands moved back to my hair, yanking my head backward so that I was forced to meet his gaze. I moaned at the sharp pain that electrified through my body. The fucking sway he commanded from me.

His head dipped down into my shoulder. He dragged his nose along my collarbone and then slowly over to my neck. His fingers hovered over the button at the back of my neck that held my dress up. He swirled it temptingly, as if waiting for me to tell him to stop. I didn't.

His mouth moved to my ear. "Say yes."

I said nothing.

"Tell me you want me, English."

I closed my eyes as he nipped on my earlobe. "I hate you."

His laugh was gravelly against my ear. "Then tell me to fuck off. Walk away right now."

"Bastard," I croaked.

"Call me whatever you want," he said, pulling back just enough to gaze at me. "Just say yes."

I bit my lip. Anguish at the implications of that word. At how fucking bad I wanted this. I closed my eyes as he sucked on my bottom lip, nearly groaning again.

"English..."

"Yes," I finally gasped out against his lips. "Yes... fuck, yes, Court."

That smirk returned, and I was tempted to slap it off of his fucking face again. But he was having none of that. In that moment, Court Kensington was in the room. He was in complete control. This wasn't the man child I'd had to deal with after he was arrested. This was the *man* who could very easily be running an empire. I could see it in the smile and how he moved and the way his body just radiated power. This was the Court Kensington hiding beneath his mask. And it was fucking sexy as hell.

"I knew it," he said, backing me into the wall. "I wasn't wrong last week, and I'm not wrong now."

I swallowed. "Fine. You're not wrong. I wanted to kiss you."

His smile just grew. "Then kiss me."

He didn't wait. He tipped my chin up and fitted his mouth to mine. Our lips tangled as they moved together. As if neither of us could get enough. My hands moved up into his hair. That fucking unruly hair that I'd had to bring someone in to tame for interviews. And god, it was thick and full and fucking perfect. It was better mussed than ever in order. Just like the rest of him.

His hand returned to the button on my dress that held up the backless top. He flicked it open as if he'd done it a million times. The material fell to the skirt, baring me from the waist up. A tiny zipper in the back was the only thing keeping me from being completely naked.

"Fuck," he ground out as his hands slipped down my body.

He grasped my breasts in his large palms. He kneaded them as he grew acquainted with me. He pinched one of my nipples, and I gasped against his lips.

He pulled back with a cocky smile. He pinched me again. He wasn't being gentle, and fuck, I liked it. Heat shot straight to my core.

My back arched off of the wall with the next pull between his fingers. I bit my lip to keep from crying out. But then he replaced his hands with his mouth, sucking my nipple in, his tongue laving across the erect peak. I couldn't stop it then.

When he dragged my nipple between his teeth, a sound like a whimper escaped me. I couldn't remember ever making that noise before. It was as if something had unlocked in me. I was out of my body. I wasn't even Anna English. In that moment, I belonged to Court Kensington.

Court didn't know the difference. Didn't know that I hadn't made noises like this. That I was unraveling right before his eyes. He just moved to my other breast and made me cry out all over again.

His hands slipped behind my dress, found the spare zipper, and yanked it down. The pink material made a puddle at my feet. Leaving me in nothing but a nude thong and bright white high heels.

The bastard was still fully dressed. Though I could see his erection straining against his suit pants. I reached out to get acquainted with it, but he fell to a knee in front of me. He grasped the edges of my thong and dragged them down my legs. I stepped out of them and opened my mouth to say something. To stop him? To urge him on? Fuck knew where my head was.

But he wasn't looking up at me. He just grasped one of my legs and lifted it up onto his shoulder. My only anchor was my back against the wall and one measly high heel. How much had I had to drink earlier?

Fuck.

His face was level with my pussy. And he didn't wait for me to urge him on. He ran his hand down my inner thigh and up to the lips, where he spread me open before him. I clenched tight at his fingers on me, swishing through the wetness that was already there and then pressing up into me.

"Oh fuck," I cried out.

Two fingers without hesitation. No waiting for me to be ready or easing me into it. He just took it.

Then his tongue touched my clit. I thought I was going to

black out. That my high heel wasn't going to hold me up. My body shook as he rolled his tongue around my most sensitive area. He increased the pressure, sucking and then biting my clit. I tried to pull away, to resist the intense sensations coursing through me. But his free hand slammed my hips back against the wall. He braced me with his forearm against my lower abs. There was no escape. And for some reason, that made me even wetter. I wanted to escape, and I wanted to stay precisely where I was for all of eternity.

"Court," I groaned. My fingers ran through his hair. "Please, please..."

I didn't even know what I was begging for. If I wanted him to continue or if I wanted him to stop. I'd never come from oral. It sounded insane, but I'd dated selfish douche bags in college, and then Josh had always been so impatient to fuck me. We'd just skipped foreplay most of the time.

Court was having none of my squirming. He wouldn't let me get away from this.

"I like it when you say my name. Say it again."

"Court. Oh fuck, Court."

Then he curled his fingers into me while sucking. I didn't know if it was how he had me braced so I couldn't get away from the orgasm or the way he demanded me to use his name. But something clicked in me. I hit a wall and waves rolled through my body.

"Oh fuck. Oh fuck. Oh fuck," I said on repeat as the climax struck me like a tornado, fast and unforgiving.

Court licked me one more time just to watch me jump and then removed his fingers from inside me. When he set my leg back down, I nearly collapsed. My legs gave out.

He chuckled as he caught me and then effortlessly lifted me into his arms.

"I don't think I've ever made someone actually fall over," he said with that sure grin on his face.

I didn't know if he was even telling the truth.

He set me on the couch where I tried to control the shaking in my legs. Then he disappeared for a minute. My mind was blessedly blank. Everything was still pulsing in my lower half, and I was too blissed out to consider what the fuck he was doing.

When he returned, he dropped a condom on the coffee table. He held out his hand for me.

"I should take these off," I said, nodding to my shoes.

He laughed. "Not a chance, English." He hoisted me back to my feet and then put my hands on the buttons of his shirt. "Take this off."

I arched an eyebrow, but my fingers were already moving. I plucked each one out individually before letting the shirt drop off his shoulders. Then I moved to his pants, unbuttoning them and then dragging the zipper to the base. He stepped out of the pants, leaving him in nothing but black boxer briefs.

For a moment, I salivated at the sight. I never gave blow jobs. Like... never. What the hell was I even thinking?

When I didn't move forward, he freed his dick. My eyes rounded. I'd seen big dick before, but fuck. How was this even fair to humanity? To be this fucking hot and charming and have money *and* have a huge cock? Like... fuck everything in life.

He laughed at my expression. "Come here."

I stepped into him, reaching forward and taking him into my hand. He grunted at the first feel of me. But his hands moved into my hair. They were pulling the tangled mess of Hollywood platinum-blonde hair up into a makeshift ponytail. He had control with all of that in his hands.

"Lean over the couch arm."

"Excuse me?"

"I'd have you suck me off, English, because fuck knows that I want to see it sinking in and out of that goddamn mouth that yells at me," he said, pulling my hair back so I had to look at him. "But I want to fuck you. Right now. So, bend over the fucking couch."

I bit my lip. The bastard. I wanted to argue. But we were a bit past arguing.

I didn't recognize the person who did what she was told. I was so used to issuing orders, expecting people to do what I said, that I couldn't even believe I was following his as I turned and bent forward at the waist over the arm of the couch.

My ass was high up in the air. He still had a tight grip on my hair. So tight that my head was pulled back, making my back arch and giving him an even better view of my ass.

"Just like that," he said and then released my hair to fan around my head.

His hands roamed my ass, getting to know it like he'd done with my breasts. He slapped his hand against one ass cheek.

I yelped and glared back at him. "I'm going to fucking kill you."

He smacked the other cheek as he reached for the condom and rolled it on. "Whatever you want, babe. But you're mine right now."

I ground my teeth at his words. His filthy words. I hated him as much as I wanted him right now. It made no sense. None. And yet, I couldn't stop the want. The way he silenced everything else. All the voices in my head went perfectly still. Even as he slapped his open palm against my bottom, making it sting. Even as I was bent over, head down, ass up, with him ready to fuck me like I'd never been fucked.

Then he gripped my hips as he aligned his cock with my opening. I tensed just a moment, but he laid a hand along the small of my back. And everything released again. With no warning, he thrust deep into me.

I gasped as he hit into me as hard and fast as he could. No coaxing, just his cock deep into my pussy. If I wasn't so warmed up from him going down on me, he definitely would have stretched me past the point of pleasure. Instead, he filled me up, almost to bursting, and still, I pushed my ass harder against him, desperate for more.

"Like that?" he asked and then pulled back and slammed back down onto me.

"Oh god," I cried out. "Court, please..."

"Harder?"

I whimpered as he did it without waiting for my answer. I wanted it just like this. I wanted it punishing. I wanted him to impale me until there was nothing left of me but that point in my body where he drove into me. I wanted to forget why I was mad. Forget everything.

He grunted once behind me. His fingers dug deep into my hips as he pinned me to the couch with his cock. The only sound was our bodies smacking together. A thin layer of sweat beaded my skin. And though tears tinted my lashes, I didn't know if it was the pain of him fucking me as hard and fast as animals...or the release of all the emotions from the last week.

But it didn't matter. Another orgasm gradually began to build in my core. I couldn't believe it came on slowly, considering he fucked me relentlessly. Taking out his anger on me as much as I was taking it out on him. Maybe we were both using each other. I couldn't even think of the implications of that.

"Close...close," I got out.

"Me too," he cried.

I dug into the couch cushion and screamed into it as he drove deeper and deeper, rocking my body forward with each thrust. And then it hit me. Like a tidal wave, dragging me under through the current and battering my limp body around with the force of the momentum.

My climax triggered his. He drove into me one more time and then cried out. I could feel his release inside of me, and then everything began to go fuzzy at the edges. As if I was close to a blackout at any moment.

After a minute of heavy breathing, Court gently pulled out of me and walked to the bathroom. Look at him, being gentle now that he was done punishing my body with his cock.

I sat up. My head felt heavy as I dragged on my underwear and plopped onto the couch we had just defiled. I closed my eyes, wondering if I was about to pass out when it clicked, what we had just done.

I'd fucked my client.

Or...he had fucked me.

I'd asked him to fuck me.

My eyes flew open in a panic. I had...I had rules. This wasn't supposed to happen! I'd wanted it to happen. I'd wanted to forget about Josh and what he'd done to me. And Court Kensington was hot, my type, and all too willing. But I still shouldn't have broken my number one rule. Not for him. Not for anyone.

I scrambled back into my dress and reached for my purse when he came back out of the bathroom, completely nude.

His brows furrowed. "You're dressed."

"Yes. Well, I have to go home."

"You don't have to rush out of here. You can stay the night. I'm not a dick."

I laughed once, sharp and unforgiving. "No, you misunderstand me. This is never happening again."

"English...wait..."

"You're a client. I don't get involved with clients."

"What the fuck do you think just happened?"

I shrugged one shoulder, compartmentalizing everything, like I had my entire life. "A mistake."

Then before I could see his wounded expression, I turned and walked out of his apartment. I wondered who exactly I was trying to convince. Because it certainly hadn't felt like a mistake to me.

PART II

TURN THE TABLES

7

ENGLISH

I needed to tell someone.

But I couldn't tell anyone.

Not even Lark. Not even Whitley or Katherine. No one could know about this. No one could find out what Court and I had done.

I'd most certainly lose my job as his publicist. And I'd fucking deserve it. But where I was with the press, it would be a field day. Fuck, I could not even imagine what would happen if it was leaked. My brain hurt too much to consider it.

I spent the next day cooped up in my apartment, ignoring my phone. The primary was about a week away. I needed to get on top of things. Figure out what Court could be doing to better his reputation and help his mother win the nomination. But I couldn't bring myself to focus on it.

I needed to snap out of this really fucking quick or else... I wouldn't have a job regardless.

The middle of the second day, I finally dragged myself out of bed and got myself together. I could do this. I could get Court a schedule. I could go to his place and see him and act just like we'd been acting toward each other for the last three months.

Yep, I could do it.

After I finished blow-drying my hair and pulling clothes over all the little bruises Court had given me, I reached for my phone to text Court and let him know I was coming over. But there was already a text on the screen. A text from Josh.

So, this is how you repay me?

I furrowed my brow and opened the link.

"Motherfucker!" I cried.

The picture of me and Court that bastard photographer Jeremiah had taken was in the fucking tabloids. I was in that ridiculously sexy pink dress. I'd just grabbed him to pull him into the cab. But the angle was perfect. It looked like I was hanging on his arm. As if I were his arm candy. My eyes were wide with alarm, as if we'd been caught. The headline read, *Josh Hutch's Wife Already Moving on with Mayor's Son?*

I didn't even have a name in the headline. Motherfucking fucker.

"Fuck, fuck, fuck," I groaned.

I texted Winnie to ask her to look into who had the originals of this and how far it had gone. She knew enough people to see if we could have it retracted or clarified. I knew what I needed to do. I needed to track down that photographer and break his fucking legs. You did not go back on a deal with me.

After I took a deep breath, I decided that I would have to do immediate damage control with this. Which meant I'd have to give them something. It only took ten minutes after Winnie sent me the editor's details before I was on the phone with the woman, Mandy, who had written the article. Fucking blood-sucking journalist.

"Mrs. Hutch, what a surprise," Mandy, said.

"I'll give you an exclusive if you take it down and print a retraction."

"Right to business, I see."

"You and only you. Take it down. Print a retraction, and you get a half hour with me in New York City. I'll tell you my side."

"I don't see why I should print a retraction when you were obviously together."

"A half hour," I repeated, firm and unyielding.

She huffed. As if she had been waiting to catch me in an explanation. I had no intention of giving her something that she could twist.

"An hour," she demanded.

"Fine. Take it down now. Write up your retraction within the hour, and you have a deal."

"Done. Nice doing business with you, Mrs. Hutch."

"And for the record, Mandy, it's English."

Then I hung up on the bitch and flopped back onto my bed. Never mind. I wasn't going anywhere *near* Court Kensington until this was taken care of. His mother would kill me if she thought that any of what had been written was true. She almost hadn't hired me because I was pretty. She'd worried I was Court's type and that he'd charm me. Fuck everything for her being right.

I was going to have to tell Leslie. That was the only way to make this blow over. She couldn't hear it from the tabloids. I immediately texted the mayor's assistant to make the appointment.

And all this time... Josh texted me and called me and left voicemails.

On the fifth call, I picked up the phone.

"What do you want?" I demanded in frustration. "I'm trying to work here."

"Finally, you answered," Josh said on a sigh.

"Yes, but I don't want to talk to you. I already told you all I had to say."

"So, you call me to tell me you want a divorce and then get

back at me by sleeping with someone else and expect me not to want to talk to you?"

"I really don't care, Josh."

"So, you did sleep with him."

I breathed out through my nose. I was not going to talk to my husband about this. He had no reason to know that I'd slept with Court. I had no intention of discussing the best night of sex in my life with him.

"He's a client," I bit out.

"Yeah, well, you wouldn't be the first publicist to sleep with a client."

"I have rules, Josh."

"Never stopped anyone else."

"Thanks for reminding me that you fucked Celeste. This conversation is over. I have more important things to deal with today."

"Look, I get it. You found out about me and Celeste. You were mad. I know how you are, English. Your temper runs hot as fire. It ignites like an explosion and ricochets in every direction. You were mad at me and then did something drastic to get back at me. I don't blame you."

I did have a hot temper. I'd gotten it from my dad. Unfortunately. But I didn't want to let him know he was right.

"Josh, he is a *client*."

"I don't believe that you didn't sleep with him, English. I know you too well."

"Well, I'd love to listen to your guilty conscience all day, but I have things to do."

"Let's just move past this. You got back at me for Celeste. And now, we're even. You got it out of your system. So, now, we can move on."

"Move on?" I asked, cold and hard. "You fucked your costar behind my back. The only thing I'm moving on from is you."

Then I hung up the phone and fell back onto my bed again.

I'd have to get up in a few minutes to prepare for my meeting with the mayor, but right now, I needed the time to wallow. Because as mad as I was with Josh, I still loved him. Or at least the man he'd been and the relationship we'd had. I was going to need more time to grieve this before I could think of being okay.

My meeting with the mayor went about as well as expected. She worried that my breakup with Josh would hurt the campaign. Lark had reassured her that it wouldn't. But I wasn't so sure. I'd told her that I was fine and still on my game, but I knew that I wasn't. I needed more time. And we didn't have time.

At least the meeting had been productive, and I'd figured out the next steps with her regarding Court's publicity, going into the primary. Which meant I had a list of events he could attend and the one mandatory victory party. From what I'd grasped, his mom didn't want the reminder of his arrest at the primary events. So, it might even be better for him not to attend. And just to keep him out of trouble until the party.

I steeled myself and texted Court. It was the first communication we'd had since I left his apartment.

> *Here's the list of events your mother is attending. She wants you to keep your head down and try not to get any more media attention. But she would like you at the victory party. If you haven't seen the tabloids, our picture from that pap was in it. I'm handling it.*

I sent it off with the list from his mom and then headed back uptown to start digging into what I could do to help make him more of the golden boy of the Upper East Side. Maybe I should brainstorm it with Winnie. She might have other ideas.

Before I could give her a call, Court responded.

Fine. All right. We're just discussing work?

Work is all there is.

We should meet to discuss this.

Meeting him would be a disaster. It was too soon. I couldn't even be near him. I knew myself too well.

I'm busy, dealing with the tabloids.

English...

I tucked my phone away. I didn't want to answer that plea. I knew what he wanted. But I couldn't give it to him. We had work to do. That was all.

I'm going out. Probably going to do something stupid.

I glared at the text message from Court. A week had passed. I'd managed to avoid him that long. I'd spent the week curled in my bed, thinking about the fact that my husband had cheated on me and I was divorcing him. I'd even initiated the process. A process I knew was going to be a huge pain in the ass.

I'd started my divorce proceedings so that I wouldn't have to think about Court. My own client. Who I should be seeing regularly to keep him out of trouble. And now, he was sending me texts like this.

You're an idiot.

I need a babysitter. I've been told that I'm impulsive.

Damn if that wasn't true.

You need a sedative.

The primary is Tuesday. Wouldn't want to ruin that.

I knew he was goading me. And still, I wanted to head out and make sure he didn't do anything else reckless. Also, I wanted to see him. Even though he drove me batshit crazy. But I also couldn't see him. In no way, shape, or form.

Still, I was half-tempted to do it. Just to forget about Josh again for a few hours.

Then, another text came in but this time from Winnie.

SOS! Call me!

I dialed Winnie's number. "Hey, what's up?"

"Ugh, English! Thank god! Anisa Union is on *The Tonight Show* tonight. We prepped her. She was totally fine, on point, no issues."

"And now, she's having a meltdown?"

"Yes!" Winnie gasped. "We don't have anyone else in New York. I know that you're not on staff like you were, but I'd owe you a huge favor if you could go over there and calm her down. Give her a fucking Xanax, tell her she's going to do great, and get her through this interview. This is make-or-break-it for her upcoming movie."

The universe was handing me an out.

If I did this, then I wouldn't have to go see Court. I could deal with someone else's problems other than my own. And that was what I was good at anyway. I could get some hopped-up movie star to chill long enough to conduct an interview. No sweat. That was nothing.

"I've got you covered, Win. I'll head over there now."

"Thank you, English. You're a lifesaver."

"I'll call in that favor one day."

Winnie laughed. "No doubt. I'm sending you the information and letting Anisa know you're on your way."

"Thanks."

I dashed into my closet, changing into my favorite black dress and heels. I added some eyeliner and a dark red lipstick. I had to look the part.

This was why I did the job. It was the rush. The reminder that I was *good* at this. Court Kensington was an experiment for me and the agency. He was not the be-all, end-all of my career.

So, I texted him as I was on my way to Rockefeller Center.

Can't make it. Dealing with another client.

Another client?

Yep. Just try not to get arrested.

English...come on.

Good night, Court.

8

COURT

English was avoiding me.

Which had been fucking fine for the first few days. She'd bailed right after we fucked. I'd thought her excuse was just that... an excuse. How could she not want to do that again? Fuck, it'd been amazing.

But it hadn't been an excuse, apparently. She'd redirected all my attempts to contact her. She'd given me some bullshit work to do for the week leading up to the primary. She'd made up some extra clients in the city to keep her busy. I hadn't even seen her since that night.

I knew I'd see her tonight. She had to be at my mother's victory party for the primary she was surely going to win. I'd kept my head down and done all the things I was supposed to do. I wasn't a liability. Blah, blah, blah.

I'd seen it time and time again. I'd been to enough victory parties to know how they went down.

I'd made sure that someone saw me voting. I'd even answered someone's question with a goddamn smile at the polling place. English hadn't even had to tell me what to do. I could be the Kensington poster boy if I tried. Just trying was overrated.

Now, I stood with my mother at her campaign office. She'd just come back from a rally where she encouraged people to vote. She'd had an entire fucking parade for her entrance into the polling booth. To vote for herself no less.

"Stop pacing," I ground out. "If you win, you win. If you lose, you lose. You've done everything you can."

She narrowed her eyes. "I can always do more."

But she stopped pacing.

"You're coming to the party tonight? It would look good to have you onstage with me for the win."

"Unlike the last month where you wanted me nowhere near your events?"

Her eyes hardened. "I would have loved to have your support. But at that time, it wasn't advisable. We'll see if everything Anna has done is valuable."

Anna. I almost laughed. I'd gotten so used to calling her English that Anna almost felt strange. "English is great at her job. Even if she drives me crazy."

"Good. That means she's keeping you in line."

I kept a tight rein on what I wanted to say to *that* comment.

A knock sounded on the door. Thank fuck for that interruption.

"Come in," my mother called.

The door opened, and a face appeared. A face I hadn't seen in months.

"Penn?" I asked in surprise. I stepped forward and shook my younger brother's hand. "I didn't think you were back from Paris."

He'd disappeared at the start of the summer. Literally left the day after my arrest with no intention of returning until the semester began at Columbia, where he was a philosophy professor. I didn't blame him one bit for ditching the summer campaign season.

"Just got back today," he said.

"What a surprise," our mother said with a genuine smile on her face. "I hope you voted."

Penn pushed the door open a little wider. "We both did."

And standing there in a green sundress was Natalie Bishop. She grinned up at my brother as if he was the only one in the room. The center of her entire universe. I wondered what that felt like.

"Hello, Mayor Kensington," Natalie said, taking a step inside. Penn closed the door behind her as her gaze shifted to me. "Hi, Court."

"Natalie," my mother said with raised eyebrows. "Were you both in Paris this whole summer?"

"Actually," Penn said, taking Natalie's hand in his, "we have something we wanted to tell you both."

Natalie held up her left hand. "We got married."

My jaw dropped open. I didn't have to look at my mother to know that she was making the same face. I jumped in before she could say something stupid.

"Fuck! Congrats, man." I held my hand out for him again and shook it. Then, I dragged Natalie in for a hug. "You're family now... Natalie Kensington."

Natalie flushed. "I suppose I am."

"When did this happen?" our mother asked, shock evident in her voice.

"In May, in Paris," Penn said.

"But... it's not legal in the States if you were married in France," she said, calculating something in that quick mind of hers. "You'll need a ceremony here."

Penn grinned. It was a Kensington grin that said he'd already figured that out. "We actually went to the courthouse this morning to make it official here."

"I guess we have two wedding dates now," Natalie said with a strained laugh.

I could see that she was trying to hold it together in front of our mother. I knew they had fraught history. But who fucking cared? Mommy dearest was going to have to get used to it now. Penn never did anything this rash. It was fucking great.

"A reception," my mother blurted out. "You'll let me throw a reception."

Penn and Natalie exchanged a glance. They'd already discussed this, too. That made sense if they'd had all summer to plan out this attack.

"We'd love you to," Natalie said kindly.

"Wonderful," she said. "Just wonderful."

Then, she stepped around her enormous desk and came to face her son and daughter-in-law. To my surprise, she pulled Natalie into a hug.

"It'll be great, having you in the family."

And she sounded sincere.

Natalie swallowed and nodded her head. "Thank you."

"What this means is, we need drinks," I insisted. "Have to toast the newlyweds."

My mother and Penn rolled their eyes at the exact same time. But Natalie just laughed.

"That sounds like a good time. Right, Penn?"

Penn shrugged. "I could go for a drink."

"Have one at the victory party tonight," my mother said. "We'll have two things to celebrate then."

"Oh right, the party," Penn said. His eyes cut to mine, and he arched an eyebrow. "I forgot."

"You'll have to be there to show off that pretty diamond to everyone," my mother insisted.

She tugged Natalie aside and began to discuss stuff for the reception. Already, Natalie looked overwhelmed.

"So... getting married without all the fanfare during campaign season. Nicely done, little brother."

He shook his head. "How have you been? Dealing with the arrest all right? I didn't hear much while I was gone. Charges were dropped?"

I shrugged. "Charges were never officially filed. Mom thought they were going to come back with questions for us. It was in a lot of the papers that I was getting charged. But it never panned out. Mom did the only sensible thing and hired me a publicist. Can you believe that I get to play the part of the golden boy of the Upper East Side?"

Penn snorted. "How is *that* going?"

"Surprisingly well. English is really good at her job."

"English? Anna English?"

"Yeah. You know her?"

"She's friends with Lark. I met her a few times when she was at Columbia for her JD. I thought she lived in LA."

"Yeah well, Mom wanted the best."

"Huh," Penn said. "Interesting. Well, it's good to know you're in the right hands. I can't imagine anyone making you look like the golden boy of anything."

I laughed. "Me either."

"Should we go get a drink? I think I have to rescue Natalie before she decides to divorce me on our second wedding day."

"I'm down."

I was surprised that he even wanted to go out to get drinks with me. Before he and Natalie had gotten serious, he wouldn't even talk to me. All we had done was egg each other on and yell at one another. But... it was good to have my brother back. He was the only other one who knew what it was really like to grow up a Kensington. That it wasn't as glamorous as it might seem. Instead, it was a world of fucked up bullshit. And we were the pawns being moved around the board, no matter the damage.

We might have gone overboard.

Celebrating was an official sport on the Upper East Side.

Natalie dramatically rolled her eyes as we crashed into the cab that took us uptown to the primary victory party. "Can't you boys hold your liquor?" she asked with a laugh.

"We drank a bottle, love," Penn said, nuzzling into her neck.

She giggled and swatted at him. "You're the worst."

"If you say so."

"Fuck, stop," I groaned. "You're so in love. It's disgusting."

Natalie elbowed me in the ribs. "Oh, shut up, Court. If I have to deal with your drunk ass and properly get you to Percy Tower for this party, then you can deal with our cuteness."

I held up my hands. "Fine. Continue if you must."

I wasn't even upset. I was too pleasantly intoxicated for that. Plus, I was glad that Penn was happy. After all the shit he and Natalie had gone through, I could only wish them the best.

We pulled up in front of Percy Tower and headed into the ballroom where the party was already underway. Natalie pushed our way through the crowd and miraculously to the bar. Damn, she was a good woman.

I took whatever she'd offered me, and then we meandered back to the stage area. I could see most of my friends were congregated together—Lark and Sam, Katherine and Camden, Gavin and Whitley, and... English. Our eyes met across the short distance. She looked away first, returning to her conversation with a frazzled Lark.

"Should we go over?" I asked, gesturing to the group.

Natalie stalled when her eyes settled on the lot of them. "Um, you know, I think I'm going to pass."

"I thought we were going to deal with this," Penn said.

"Yeah, but maybe not today. I don't know what Katherine is going to do."

"Nothing," I said. "She's so far up Camden's ass."

Penn frowned. "You're right. Maybe not today."

Natalie visibly relaxed and took a sip from her glass of whiskey. "So, this is an election party."

"Pretty disappointing, huh?" I asked.

She shrugged. "It's not as glamorous as I thought it'd be, considering the Upper East Side."

"That's the election night party," I told her. "Ballgowns, tuxedos, the like."

"Ah, more in line with what I'd guess."

My eyes drifted back over to my group of friends. English laughed at whatever Sam had just said. Then, she looked briefly in my direction and excused herself. Now, she was walking straight over to me. Which made no fucking sense. She'd been avoiding me like the plague, and *now*, she wanted to see me?

English's smile wasn't fake when she appeared before me. "Well, we made it," she said with exuberance. "The election results so far look favorable. It seems we held the damage to your mother's campaign at a minimum."

I arched an eyebrow at her. "That's good."

"Lark is getting a few days off after this. So, I think you'll be free, too."

"Sounds like a riot."

Penn laughed and held his hand out. "It's English, right? You're the one who has had the unfortunate job of keeping my brother in line?"

They shook.

"Yes. It's good to see you again, Penn."

"And this is my wife, Natalie. I don't believe you've met."

"Wife!" English exclaimed.

Penn laughed and ran his hand back through his hair. "Yeah. Long story."

Natalie stepped forward. "So nice to meet you."

"You, too. I've heard so much about you."

Natalie winced. "All good things, I hope."

English shrugged. "You caught Penn Kensington. What more could a girl want?"

I narrowed my eyes at her. Really? *Really?*

"Meanwhile, I've only heard good things about you," Penn said. "Court said you're the best in the business. That you're really keeping him in line. Glad that we have you working for us even if it takes you away from your life in LA. It takes a real professional to deal with Court."

Our eyes met in that second. As if she couldn't believe I'd said that about her. As if it couldn't get more awkward than being complimented on her professionalism after what had happened between us. As if she couldn't *not* look at me.

English cleared her throat and turned back to Penn. "Yes, well, not much of a life in LA anymore, to be honest. And… I'm always up for a challenge."

As was I.

"Well, I should get back," English said, nodding to Lark. "I just wanted to let you know that we have a break now that the primary is over. I'm going to figure out the plan of attack for the general election. We can go from there."

"Sure, English," I drawled. "Whatever you want."

She nodded her head and smiled at Penn and Natalie. "Really great seeing you two again."

The minute she was out of earshot, Penn rounded on me. "What is going on?"

I took a sip of my drink. "What do you mean?"

"Is there something going on between you and English?"

"No."

She'd made it pretty clear that nothing was going on.

"Are you fucking your publicist?"

"Presently?" I asked sarcastically, leaning into it as a defense mechanism. "Nope."

"Jesus Christ," Penn said with a sigh. "Please don't fuck this up."

My eyes traveled back to English and the short black dress she was wearing. The heels that made her calves and ass look spectacular as she walked away from us. Walked away from me… again.

"Don't worry about that," I said with disdain. "I'm just a client."

9

ENGLISH

Leslie Kensington won the nomination.

And it felt damn good.

I understood in that moment why Lark was her deputy campaign manager. Why she put in the long hours and gave up sleep and food and time. It felt sweet. And it made everything I'd done with Court feel worth it, too.

Or at least, *most* of what I'd done with Court.

God, I just needed to shake what had happened. We had three more months together. I still had a lot of work to do to undo years of his bad reputation. It would be hard to start with. If we kept up like this, it would be nearly impossible.

I'd taken the time that I needed away from him. I would need a lot longer to grieve my relationship with Josh. But I couldn't keep putting my life and my career on hold. Three months was all I had left. If I could keep Court out of trouble that long and make people see a sliver of what I wanted to see... I thought I could pull it off.

"English, you're supposed to be celebrating," Lark said, appearing at my side. "Not moping at the edge of our party."

I forced a smile on my face. "Just stuck on work. You know how it is."

"I do. In fact, I'm so exhausted that I think I'm hallucinating. Sam and I aren't going to survive this party long."

"You haven't slept in two weeks. You should go home with Sam."

She smiled as she found Sam's gaze. He winked at her. "Maybe you're right."

"Now, I don't think you're talking about sleep."

She laughed. "Maybe not."

My eyes drifted to Court, who stood next to Sam. He'd migrated to our circle an hour ago after leaving his brother behind. It was truly unfair that he looked so damn good, even when he was wasted drunk.

The second he shifted toward me, I looked away. Jesus, how old was I?

Lark gave me a suspicious look. "Are you okay?"

"Eh," I said reluctantly.

"You seem out of it. How are things with Josh?"

I shrugged. "Don't really want to talk about him. I'm filing for divorce."

Lark cringed. "I'm sorry, English. I really thought Josh was it."

"Me too," I whispered.

"I'm not going to say there are other fish in the sea because that's bullshit. But you're beautiful and smart and funny and successful. This isn't the end. It's just *an* end."

"Thank you, Lark," I said around a lump in my throat. "The whole thing is just a bit of a nightmare. He doesn't want to get a divorce even though he's the one who cheated. I hired an attorney back home, but fuck, I hate the whole thing."

"No judge is going to see that he cheated in the tabloids and say that you're not separated. He's just fucking with your head."

"You're right." I needed to do some classic English compartmentalization. I needed to treat Josh just like any other douchebag client. Except bury him instead of try to save him. "You're a lifesaver."

"Always here to help."

"Now, I need another drink, so I can forget about this conversation."

Lark laughed. "I think I'm going to find Sam and get out of here. Get drunk with Whitley and Katherine and the guys. It'll be good for you to cut loose."

I nearly choked. Cutting loose was the last thing I needed. I'd done that, and I was still uncertain about the results.

Lark patted my shoulder once and then walked over to Sam. He oriented himself to her movements. He took her hand and kissed it, nodding along to whatever she was saying. Then he smiled a genuine smile and tilted his head toward the door.

I could feel Court looking at me. His gaze sliding down my face and over my shoulders, down my black dress. It was so intimate that I could practically feel his hands on me. But I wouldn't meet his eyes. I still watched Lark and Sam as they disappeared through the crowd. Then, before I could make the mistake of looking at him, I turned away and headed to the nearest bar.

The victory party was well under way. Leslie had given her speech ages ago, and I hadn't seen her since. Everyone was drunk. And either I needed to join them or I just needed to leave like Lark.

Except going home to an empty house sounded less than ideal.

I stepped into the short drink line. Thankfully, it didn't take too long before I ordered.

"A shot of tequila and a gin and tonic. Light on the tonic."

The bartender frowned. "We're not doing shots."

I slipped a twenty into the tip jar. "I'll take a shot of tequila and a gin and tonic."

She shrugged and began to pour.

"Make that two shots."

"Court," I murmured.

He grinned that wicked grin and tossed a second twenty into the tip jar. "English."

"What are you doing?" I hissed.

He shrugged. "Enjoying myself. It is a victory party after all. We're here to celebrate."

The bartender placed the two shots before us. She plunked down two limes and gestured to the salt.

"Shall we toast?" he asked mischievously.

"To what?"

"The primary victory, of course."

"Of course," I said, perfectly neutral.

He reached for the shot of tequila and held it aloft. I mirrored his movements, wondering exactly how drunk he was. He was practically swaying on his feet. It took *a lot* of alcohol to make someone like Court Kensington sway.

"To another three months," I muttered as we clinked our plastic cups together.

He grinned like the devil he was and then tipped the shot back into his mouth. I took a deep breath and then followed suit. The tequila burned like the fiery pits of hell all the way down my throat. I managed not to cough. But I reached for the lime like a drowning man searched for air.

I sucked on the sliver of fruit, letting the lime juice soothe my throat. Court just watched. He didn't even bother with his own lime. So, I stole his, too. He quirked another smile in my direction.

"A little too much for you?" he asked softly.

"Tequila is the worst," I told him, tossing the second lime. "But it does work the best."

"Hmm," he muttered.

I grasped my gin and tonic and stepped away from the bar.

This was good. This was fine. We could talk like regular adults and be around each other and not rip each other's clothes off. It was... functional. Sort of.

Court's hand came to my elbow. "Can I talk to you?"

Fire skittered from my elbow and all the way through my body. Okay, maybe less than functional. He shouldn't be able to cause that reaction just from touching me.

"Can't we just get drunk and celebrate the victory?" I asked, half a plea.

"Yes. But first, come with me."

I should have protested more.

There was exactly one reason why walking out of this room and being alone with Court Kensington was a bad idea. And it had something to do with being bent over the couch at his apartment.

I shivered at the memory.

"Cold?" he asked as he pushed open a side door that led backstage.

"No."

"I was going to be gallant and give you my jacket."

I narrowed my eyes at him. "You're not a white knight."

He shrugged. "Even villains can be generous."

I had nothing to say to that.

He gestured for me to enter first, which I did despite my better judgment.

"Where are we going?" I asked.

He took my hand and pulled me down the empty hallway.

"I've known Camden my entire life. You think I don't know his hotels like the back of my hand?"

"How well do you know the back of your hand?"

He grinned at me. "You're cheeky."

"You're drunk."

"Guilty," he said with a glint of light in his blue irises. He stopped in front of a dark door. "Here we are."

"And where is here?"

He jiggled the door, and when it didn't immediately open, he pulled out a credit card and swiped the lock.

"Court! What are you doing?" I gasped. "Isn't this illegal? Breaking and entering?"

"My best friend *owns* the hotel, English. Who is going to press charges?"

I grumbled under my breath. He had a point. But Jesus Christ, could he go a week without doing something illegal?

He pushed the door open and flipped the lights. I nervously checked behind me before following him inside. I'd been on enough film sets to know what this room functioned as—a green room.

I stepped inside, my eyes wide as I took in the space. It was nicer than most of the on-site locations I'd been to. With fancy couches and chairs, a few secluded desks, and a full kitchen. I could see what it would look like when the place was full of creatives, buzzing with people and energy and, most importantly, food. Lots of food.

"This feels like home," I admitted.

"Yeah, it's mostly film stars and politicians and dignitaries and the like when they have business in the city," Court said. "I thought you'd like it."

"Why?"

"Okay, I just wanted to get you alone."

"Ah. Well, I suppose you've succeeded," I said with a shrug. "And now, we can go."

"Come on, English," he said, reaching for me.

I sidestepped him. "We have three more months to work together. We have to be professional."

"We weren't the other night."

"That was a lapse in judgment. I had never slept with a client before. And I'm never doing it again," I said as sternly as possible. "I was upset about what had happened with Josh, and I took it out on you."

"I didn't really mind."

"Yeah... I might have noticed that."

He stepped closer to me. My breathing hitched. There was something in just that small movement as he got into my personal space, and I looked up into those baby blues. Fuck.

"I don't think you minded either." His fingers brushed a stray hair out of my face.

I swatted him away from me and took a step back. I rasped in a sharp breath that felt like I'd just been dunked in a bucket of ice water.

"Be serious," I said.

"Be a little less serious. We had a good time. Let's do it again."

"So, that's why you brought me back here." I'd already known that. I'd come anyway. But now that I was here, I couldn't do it.

"Don't act like you don't want it, English. I know that you do."

"You don't know anything about me," I snapped back.

"Sure I do."

"Okay. What's my middle name?" I laughed. "What's my first?"

"Anna," he purred, stepping forward.

I shivered again at the way he'd said my name. My first name. No one called me Anna. Not my parents or my boss or my friends. Just people who didn't know me. And now, apparently, Court Kensington.

His eyes assessed my reaction though. "Anna," he said again, drawing out the word like a caress. "See, I know the important things. Like that little whimper you make when my tongue touches your clit. Or..."

I held up a hand and swallowed. “I get it. But... no. I don’t want that.”

“You’re such a good liar,” he said, tilting his head as he examined me. “I almost believe you.”

“It’s the truth.”

“How often do you lie a day?”

Too many. My entire job was lying to people. I couldn’t even get through a meal without lying to someone.

“I’m convincing people you’re a good person. How often do you think?”

He laughed. “Enough.”

“But I’m not lying about this.”

“Yeah, sure.”

But he didn’t believe me. Fuck, I was a good liar, but I didn’t even believe me. Fucking Court Kensington had been the most amazing high I’d ever been on... and I had grown up in Hollywood.

He stepped closer. “Do you want to have sex with me again?”

“No,” I lied.

Court laughed. “Lie. I’m getting better at detecting them. Did you have a good time when we fucked?”

I gritted my teeth. “If I say yes, will it make your head bigger?”

“Can it get any bigger?”

I snorted. “Now, that is something I know. It cannot.”

“Is this why you’ve been avoiding me then?”

“I haven’t been avoiding you. I’ve been busy.”

“Another lie, Anna.”

I took a deep breath and let it out. “Look, you might have a lot of one-night stands. You probably fucked around the whole time you were with Jane. From what I hear, you two weren’t even that serious. This is all your MO. I get it. But this isn’t me,” I said with a shrug.

Court took a step back. Something in his face shuttered. As if my words had hit home, and his fun, lighthearted, drunken persona evaporated.

"Okay. Yeah, fine. Don't want to compromise your integrity," he drawled. Somehow, he'd reverted into that Upper East Side prick I'd first met.

"I… yeah," I said, off guard.

"No problem."

"Court, are you taking this seriously?"

"If that's what you want, English," he said, a bite on my name, "then fine. We can be professional."

And suddenly, I felt as if I wasn't on solid footing. I didn't like the way he'd said my name. I didn't like the way he'd somehow flipped it around. As if I was the person doing something wrong.

But before I could say anything, he wrenched the door open and walked through it. Leaving me alone in the green room, wondering what the fuck had just happened.

10

ENGLISH

I still had no clue what had happened that day in the green room. But I must have gotten through to Court because he'd been nothing if not professional from that moment on. Stiff and unyielding like he'd never been before that. I'd take that over the possibility of sleeping with him again.

We were on a schedule now. I'd agreed to help Winnie out with any of her New York City clients if she needed them. And thankfully, that kept me busier now that Court was mostly out of the water. We still had events planned in the upcoming months, but I'd taken a step back. The press had worked in our favor. Moving too fast wouldn't garner more favor. It would just look desperate.

Kind of like this fucking shark in front of me.

"Hour's up," I ground out as my alarm went off.

"I feel like we just got started," Mandy said with a grin.

I hated that I'd had to agree to do this interview to get that picture of me and Court taken down. Of course, the picture of us together had run for less than an hour and had gone viral. Because nothing was ever much removed from the internet.

I pressed the button on her recorder. I knew all the tricks. I'd employed them myself.

"Have a good day," I said, standing and reaching for my purse.

"I'm surprised, you know."

I frowned and ignored her. I wouldn't rise to the bait.

"That you're sleeping with Court. That he's just a 'client.' " Mandy put quotes around the word.

I glanced down, wondering where the second recorder was. I glared back at her. "I said, one hour. We talked about Josh. We're through."

She laughed and held her hands up. "Can't blame me for trying."

"Can't I?" I asked.

"Nice doing business with you."

I gritted my teeth as I ventured out of her office and out onto the Manhattan streets. I hailed a cab and felt like I hadn't breathed the entire time I was inside. The interview had gone well. Well enough at least.

I knew how to control the situation, but I wasn't used to being the one answering questions. At least, not unless I answered them for clients. I'd almost thought that I should have Winnie out here for this. But it felt ridiculous. I was more than capable. I just wasn't... objective about Josh like I was about the douchebags who fucked around on my clients or vice versa.

I probably should have told Josh that I was doing the interview. It'd have been the considerate thing to do. Speaking to the press was taboo. I doubted he ever considered that I'd do it. But... it hadn't actually been for me. It was to protect Court. He was a client, and that picture could do lasting damage to the campaign, which was the whole reason I'd been hired.

I needed to shake the interview off. I had another one

planned in Greenwich Village. And unfortunately, it was going to be even worse than the one with Mandy.

This one was with my sister.

Taylor English sat with her back to the rest of the coffee shop. Not smart or anything I'd ever do, but I could pick her out by her long black-to-blue-tipped hair that was gently curled at the ends. She looked like she fit in at The New School with a sketchbook open on the table and another notebook opened that she was scribbling notes into. She had three half-finished cups of tea—because she didn't drink coffee—and a small scone. I was sure it was vegan. She'd picked that up a few years ago after doing an art project on slaughterhouses.

I ordered a latte and then headed to her table.

"Hey, Tay," I said, managing a smile as I plopped into the seat opposite her.

"Oh," she said, looking up at me. "Hi, Anna."

"How's school going?"

Taylor made an indistinct noise. "I don't know. It's only the second week. We've just been going over the syllabus in every class."

"Right. I remember those days. So... this is just... recreational?" I gestured to her notebooks.

She slammed the sketchbook closed and shoved it into her messenger bag. "It's nothing."

"Okay," I said, frustrated. This was how it always went with Taylor.

"So, like, did Dad send you to check on me?" Taylor asked. Her ice-blue eyes mirrored mine even if she looked nothing like me otherwise.

"Yeah, so? I'm here."

"I don't need a babysitter."

"That's good because I have enough people to babysit and only one sister."

She wrinkled her pert nose. "Oh yeah, your *clients*."

It came out as a sneer. She wanted to offend me. So, I was purposely not offended.

"Yep. Always pretty busy at work."

"I don't know how you even work there."

We'd had this conversation before. My dad hated my job, too. It had clearly rubbed off on Taylor. I didn't need to justify it to them. But it would be nice for someone in my family to be proud of what I'd accomplished.

"Pretty easy. I'm good at cleaning up messes."

"Just not in your own life," Taylor quipped.

I nearly bit right back at her. But it was true. Look at Josh. We were in the midst of a divorce. Meanwhile, he was trying to drag me through the wringer because he didn't want the divorce. And then there was Court, which I had no idea how to fix or if we even needed to be fixed. Plus, my family… which, as much as I'd tried, I had never been able to figure out.

I shrugged one shoulder. "Sure."

"You know I don't need you checking in on me."

"Okay."

"So, don't bother," Taylor said huffily.

"All right," I said. "I do care though, Taylor. I'm not just here because of Dad."

"This is supposed to be my new start," Taylor said with a sigh. "I don't need anything to make me different here."

I glanced around the coffee shop. Everyone looked a little *different* here. A little less Hollywood, a little more New York City. Dark and haunted and tortured. Angsty, edgy, and artistic. The darkness to my light. I'd always fit in in LA. Maybe a little too well. But New York seemed to favor Taylor. I understood wanting to fit in.

Then my gaze snagged on the TV. A face appeared that I recognized—Jane Devney.

Court's ex-girlfriend and her Upper East Side alias. Her real name was Janine Lehmann, and she was a dual German-

French citizen who had stolen more money than God from banks all over the world. All with the force of her personality. She had conned Court for two years while they dated and stolen I didn't even know how much money from his trust fund.

The very reason that I had been hired to help Court's image.

I leaned forward to read what was scrolling across the bottom of the news channel.

Jane Devney, pseudonym to Janine Lehmann, refuses a plea deal and pleads not guilty to charges of grand larceny and fraud. A court date has been set for December 10.

"Fuck," I spat, jumping to my feet.

"What?" Taylor asked. She turned to look at the television. "What's going on?"

"I have to go."

"Go? Where are you going?"

"Work," I said, grasping my bag. "I have to get back uptown. We could meet up again... later."

Taylor rolled her eyes. "Don't bother. I know that work comes first."

And it did. It had to.

"Maybe you'll understand one day. Maybe you won't," I said with raised eyebrows. "Enjoy school. Keep your head down."

"Whatever."

I wished there were a way to make this better between us. But it certainly couldn't happen over forced coffee. And it wouldn't happen when I had to deal with Court first. He was the priority. No matter what was going on with Taylor.

I dashed into the first cab, stealing it from another couple who yelled at me. But my need was great. I called Court and texted and called again. He never answered. I knew he was out with Gavin for their weekly lunch, which mostly consisted of drinking. But he should have his phone on him. The last thing I wanted was for someone to ask him about Jane without him knowing about it, without me talking with him first.

"Fuck, fuck, fuck," I murmured. I leaned forward. "Can we go any faster? I can pay."

The woman shrugged and turned down the next alley. Soon, we were zipping through the streets. She drove like a maniac, but right now, that was what I needed. I felt frantic. It was the worst time of day for me to be in Greenwich Village when I needed to be in Midtown.

It was an interminable amount of time before the cab screeched to a halt in front of the St. Regis. Thankfully, Court had a routine, and he lunched here every Wednesday. King Cole Bar was a staple for the business types. Dorset & King, the oil company Gavin ran in the city, had their New York headquarters nearby. Occasionally, they went to The Mark or Casa Lever, but I remembered Court had said something about St. Regis, and I was betting on it since he hadn't fucking returned my call.

I walked through the lobby and straight into the restaurant and bar, bypassing the receptionist, who looked put out.

"Excuse me, miss. Can I help you? Do you have a reservation? Are you meeting someone?" she asked, hustling behind me.

"No. I'm fine. Thank you."

Then, I continued forward as she followed me. Everyone looked alike here. So many two-thousand-dollar business suits and musky cologne. Don Draper from *Mad Men* could have stepped straight into this place. There was not a single other female. It was disorienting.

Then, I found Court sitting opposite Gavin. They had dirty martinis in front of them. Gavin laughed at whatever Court had just said. There were four other men with them, who I'd never met before. Though one of them looked familiar. I couldn't place him though. Robert something?

I inhaled and then exhaled. At least I wore a sensible black dress and heels. I couldn't appear frazzled to these men. They ate that for breakfast.

Gavin's cunning eyes saw me first. He ran a hand back through his reddish brown hair and then jumped up. "English, love!"

"Gavin King." I winked at him. "Just look at you."

Court whipped around. His eyes narrowed in confusion. I hadn't interrupted his guy time like this since I investigated his monthly poker game with Camden.

Gavin stepped around the table and drew me into a hug. "To what do we owe the pleasure? You look smoking hot. Has anyone told you that today?"

I laughed. "Actually, no, they haven't."

"I'm not saying that I'm happy that you'll soon be single," he said with a wink. "But… when you're ready to date, you know who to ask."

"Is that right?"

Court's frown deepened. "I wasn't expecting you."

Gavin smacked Court's arm. "Fucking manners, Kensington. Shouldn't we introduce her around?"

"Oh, that's not necessary," I said, all business. "I'm just here to steal Court away from you all."

"Why?" Court asked suspiciously.

"When a beautiful woman asks to steal you, you don't ask why," Gavin said with a laugh.

Court looked like he was going to object, but he gracefully rose to his feet. He looked… stupid good in a gray Tom Ford suit. He tugged his jacket forward, pulling it taut against his broad shoulders and buttoning the top button. He grasped the martini in front of him and drained it.

"Gentlemen," he said casually. "Business awaits."

They laughed and said their farewells. He shook hands

with the familiar-looking guy—Robert something—and then Gavin.

"Poker tomorrow?" Gavin asked.

"I'll see you there."

"Don't have too much fun."

Court shot him his inimitable grin. "Don't I always?"

Then, he gestured for me to precede him out of the restaurant. I glanced left and right, making sure no press had flagged him down before me, and then hustled him into his awaiting black car. I didn't relax until the rest of Manhattan fell away with the snap of the car door.

"What's going on, English?" he asked curtly. "I thought you had planned to let me live my life how I saw fit. That was a rather important luncheon."

"Jane," I whispered, hating it.

He froze. His entire body stiffened. "What about Jane?"

I swallowed. Fuck, I hated this.

"She refused a plea deal. They just scheduled her trial for December 10. I'm sorry, Court. I had to get you out of there."

11

COURT

I had no words.

I couldn't believe that Jane hadn't taken a plea deal. She wasn't stupid. In fact, she was incredibly smart. That was how she had swindled her way into my life and the Upper East Side. She couldn't think that a trial was going to be more favorable to her. If they kept digging through everything she had done, it could only get worse from there.

And even though she had wrecked my life—used it and abused it and completely fucked it all up—for a moment, I wanted to protect her. Tell her not to do this. But I couldn't do that. I couldn't speak to her.

Not that I'd even know what to say to her. But it would look horrible.

I hadn't seen her since the night of Natalie's party when we were arrested together. Jane had gone catatonic. She hadn't even told me what was going on.

Though she had confessed to someone at a later date that I'd had no clue about what she had been doing. I was thankful that she'd admitted the truth. And wondered why the hell she'd done it. Any of it. Why me?

"Court, say something," English said gently.

Too gently for her. She wasn't gentle. She was fierce and hard and determined. Not… this.

"Why didn't she take the deal?" I asked, my eyes cold and empty as I turned to look at her.

She straightened at that look. "I don't know. I just heard about it on the news."

"You haven't even heard it from a lawyer or the source or anything?"

She shook her head. "I wanted to get to you as soon as possible. I figured if we just got you out of the public eye, then we could formulate what we were going to say while we figured everything else out."

"God," I groaned. "Just… who the fuck is representing her? Are they even doing their fucking job if they told her not to take the plea deal?"

Her head tilted slightly. I could see something shift in her expression. This wasn't what she had been expecting from me. After her assessment of my previous relationship at the primary victory, I shouldn't have been surprised. I didn't correct people's initial judgments of me. It was easier to let them think the worst.

"Does it matter?" she finally asked.

I turned back to face forward. "I guess not."

She opened her mouth like she was going to say something. Maybe offer me an apology. But I didn't want to hear it.

"Let's just get back to my place and then talk."

She closed her mouth and didn't say another word until we pulled up in front of my building. I couldn't believe that there were already two or maybe three news people with cameras set up in front of my apartment. It had been months since Jane and I were arrested. Why did they even care?

"If any press approach us, just say *no comment*," she said before pushing the door open.

We stepped onto the sidewalk and were immediately accosted.

"Court, we just heard that Jane Devney refused to take the plea deal. Can you comment on why she did this?" a reporter asked.

"Are you going to be at the trial?" another asked.

"Have you spoken to her about her thought process?" the first one butted back in, shoving the microphone in my face.

"Let him through," English snarled. She was a force, walking through the press with her head held high and her gait exaggerated. "No questions. Just let us through."

"Court, can you tell us how you feel about Jane's impending trial?"

"No comment," I said brusquely and then followed English into the building.

She hurried forward as if the press was going to come after us and jammed her finger on the elevator button. We stepped in together. I sighed and slumped back against the wall when the doors closed. But she was a ball of anxiety and energy, impatiently tapping her foot as we soared upward.

When the doors opened into my apartment, she marched inside like a drill sergeant. And I went straight for the wet bar.

"Can't you do anything but drink?" she snapped irritably.

I ignored her and poured myself a double.

"I need you sober right now."

I held the glass up to her and swallowed half of it in one gulp.

She narrowed her eyes and began to pace. "We're going to have to figure out what the hell to do about this. We need to get our story straight. Then, we're going to need to plan an interview with a sympathetic journalist. Probably do something drastic that puts you in the spotlight in a positive way."

"English, could you just stop for one minute?" I asked as I sank into the couch.

She stilled and looked at me, as if just realizing where we were. She hadn't been here since the night we fucked. Her cheeks flushed, and she looked away.

"Can you find out what happened?"

She nodded. "I'm already on it. I was texting with a few people who could get me an in on the situation. I should have answers before we leave again."

I blew out a breath. "Has my mother been informed?"

"Yes. I spoke with her assistant." She frowned. "And Lark."

"You did all that when we were in the car?"

She shrugged one shoulder. "It's my job."

She'd been all high focus while I'd been silently freaking the fuck out.

"How do we fix this?" I managed to get out as I finished my drink and set it down on the table.

"The important thing is that we get ahead of it. Two, maybe three press people downstairs, we can handle. We need to get a statement out as soon as possible. Something short and sweet and sympathetic. And then we need a big splash. Something that screams golden boy."

I snorted. "Good luck with that."

"I can put together an interview and photo shoot. I think that will help, but it's not enough. It's not flashy. Like when we had the charity donation—that was flashy."

"You want me to give away more money?"

I didn't care about the money. The donation had been a good idea. No, a great idea. I'd played lacrosse my whole life. Had even played at Harvard. But I never would have thought of funding the rec league in the city.

"I mean... no. I don't think that would work here."

"Then what?"

She paused, turning slowly to face me again. She put her index finger to her lip and touched it there one, two, three times. I could see her considering. And all I could think about was how I wanted to drag that bottom lip into my mouth. Fuck, I needed to think of something else. She'd made her position perfectly clear.

"I have an idea," she mused aloud.

"Why do I have a feeling that I'm not going to like it?"

"I don't think it matters. We need something big. Something that will make people look twice."

"My feelings don't matter. Got it."

She narrowed her eyes. "That's not what I meant. We'd never do anything you weren't expressly comfortable with. But comfort is a degree when it comes to maintaining an image."

"Okay. What's the idea?" I asked, certain that explanation only made it worse.

"You go back to working for Kensington Corporation."

My back stiffened. "No."

"Just think about it. We can pitch it as the prodigal son returns to his company. A destiny or fate sort of thing. We can say that you're on the road to taking it back over. Following in your family's footsteps. It's a perfect picture of the golden boy of the Upper East Side."

English was so smart. But sometimes, she asked all the wrong questions. Always the *what*, but never the *why*. But my feelings were irrelevant. She had made that clear.

"I see the picture you're painting. But no one will buy it. I left the company five years ago and never looked back," I told her.

"They'll believe whatever the fuck we tell them to believe. You a have bachelor's in economics from Harvard. You stayed to get an MBA and worked for the company for a couple years. We'll say you left to pursue your own endeavors, to get your own experience, and are ready to come home."

I narrowed my eyes. "All of that is bullshit."

She sighed. "Fine. Then give me something better. Give me something that spells *golden boy*. That says they don't need to ask you about your ex-girlfriend who is going to be on trial for grand larceny!"

"I don't know," I grunted.

"I'll take anything. If this were Hollywood, I could invent things that made you look good. But the Upper East Side is different than Hollywood. No one would believe a charity benefit or a trip to a third world country. We can't spin it so that this is somehow for a role. We can't give your mother an illness because we're working in her favor. Court, it has to be something big."

There was something. But it wasn't big enough. And… I didn't want anyone to know anyway. It belonged to me. In a way that little else did.

I set my jaw. But fuck, I didn't want to work for the company. I could give her this thing I'd held back. Put the last piece of myself on display for the media. I just didn't want to. It would be worse than going back to Kensington Corp. and dicking around with investments for a few months.

"There's nothing," I lied.

She frowned back at me. As if she could see *my* lie this time.

"I think this could work. If you're willing," she finally said.

"Fine," I said on a sigh. Serving up my life on a silver platter. "I'll do it."

12

ENGLISH

I knew that Court didn't want to go back to work for Kensington Corporation. But once he was all in, he was all in.

We'd met with his mother, who had been ecstatic about the decision. She'd wanted one of her boys to take over the company ever since their father died seven years prior. But neither of them had had any interest. Leslie saw this as the first step toward that dream.

She'd even spoken to the board for us and secured him a position. I didn't even really know what they did precisely. Something to do with investments and banking. They made a lot of money. That was for sure.

Court would have a corner office on the top floor. Apparently, it had been vacant for years, as it was reserved for a Kensington. I wondered how long it would have stayed open before they decided against that. But I was glad for it now. It would look better to do the announcement tomorrow out of his office, which I'd hired an interior designer to whip into shape.

"What do you think?" I asked Court as we walked around the space with the designer.

Court shrugged. "As long as I have an enormous desk and a full library, then I'll be happy."

The interior designer took notes. "I wasn't sure about the library, but I'll have my people in right away to begin."

"It will all be ready by tomorrow?" I asked.

She nodded. "Definitely. I'll have the entire staff on site, working all night to get this set up. Anything else?"

I checked my watch. "No. We're running late. Come on, Court. We need to get to your next appointment."

He stood in the center of the room, gazing out the enormous glass windows to the city streets below. He was in a black suit and blue tie that matched his eyes. His demeanor seemed to shift in the space. It was as if I was seeing the man who had bent me over the side of the couch and held my hair back so I'd arch into him. The commanding man who could run this business if he chose and not the one we were pretending could.

"This will do," he finally said.

Then, he turned to face me. Strong, assertive, powerful. *This* was Court Kensington.

He smiled at me. My knees went weak. All my own bluster and strength fled in the wake of that smile.

"Shall we, English?"

I nodded.

But he led the way out.

Evelyn Rothschild obliged us with a second interview for her society magazine. I was pretty sure that she would do anything to get at Court again. Our first interview had been a tour of Kensington Cottage in the Hamptons. A chaste affair where I'd dressed him like a prep-school knockout. All class and charm. The video had gone viral, plastering his pretty face all over the internet.

Evelyn had wanted to see more of him. I'd cashed in that favor.

"Remember, keep it casual. Stick to the prepared questions," I told her. "Your readers will eat him up."

"I know how to do my job," she said with that Cheshire cat smile that said I didn't really want to get in bed with her.

"I'm well aware."

"But off the record, was he really involved with his ex's schemes?"

I narrowed my eyes at her. "If you ask him that, I will pull this entire shoot and blacklist you from celebs in all of New York City."

"You don't have that sway," she bit out.

"Try me," I snarled.

Fear pricked at her. It helped that I was at least six inches taller than her and could stare down at her over my nose.

"I wasn't going to ask," she said hastily. "It was just a joke between two girls."

I was saved from answering by the appearance of Court Kensington. Evelyn wasn't the only one who stared helplessly as he stepped into the room as if straight off of the cover of *GQ*.

I'd hired the same hair and makeup team as his last interview. And I'd brought in a stylist who had combed through his closet and brought in a few complementary pieces. Inherently, I'd known that he was going to look good... the best. He had to look the best for this. But I hadn't prepared myself for it.

For the dark hair that had been perfectly styled. None of his messy waves from him running his fingers through it. I couldn't even tell that he had makeup on, but whatever they'd done highlighted all the best features. Especially those blue eyes. They were usually such a radiating ocean blue. But now, they seared me with their intensity. The dark, mysterious depths of the ocean. Waves crashed in those eyes, and I was the one pulled under by his current.

He had a few outfits, but we'd started him off in a debonair three-piece navy-blue suit that the stylist had taken one look at and actually shrieked with delight. It had been handmade from Savile Row in London, fit to his incredible form, and paired with brown oxfords that likely cost more than my parents' house back in the Valley. The full effect was dazzling.

Neither of us spoke.

He just arched his eyebrow. "I'll take that to mean I look all right."

Evelyn cleared her throat. "Yes. You look wonderful." She coughed again. "Let me introduce you to the photographer."

"By all means," he said. His attention shifted just briefly from Evelyn up to me, and he smirked.

I knew what that look meant. And it made me want to gouge his eyes out. The cheeky little shit.

I took a deep breath and then followed them over to where the photo shoot was taking place. Evelyn had whipped all of this together in two days, and it looked good. Exactly the kind of Upper East Side sophistication I'd wanted. And as he stepped into the space, he took over the room. God, when he tried, it was as if he were a different person.

The photographer, Alejandro, started in on his subject. He was a professional. The best we could get on short notice. But after only a few minutes in Alejandro's care, all my fears evaporated. Not only was Alejandro exceptional at his job, but Court also acted like he had been in front of a camera his whole life.

It made me wonder what Court could have done with his life if he'd just cared an ounce more. If he'd planned to use his MBA. If he'd liked anything as much as drinking and partying. If he'd just tried.

I'd grown up with a whole lot of nothing. I'd had to claw my way up the social ladder. I'd faked my way into parties and meetings. My ability to lie like a pro had always come in handy. And still, even when I belonged, I kept reaching for more,

more, more. I wanted everything and then some. I wasn't content with success. I had to have it all.

And yet, I had always been attracted to these kinds of guys. The ones who were the hot fucking assholes. The gorgeous model in LA who thought his looks and cocaine habit would make him a star. The party-hard rock star who could make out only three chords but had *the look*. The douche actor who had been in three commercials and thought he would be the next Brad Pitt just because a few people had said he looked like him.

I'd thought it was a miracle when I met Josh. He was different. He was going places. Sure, he partied with the rest of us, but he was never out of control. And he'd made me want to rise to my full potential. I had already been working for Poise, but the years with Josh was when I hadn't just climbed; I'd soared.

It was still hard to believe that he'd been stupid enough to sleep with Celeste. To ruin it all.

I shook my head to clear my thoughts. I didn't need to think about any of this. Not about the ex-douchebags or Josh or even Court. Because that wasn't happening again with Court. I was forcing ambition on Court Kensington. It wasn't the same thing as him having any himself.

Court changed his outfit for the third time, and we moved into another space. This with a plain white background. Just Court and the camera.

I'd been working through most of the photo shoot, but when he came back out in a black suit and light blue shirt with no tie, my eyes lingered longer than they should have.

They lingered.

And lingered.

I slipped my phone back into my purse and watched the magic. It was unfair how attractive he was. Just unfair to the rest of humanity.

"Okay," Alejandro said in his thick accent. "Now, take the jacket off."

Court's eyes slipped to mine. I didn't say anything. Didn't stop him. But my mouth went dry as he casually removed his jacket and slung it over his shoulder as if he'd done this his whole life.

"Excellent. Now, the shirt."

"Wait," I said, my throat tight. "We didn't agree on shirtless. This is a business shoot."

Evelyn shrugged. "One or two couldn't hurt. The readers will die for it."

Court waited. His eyes back on me. "Your call, English."

I frowned. I didn't want him to do the shirtless shoot. I wasn't sure that it gave the right appearance. That it said what we were going for. But at the same time, I wanted to see him shirtless. My mind had been wandering there the entire time I'd seen him in those suits. Who wouldn't be wondering the same thing?

"Just one," I told Evelyn. "Don't use any more than one."

She nodded hungrily. "All right. Just one."

I nodded at Court. My throat bobbed. I had to watch him unbutton each individual button on that shirt. Slow, methodical, and so, so tempting. Revealing every inch of powerful chest and abdomen.

I shifted uncomfortably as I remembered how eager I'd been to get to that six-pack and run my hands lower. What exactly I'd wanted to do... and actually done after that.

He stripped out of his shirt and effortlessly tossed it off to the side. I heard Evelyn suck in a breath. I already wasn't breathing. It was an agonizing few minutes as Alejandro worked his magic.

Then, he rose to his feet and nodded. "Perfection. We have what we need."

"Great!" Evelyn said. "That's a wrap."

And over her short head, Court's attention returned to

mine. Our eyes said everything and nothing, all at once. Desire smoldered there. And I wasn't sure that mine didn't answer.

I hated the arrogant prick who thought he could take what he wanted in that moment. And I wanted him all the same. The heat pooling in my core was enough to say just how much I fucking wanted him.

Court broke the contact, reaching for his shirt and slinging it back on. Evelyn bustled over to him, talking in hushed tones and giggling like a schoolgirl. He righted his shirt and then jacket. But his smile was as genuine as I'd ever seen it as he indulged her. And I had to watch.

The interview was short and scripted. She'd done exactly what she'd said she would do. And for that, I was grateful. I was still reeling from the photo shoot and the new vision I had of Court Kensington stripping in front of me.

"Well, thank you so much, Mr. Kensington," Evelyn said coquettishly as I waited nearby to vacate the building.

"Please, Evelyn, call me Court."

She flushed. "Court. Of course."

"Actually, do you think I could get your number? It'd be nice to have it in case we need to meet and go over the interview again."

My eyes rounded in shock. Was he... asking her out? In front of me?

Evelyn giggled again. "I think I have a business card here somewhere." Then, she produced one so swiftly that I was certain she had been waiting for the moment to hand it to him all along.

"A pleasure." He dipped down and kissed her hand.

"As always, Court."

Then, he smiled indulgently again and walked back over to me. "Ready, English?"

A frown had taken up residence on my lips, and I carefully

pulled it back into neutrality. "Yes. Let's get out of here. We need to prepare for the announcement still."

We stepped out of the photo shoot and into an elevator. Court swiped the business card back and forth across his palm with a shit-eating grin on his face.

"So, you think I have a chance?" he asked me.

"With what?"

"Evelyn."

I arched my eyebrows at him. "Seems too easy, if I'm being honest."

"You think so?"

His eyes smoldered on me. So bright and all-knowing.

Bastard.

"I think we should concentrate on the announcement tomorrow. That matters more than your dating life."

He laughed, cool and calculating. "I think I'll still call her."

"You do that," I said, feigning indifference.

"Unless there's a reason I shouldn't."

"Besides her being a journalist?"

"Besides that, yes."

"Can't think of anything," I said plainly.

He smirked. As if he knew exactly what I was thinking. And then slid the business card into my purse and not his pocket.

13

COURT

The office was abuzz, and yet it was all white noise. Just a whirl of activity that I couldn't process. Camera crew setting up for the shot, lighting blinding my new desk, hair and makeup floating about, a flurry of very important people for the company chattering behind the spotlight. It all felt... surreal.

I couldn't believe we'd whipped all of this together in a matter of days. The photo shoot and interview that would release, following this announcement. The interior designers had practically re-created my father's office down to the desk I stood before and the circular rug under my feet.

It made me want to vomit.

Had someone given them a picture? It had to have been deliberate. It was too coincidental. I suspected my mother od tampering. It wasn't English's style.

The world felt as if it were dropping away under my feet. I was going to hyperventilate. I hadn't had a panic attack in years. I'd been sober too long. I needed a drink. I needed... something.

Then, a figure emerged out of the mayhem. Penn stepped

forward and stood next to me in the glaring light. He reached his hand out. A gesture of goodwill. I shook his hand.

"How are you holding up?" Penn asked.

I released his hand and then straightened. I needed to leash this. I'd thought I had it under control. That his ghost couldn't touch me.

"Well, I didn't ask for Dad's desk," I said hoarsely.

"Mother's handiwork?"

"Who else?"

"Can I ask why you're doing this?" Penn asked hesitantly.

I could see that my little brother thought I was insane to fall back into the Kensington mold that I'd done my hardest to avoid. He meant well. Even if it wasn't helpful in this moment.

I shrugged. "I'm helping the campaign."

"You don't care about the campaign or if our mother wins it."

He wasn't wrong.

"Eh… maybe."

"But why? I can't figure it out. It's not in your own self-interest."

"Are you saying the only things I'm capable of are in my own self-interest?"

Penn tilted his head. "I'm a moral philosopher. I think that about nearly everyone, but I know that about you."

"If you know everything already, then does it even matter? It must be in my own self-interest," I responded blandly.

I'd thought it would be good to have Penn at my side. We'd spent so many fucking years arguing that it was nice having a brother again. Except for this bullshit.

"You left after Dad left and never looked back. How is this your own self-interest?"

My mounting anxiety hit a peak, and Penn was the only one standing in its wake. "Don't pretend you know or care what I went through after Dad died," I responded low and feral.

Penn took a step back at my anger. "Ah… so, you're still in there."

"You're the one bringing up the past like you always do."

"Some people find the past illuminating for the future. I guess I should have as well," he muttered. "I'm heading off to the Hamptons for the weekend with the crew. Good luck with this madness."

Then, before I could respond, Penn strode straight past the camera crew, our mother, and out the door. He'd never had much tolerance for me, let alone Kensington Corporation. Apparently, I'd hit the max for him.

"All right," English said. She strode toward me with her fake business smile plastered on her face. "Good to go?"

"Sure."

She kept that smile on her face, even as her eyes softened. "Everything okay with Penn? That seemed kind of intense."

"You've met my brother. All conversations with him are intense."

"True. Are you still feeling confident? You seem a bit… pale."

I wanted to tell her. It was my father's desk. I didn't want his desk. But what the fuck could she do about it at this point? She wasn't going to cancel everything we'd set up because the desk was familiar.

"Just a lot of lights," I lied.

She frowned and then leaned forward, turning us so that no one else could see what we were saying. "Court, are you sure you want to do this?"

"Yeah."

Her face was deathly serious. "That is not very convincing. I can stop this right now. No questions asked. I told you that we'd only do it if you were comfortable."

"Comfort is a degree," I threw her words back at her.

"Tell me if you want an out."

"We already did the interview... and everyone's here."

"So?" she asked with a straight face.

"This is going to help, right?"

"Yes," she said automatically.

"And it's not permanent or forever."

"No job ever is."

I nodded, feeling some of the weight come off of my shoulders. "I'll do it."

She nodded. Confirmation enough for her. "All right. Then, it's showtime." She nudged me with her elbow and smiled brilliantly. A real smile this time. "Show them that Kensington charm."

I watched her ass until it disappeared in the burning lights. Then, I straightened my tie and waited for my cue.

Twenty minutes later, my announcement was over.

I was officially working for Kensington Corporation. I'd shackled myself to my father's legacy. Bound myself to this life, as if signing a contract with the Devil himself.

Afterward, everyone congratulated me as if I'd done something heroic. Instead of just rejoining a company that I'd avoided like the plague for the last five years. We might be spinning the story to say that I was some golden boy or that I'd returned to my destiny. But I didn't believe in destiny or fate or any of that nonsense. If I did, then I probably deserved to be six feet under, just like him.

My mother reached for me as soon as it was over. She patted my shoulder. It felt like her version of motherly affection. "Congratulations, Court. What a great speech."

My mouth went dry, but I stood strong and imperious. "It was time to take back the mantle."

It was a lie. We both knew that I was only doing this

because of Jane's trial. But I seemed to be the only one who remembered or cared.

"This will be a wonderful new direction for the company. I look forward to seeing the budding future," she said.

English slipped through the row of sycophants and to my side. Her hand grazed mine in comfort and acknowledgment. She put herself between me and the rest of them. Even between me and my mother. Something my mother noted with clear disapproval. But this was what she'd hired English for. To make me look good and to protect me. My mother had probably never envisioned that English would be there to protect me from *her*.

"What a great announcement. So excited that this is going to be out in the world," English said smoothly. "Now, I'm going to get my client out of here. He's had a long day." She whirled on me. "Court."

I nodded. "Yes, it's time."

I shook hands with the few closest men. I smiled at my mother, who looked like she wanted to shake me, tell me that I had to stay and schmooze these men and then hopefully knock some sense into me. But English was giving me an out, and I had every intention of taking it.

Neither of us spoke. Not in the hallway on the top floor of the company. Not in the elevator or through the lobby or out the front door. She didn't say a word until we got into the black car she'd secured for the last few days.

"It worked," she whispered. Her perfectly straight-backed posture evaporated, and she sighed in relief. "It worked."

"Don't you think that's yet to be seen?"

She had her eyes closed and was slouched back in the car. She shook her head. "No. I can just tell."

"How?"

"Years of experience," she murmured.

"Well, that's a relief." I loosened the tie at my throat and then pulled the damn thing off, chucking it across the car. Next came my jacket. I tossed it onto the floor without care. Then, I popped the buttons of my sleeves and began to roll them up to my elbows.

English's eyes were open now and watching me. Those bright blue eyes scouring my skin.

"What now? Are you dropping me off at my place?" I asked her. "What are you doing for labor day weekend?"

Her lips pulled down at the question. It made me think that she must have originally had plans with that cheating douchebag husband of hers before it all came out.

"Nothing," she finally said. "Lark said I could meet them in the Hamptons if I wanted, but I think something serious is going on. Something with the crew, and I don't know all about it. I'm welcome, but I'm not welcome."

"So, what are you going to do?"

She shrugged and pushed back into a respectable seat. "We are going to go get a drink."

I arched an eyebrow. "*We* are, huh?"

"Yes, after everything we just went through, I think we could both use a big fucking drink. Like giant house margaritas." She tipped her head back. "Fuck, I used to go to this place down the street from my place in LA when I was underage. The place made the best margs this side of Mexico. Tequila and cocaine and lots of stupid, stupid behavior."

I laughed. I couldn't help it. "You did cocaine?"

She grinned sheepishly, her eyes meeting mine again. "Well, I wasn't a saint. Gave it up around the time I started working for Poise. But sometimes, it's still hard around clients. It was a way of life. Drugs, sex, and rock and roll. A total cliché. I was so Hollywood."

"Little Miss Anna English," I said in disbelief. "I never would have guessed."

"I'm an enigma. I bet you still do cocaine," she said with no accusation in her voice.

"Sometimes. The Upper East Side has its drugs, sex, and rock and roll, too."

"No cocaine," she said with a sigh. As if she could still taste the euphoric high. "I hear it's addictive."

I snorted. "I have heard that before."

"Just a drink. A few drinks. You in?"

Was I in?

"Fuck yes, English. I know someone who is having a party tonight. We could get drinks out and then head there."

She nodded, coming back to herself, as she seemed to just realize that she'd opened up to me. "I'd like that."

14

ENGLISH

We found margaritas.

And tacos and chips and salsa and guacamole.

Court insisted it was his favorite place in town. But the boy had clearly never been to a real Mexican restaurant in Southern California. Because while it felt like comfort food, it was nowhere *near* as good as home.

But they poured their drinks strong, and after three of them, I was definitely tipsy enough not to care that the tacos were subpar. At least they were tacos. Tacos were life.

I came back from the restroom to find that he'd already paid the bill. I swatted at him. "I was going to pay half."

He quirked an eyebrow. "I'm a gentleman."

"No, you're not," I told him, poking his rather firm chest. "Next time, it's on me."

"You seem to be uncomfortable with the idea of me doing things for you."

I stepped back a step. "I'm... well... I am. You're a client."

"Yes, and you do enough for me," he said evenly. "I was raised that a man holds the door open, gives the girl his jacket, and picks up the tab. Not because we're not equal. But out of courtesy. And I'm not going to stop doing it for you, Anna."

I swallowed, heat coming to my cheeks at the way he caressed my name. He hadn't called me Anna since that night in the green room. I hadn't realized that I'd missed it.

"All right," I said finally. "Then... thank you."

He smiled, all charm, and then pulled the door open to the restaurant. "You're welcome."

I might have hesitated before, but this time, I just strode through it and into the awaiting car that whisked us to his friend's party. The car pulled up to an innocuous building on Park Avenue nestled between a bakery and a designer handbag store. A doorman stood at the ready when we appeared. Court flashed him a smile as if he knew the man and then beelined for a set of elevators.

To my surprise, the party wasn't actually in a penthouse. I'd practically grown accustomed to them. Lark didn't have one, but that was a choice against her parents. The rest of the Upper East Siders that I knew had one. Even *I* did. Though... I was far from an Upper East Sider. I was Hollywood, looking in on the New York glamour and high society.

The door was unlocked when we reached it, and Court let himself in. I didn't know what I'd been expecting, but the place was massive. Completely unlike the evenly spaced doorways in the hallway. It was clear the owner had purchased multiple apartments and renovated them into one space.

"Wow," I whispered to Court as he closed the door behind us.

"Yeah. Robert's place has that effect. He's always trying to buy out his neighbors and knock down more walls. Honestly, I'm not sure how structurally sound it is."

"We'd have to ask Sam. Isn't he good at that sort of thing?"

Court laughed. "That he is. Too bad that he's in North Carolina, visiting family this weekend."

"Oh, really?" I blinked. "I thought he was going to the Hamptons."

"Seems he felt about as welcome as you did."

"Huh. Lark didn't tell me."

"You've both been kind of busy."

"True," I agreed as I followed him into the living room and through the pulse of people.

We stopped when we reached the kitchen. An array of alcohol was displayed. There was even a bartender stationed at the front. My buzz was already wearing off. Whatever he was serving, I wanted it. It had been one hellish week.

Court pointed at me. "She'll have a gin and tonic. I'll take a bourbon and Coke."

I opened my mouth to protest, but Court flashed me a smile. As if it was just another thing that he'd been raised to do. He knew what drink I liked. And he knew to order it for me. I let the protest die on my lips and took the procured gin and tonic.

"You made it!" a man crowed, appearing out of the crowd and clapping Court on the back.

Court turned and grinned at the Hispanic man I'd recognized from lunch the other day. "Robert, good to see you."

"I just heard about your announcement." Robert shook his hand. He was handsome with sun-kissed skin and dark hair, almost black, styled in the latest European fashion. He had the air of someone who could talk his way in and out of everything. "Congrats! Now, you'll get to live the drudgery life like the rest of us."

Court just laughed. "It was time."

"It fucking was, man." His gaze slipped to me. "Now, introduce me to your beautiful woman."

I opened my mouth to object, but Court was already there. "This is English."

Robert winked at me as he took my hand. "Pleasure to meet

you. Any friend of Court Kensington is a friend of mine. But he does always find the loveliest woman in the room."

"Thank you," I said with a laugh. "I remember you from something. When I saw you at St. Regis, you were Robert something. Just on the tip of my tongue."

"Ah, yes, next to a Kensington, Robert something is about as good as it gets, isn't it?" He waved his hand with a flourish. "Robert Dawson, at your service."

"Dawson! I knew it. I think we met when I was at Columbia. You're friends with Lark."

"Indeed, I am. Larkin St. Vincent is one of a kind." He grinned at us both. "Well, I know most of New York is saying their last hurrah in the Hamptons this weekend, but I think it'll pick up tonight."

"Pick up?" I asked softly. "It's already packed."

"Robert fancies himself a bit of a Gatsby," Court said.

Robert grinned at Court. "That's the nicest thing you've ever said to me, Kensington."

Court just shook his head. Suddenly, a buxom woman with a sheet of mahogany hair appeared at his side.

"Hey, Court," she said with big doe eyes accented with eyeliner.

"Poppy Arlington," Robert crowed. "You were a *maybe* on the RSVP list."

She winked at Robert. "I'd thought that I'd still be on my yacht in the Mediterranean, but I took one too many pills in Ibiza, if you know what I mean."

"Sent you back to rehab?" Robert asked with a laugh.

"As if I didn't have anything better to do," she said with an eye roll. "How have you been, Court? I haven't seen you around."

"He's working at Kensington Corporation again," Robert interjected.

Court just shrugged and sipped his drink, oblivious or purposely ambivalent to Poppy's flirtation. "Just busy."

"Ooh, taking after Daddy," she cooed. "I like."

Court's eyes narrowed at the insinuation. "Poppy, if you'll excuse us."

He took my arm and hauled me away from them.

"What was that about?" I asked.

He shrugged. "I like Robert. He's good people. He went to boarding school in Europe and loves high fashion and elaborate parties. He makes Gavin look tame," he said with a laugh. "Poppy is just..."

"Aggressive?"

"You could say that."

We meandered to the edge of the living room that had been converted into a dance floor. I eyed the crowd of people. All so rich and carefree. I needed to drink more to feel like that.

But I drifted back to Court's side. His eyes were on me. And I tried not to blush at the intensity of his look.

"Why did you let Robert think that we were together?" I couldn't help but ask.

He stepped forward and drained his drink. "Aren't we?"

I gulped. "No."

"We came here together."

"That's not the same thing."

He grinned at me and tucked a loose strand of blonde hair behind my ear. "Okay, Anna."

Anna.

There was that name again. The one that no one ever used unless they didn't know me. The one he somehow laced with so much desire.

"It's... it's English," I murmured. "Everyone calls me English."

He shrugged. "I'm not everyone."

"Court, please," I whispered, half-rebuke, half-plea.

He laughed gently as if my unease amused him. "Relax. Have a good time. I'd say we've both earned it."

I nodded. We had. Then, I tipped the drink back and drained it.

"I'll grab us another," he promised. "Don't leave."

I watched him disappear back the way that we had come. This was dangerous territory, being here with Court. It was probably pretty stupid. But I'd just figured we'd put in so much work this week that it would be worth it to cut loose. That didn't mean we had to do anything stupid. We could just hang out, especially since all of the rest of our friends were currently in the Hamptons. I'd rather do this than go back to the empty apartment, all alone again.

The music carried me away as the drink finally caught up with me. In Hollywood, I used to go out dancing with Winnie all the time. We'd ditch our respective beaus and dance the night away. Sometimes, we'd do it to keep up with clients, and sometimes, it was just for ourselves. Lark was too busy to go dancing all the time. Whitley was a hot plastic surgeon. As much as she wanted to go out all the time, it was too draining. And I still couldn't get a full read on Katherine. She was loyal to a fault, and I was just getting into her good graces. This New York life was so different. It felt good to just let loose on the dance floor.

My hands were over my head. My eyes closed as I swayed my hips back and forth to the beat. Everything else just disappeared.

Then, a hand came to my hip. My eyes flew open, and I stared up into Court's impossibly blue ones. He mirrored my movements with his own hips. A rocking that felt all too familiar.

He handed me a drink with a wink. I took it and didn't halt my movements. Neither did he. I downed the drink like it was a lifeline. Probably not the smartest thing I'd ever done.

Court moved in closer when my drink was gone.

"What are you doing?" I said hoarsely over the music.

"Dancing." He reached up for my arms, slinging them around his neck.

"This is a bad idea," I said as his hands slid down my back. "What if people see? Or... what if..."

"English," he breathed into my ear, "shut up."

I shivered all over at the caress of his lips against my ear. Just the lightest brush. I was sober enough to know that we shouldn't be doing this. That this wasn't what I'd signed up for when I agreed to come to this party. But I was drunk enough to keep dancing. To want to feel his strong hands on my hips, the crush of his body against mine, to see the intensity in his eyes.

It was just a dance. A dangerous dance. And yet, I wanted to keep dancing with him. For one thing, he was just really fucking good at it. For another... well, my brain shut off when he was this close to me.

His hands slid from my hips to the small of my back, inching lower and lower. As if, at any moment, he would slide down to my ass. Maybe even lift the slim black dress I wore and touch skin. Skin that was on fire as we drew in closer and closer. So close that I could just stand on my tiptoes to meet his lips.

At the thought, I whirled around in his arms. Not that this was better. In fact, it might be worse. No longer was I close to his tempting lips, but now, my ass was pressed firmly against his growing erection. If he tipped me forward at the waist, we'd be exactly where we'd started a few weeks ago.

His arm wrapped around my waist, pulling me flush against him. Almost as if he knew that I was thinking of bolting. I slumped back against him, letting my hands drop around his neck.

He groaned into my ear. Fire spread through my core. It was erotic. Dancing with him like this made my pulse race and my skin heat and memories flood my system. Ones that I had been purposely trying to avoid. Because thinking about the best sex of my life when I was in Court Kensington's arms was a recipe for disaster.

"Anna," he murmured against my ear. "Fuck."

I shuddered. Which only egged him on.

I needed to get away. Or I was going to give in to this. I wouldn't care what happened.

I stopped moving and wrenched out of his grip. When I turned to face him, he just looked at me expectantly.

"It's hot. I have to... get some air," I said, shuffling past him.

It wasn't a lie. I was hot and sweaty and sticky. The dancing had superheated me. Or had that been Court?

But I didn't head outside. I didn't want to be near people. I pushed through the crowd, away from Court, and toward what appeared to be a mostly deserted hallway. I could see that there was one person in line for a bathroom at the end of the hall. Perfect. Bathroom.

Then I felt a hand grab my elbow and pull me to a stop. I whipped around, only to find Court standing over me, pressing me back against the wall.

"Court, what...?"

"You said you needed air," he said with a teasing smile that said he knew it was a lie. "The balcony is the opposite direction."

I squirmed under his gaze. The way he towered over me and made my addled brain think about climbing him. I pointed down the hallway. "I decided on the bathroom."

"Why are you trying to escape me?" he breathed, inches away.

"I'm not."

"Stop lying to me. You can hate me. You can think whatever you want about me. But just stop lying. You're so hot for me right now."

My back hit the wall. His hand slid up my inner thigh, under my dress, and to my black lace thong. His fingers skimmed across the soaked fabric. I shuddered at the intimacy. Then, he slid the material aside and slicked his fingers through my own wetness.

"Oh god," I moaned, my head dropping backward.

"See?" he said, as if proving his point.

He slid his fingers out from between my legs and held them between us. Wet. Soaking wet. As if I hadn't known beforehand. Then, he did the unthinkable, and he brought those two fingers to his mouth and sucked the wetness off them.

"You taste like fucking candy."

I bit my lip hard. "Court... please... we-we shouldn't."

"Yes, oh yes, we fucking should."

And then my walls crumbled. I knew why I had been fighting this. There were a millions reasons to say no. But with Court Kensington pinning me against a wall with my wetness on his fingers and sucked into his mouth as he all but commanded my very body, how could I say no? *Why* would I say no?

I reached up onto my tiptoes and crushed my mouth to his.

Damn it all.

15

ENGLISH

The line to the bathroom had vanished by the time I came up for air. Court took my hand and dragged me into it. He kicked the door shut and yanked the bolt into place. The air was charged between our bodies. As if electricity crackled from the mounting tension of the last couple of weeks.

Our limbs tangled around each other as our lips came together. It wasn't gentle. That wasn't me and Court. It was fire and ice. It was the push and pull. It was teeth and tongue. The fight. The battle. The knockout.

"Oh god," I groaned against his mouth.

Only to have him reach under my dress and yank my underwear off. He dropped them to the ground, and I stepped out of them, kicking my heels off, too. Then he hoisted me up by my waist, dropping me onto the bathroom counter.

My hands fisted in his button-up, drawing him closer. My legs wrapped around his hips. His hands tangled in my hair. The fight continued with our tongues. A throb cut through my core. A dull roar echoed in my ears. Only this moment existed. The desperate need. The fear of getting caught. The rush of needing him right this fucking second.

My fingers pushed at his belt, undoing it with a dexterity I hadn't known I possessed. Then his pants, until the only barrier between us was his boxer briefs.

Court wrenched back long enough to release himself. My eyes rounded again. I couldn't believe I hadn't dreamed his size. That it was possible that he was as big as the image I'd had of him as I masturbated in my empty penthouse.

He searched out a condom and slid it over his length before positioning himself before me. I could already hear the people outside. A line was forming. I didn't give two fucks.

"Anna," he breathed.

But it was the only word he got out before he slid into me, hard and fast. I yelped in surprise and pain and hot, needy pleasure. His hand came to my mouth, silencing me. I knew we had to be quiet. The line outside this room might know what we were doing in here, but there was no reason to announce it to the world.

I buried my fingers in his lush hair and brought his mouth to mine. He kissed me with a vengeance. Almost a punishment for making us wait so long for this again. And fuck, did I want my punishment.

He was at the perfect height to pound into me. Our bodies smacked together. Our chests pressed tight. Not even a seam.

It was quick. It was relentless. It was exactly what I needed and wanted. Even if I shouldn't want it at all.

I'd been a fool to think otherwise. That I could suppress this want. That I could use brash words to avoid the inevitable. And as he took my pussy as his own, claimed it with a driving force, I knew it truly had been inevitable. After that first time, could I really ever go back?

"Fuck. Oh fuck," I said low and hushed against his mouth.

"Come for me. I want to watch you come all over my cock."

His words were filthy. And they triggered something inside

of me. My body spasmed, and then I had to bite down on my lip to keep from crying out as I came long and hard.

"Shit," he groaned, his eyes intent on my face.

My orgasm forced his, and he pulled me tighter to him, so crushing that I could barely breathe, as he finished inside of me.

Someone banged on the door.

We both jumped as if we'd forgotten that we were in the bathroom at Robert's apartment. That we'd just fucked in a public place and there might be other people waiting outside.

"Are you done in there?" a girl yelled. "Christ!"

"Just a minute," Court answered like a whip.

The girl didn't say another word.

He withdrew and tossed the condom as I righted my clothes, pulled my panties back on, and tried desperately to straighten my hair. I didn't look like myself in that moment. I didn't look sensible or like a hard-hitting celebrity publicist. I looked like a woman who'd had a quickie in the bathroom. A woman who had been properly fucked.

"Walk confidently out, and no one will say anything," he told me.

"I know how it works."

He grabbed the back of my head, tugging my hair so that I looked up at him. Then, he kissed me again until my knees went weak.

As my legs wobbled beneath me, he just smirked triumphantly and then pulled the door open. A half-dozen people waited in line as we filed out like we owned the place. I made certain not to look anyone in the face. It was clear what we'd done, but if I looked guilty, then maybe they'd remember rather than just write it off.

And I couldn't have anyone remembering.

We didn't say a word as we disappeared through the front of Robert's door and left the party behind. My brain was fuzzy from the alcohol and the sex. I felt almost... giddy. Which I could hardly even believe, considering my personal life the last six weeks. But I'd been in control for so long. Everything in my life had been something I had put in motion. I'd clawed my way into everything that I had. And now, for once, someone else was taking control.

It shouldn't be Court. But it was.

He tugged me into the back of the black car and told the driver to take him home. His fingers trailed through my hair.

"You'll stay with me tonight," he told me.

It wasn't a question.

"Court..."

"I don't want to hear that it's a bad idea. I think we're past that now."

"You're a bad influence," I said cheekily.

He snorted. "Says the girl who lamented the fact that we weren't going to do cocaine tonight."

I straightened and pointed at him. "I did not say that. I was the one who said *no* cocaine."

"With a wistful sigh."

"Puh-lease," I drawled. "You're the one who said you still do it."

He laughed, hauling me in for a kiss. "I love when you fight me."

I jerked back. "You're an ass."

"Yeah. Nice you caught on."

"Why do I even put up with you?"

"Do you?" he inquired with an arched eyebrow.

"Hardly. You're the literal worst."

His lips quirked up. "That is not what you were saying earlier."

I rolled my eyes. "I think it still was."

"Liar," he teased against my lips. He lifted me over onto his lap. I squeaked as my dress slid high up on my thighs, and his hands covered my ass. "Oh right, I didn't let you say anything at all."

"Yes," I muttered, currently distracted by the way my panties ground against his growing cock. "Because we were in a public bathroom."

"You didn't seem to mind."

"Again. Bad, bad influence."

His hands lifted my skirt. "We could try again. Right here."

"We're almost to your apartment."

He shrugged. "I can have him drive around the block."

I shook my head, slipping off of his lap. "You're filthy, Court Kensington. Straight filthy."

"You bring it out in me," he said, stealing another kiss.

I highly doubted that. If anything, he brought it out in me. I'd done stupid things like this in college, but that felt so long ago. Court made me act like an idiot. And worse, he made it so I almost didn't mind.

The driver pulled over in front of Court's building. I insisted that Court tip him extra after our display, which he did with no complaints. Then, he gestured for me to follow him upstairs to his penthouse.

Even though I'd been here a number of times since that fateful night when this had all started, it still unnerved me. It felt like a decision. One that I wasn't certain on making. I wanted to be here. I wanted to have sex with him. I couldn't deny that. But the rest of it... I didn't know.

When we strode into his apartment, Court went right for the wet bar. "Drink?"

I sank into a chair. "I think I'm already drunk enough."

He laughed as he poured himself a glass of amber liquid. "You have a pretty high tolerance."

"Yeah, well, you don't even seem drunk."

"I have a *very* high tolerance."

I laughed at that and then couldn't stop laughing. "Court, what are we doing?"

"Having a drink?"

"But really?"

"Why do we have to be doing anything, Anna?" he asked, drawing me off of the chair and into his lap again. I straddled him, wrapping my arms around his neck. "I just got out of a long-term relationship. You're..." He didn't finish that statement. We let the unsaid word *married* float between us. "Can't we just have amazing sex? Because fuck, it's amazing sex."

"It is," I admitted softly.

"Oh yeah?" he asked with that shit-eating grin.

"I'd tell you it's the best sex of my life, but it would go straight to your head. And we both know that your ego needs no help."

His eyes smoldered. "Best of your life?"

I mutely nodded once.

"I like that."

"I thought you might," I told him with a shake of my head. "Fuck, I'm going to need that drink." I took it out of his hand and forced down a large gulp. I coughed at the scotch as it burned my throat.

Court took it back from me and finished it. "Going to see if we can make the best sex of your life happen again."

Without preamble, he lifted me into the air and carried me into his bedroom.

Neither of us slept a wink that night.

16

COURT

I yawned and stretched on my bed, blinking sleep out of my eyes. English and I had finally crashed around four or maybe five in the morning. I swatted my hand at my phone and saw that it was already noon. We'd slept straight through the morning.

My eyes drifted over to where she lay, curled up in my sheets. Her blonde hair fanned out across the pillow. Her still-naked frame covered only by the thin sheet, but I could just make out the curves of her breasts, hips, and ass. She had one hand extended toward me as if we'd fallen asleep, reaching for each other.

Selfishly, I wanted to wake her up with my head buried between her legs and start all over again. But I knew she was sore and needed the sleep. She'd feel me every time she moved for the next day or two at least. A smile touched my features at that thought.

Another yawn hit me. I probably should just pull her against me and try to get another hour or two of rest, but once I was awake, I was awake. So, I kicked off the covers, yanked on boxers and shorts, swiped my phone off the nightstand, and headed into the kitchen.

As I brewed a pot of coffee, I went through my messages. There was one from Robert, thanking me for coming to the party. Two from Poppy, insisting we meet up later. One from Camden that made me frown.

Heard you went to Dawson's party last night with English?

Great. So, the news was already circulating. Of course, I could lie. At least to everyone else, I could lie like a champ. She was my publicist. She was there to keep me in line. All that bullshit.

But to Camden?

Yeah, the lie would never stand. He'd probably already guessed what I hadn't said.

I decided not to text him back. I'd rather talk to him in person. Plus, he was in the Hamptons all weekend with Katherine. And if Penn was back, then the tension must be high between them. Katherine and Penn had had an on-again, off-again thing for years. I still didn't understand why Camden had married her. Insisted on an arranged marriage at that. But I knew that my little brother's presence around his wife made him want to blow a gasket. Even if Penn had just come home, married to Natalie. It made me almost glad not to be there to witness that malfunction.

The last message was from my mother.

Congratulations, Court! This is just what I've always wanted for you! <attachment>

I clicked on the attachment with dread knotting my stomach. My mother and I had never seen eye to eye on what the other wanted. She'd had dreams for us, and who we were as people had never mattered much around those dreams.

The image displayed, and it was a screenshot of Kensington Corporation stocks. They'd skyrocketed overnight. I froze in surprise. This wasn't what I'd been anticipating. Me joining the company had made the stocks climb? It seemed... unbelievable. But it must have shown investors that the company was headed in the right direction. That it was more certain of the future.

And for a second, I wondered if that was true. Could I be the future of Kensington Corporation? Sure, it had all been bullshit. English had engineered it. But... this said something else. Not just that it had worked. But that others believed in me. I couldn't remember ever feeling that before.

I typed out a quick response to my mother, still shaking out that feeling. Then, I poured a mug of coffee and brought it back into the bedroom where English was still fast asleep. I set it down to cool and then pulled out the book I'd started yesterday —*Station Eleven*. It was a postapocalyptic novel centered around a traveling Shakespearean theater. Murder, the world ending, and Shakespeare. Really different and engrossing.

I fell back into the book like through a rabbit hole. Time disappeared when I was reading. As if I'd entered my fantastical world and lived out my time as the main character. Books had a certain kind of magic. An escape like no other.

Incessant buzzing coming from the other side of the room jolted me out of it. After the third long ring, I finally put the book down next to *This Is How You Lose the Time War*—a fantastic time travel novel I'd read last week—and went in search of English's phone.

It was tucked inside her small black purse, and I pulled it out to silence it. The screen lit up one more time.

JOSH

My teeth clenched. Jackass.

A part of me wanted to answer the phone. Explain in vivid detail exactly what I'd been doing with his wife the night before and tell him to fuck off.

But I didn't.

English would kill me. Literally. She had martial arts skills, and I was certain she'd act out of instinct.

I silenced the phone and carried it to the nightstand next to where English slept happily, oblivious to her husband's incessant calls. Just as I set it down, another text came through in all capital letters.

YOU TALKED TO THE PRESS? TO A TABLOID? WHAT WERE YOU THINKING? CALL ME BACK NOW! WE HAVE TO FIGURE OUT HOW TO FIX THIS!

I frowned and hastily turned the phone over. I hadn't meant to snoop. It had just fucking appeared there. But now, I couldn't shake it.

She'd talked to a tabloid about Josh? When had that happened? We'd been together every day this week, and she'd never mentioned it. Why the hell would she even do that?

I sank back into my side of the bed and reached for my phone. I searched her name, and immediately, an article popped up with the click-bait tagline, *Josh Hutch's Wife Tells All His Scandalous Secrets in Exclusive Interview.*

Wife. They didn't even list her name in the headline. As if she were someone else's property.

I clicked on the link. Half out of curiosity and half out of dread. I skimmed the story. It was a tell-all but a carefully constructed one. English had clearly played this journalist. She'd put everything together in such a way that she'd actually revealed very little. But it didn't matter. The tabloid twisted it and likely outright lied about the facts. It was bad enough that she'd gone on record to say, *Yes, Josh cheated with his costar, and yes, we're getting a divorce.*

Especially if Josh hadn't known she was doing it.

A small smile touched my features as I put the article aside. English had gone for the jugular. She was a brilliant fixer... and she could tear someone down just as easily.

I pulled my book back out and was deeply engrossed again by the time English first began to rouse. Her eyes fluttered, she reached for me, and a small noise escaped her lips.

Then she looked up at me with those big blue eyes. "Court?"

"Morning. Or well, afternoon."

"What are you doing?" she muttered, rubbing at her eyes.

"Reading."

"Is this a common occurrence?"

I resisted the urge to brush her hair out of her face. "Pretty regular."

"Huh," she said, fighting another yawn. "I stayed the night."

"Well... it's more like you stayed the morning."

She stretched her arm over her head and succumbed to her yawn. She reached for my discarded T-shirt on the floor, pulled it on over her head, and trotted to the bathroom. She returned a minute later, still barely awake but a little more fresh-faced. She ambled to her purse and fished through it.

"If you're looking for your phone, it's over here," I said, pointing it out. "It kept ringing off the hook."

She flushed and reached for it. Her face fell when she saw what I'd already known was displayed on the screen.

"What?" I asked anyway.

She shook her head. "Nothing. Just, uh... nothing. I have to... get to work."

I put the book down. "We could get breakfast first. Or... lunch?"

"No. I... fuck." She ran a hand down her face.

And just like that, I lost her.

One second, she'd been here. She'd been Anna. Mine.

The next... gone. Like a light switch.

"Don't do this," I said automatically.

Her face closed off. The publicist appeared. "Court, I... we... this..."

"Stop," I insisted. "We had a great time."

"We did. I mean, I can't deny that we had a great time."

"But..."

She nodded. "But it's... wrong on so many levels."

"It's right, English," I ground out.

I got out of bed and approached her, but she backed up a step as if I were going to attack her.

"Last night was amazing."

"It was. I don't disagree, Court. But I'm still married."

"Separated."

"It's only been six weeks since I found out about Josh. The divorce won't be final for like six months."

"Long enough for you to be comfortable enough with talking to the press."

Her eyes narrowed. "Did you read my messages?"

"I saw one when I turned the phone off. I read the rest in the tabloids this morning."

"You know nothing," she spat at me. "You have no idea how I feel about any of it or even why I fucking did it."

"You could just fucking tell me," I snapped back.

"This is a rebound."

The words cut. They hurt the most because they were true. I knew they were. And yet, we worked. But did we only work because we'd both just been royally fucked over and needed someone? Or was it just the sex? Did it have to fucking matter?

"Fine," I said. "It's a rebound."

"Can't you see that this is going to end poorly?"

"I'm not really thinking about the end. I'm still stuck on the five hours we spent together last night."

She flushed. "It's my job to think about and anticipate every future."

"And how did that work with you and Josh?"

Her hand whipped out and slapped me across the face. The last time she'd done that, we'd fucked for the first time. This time was different. She was breathing hard. Her anger a living, breathing dragon threatening to rip out of her chest.

"You have no right to say anything about Josh. You are the playboy of the Upper East Side. I was literally hired to make you look like a good person. Just because I'm fooling everyone else does not mean that you can try to fool me."

And there it was.

Right out in the open.

The same old shit. Different day.

"Have you ever seen me with another girl?" I asked her with a cold-edged fierceness. "The months you've been working for me, have you ever even seen me flirt with anyone else, except as a joke? Have you had to wake me up with a woman in my bed? Have I missed an appointment because I was getting pussy?"

She just clenched her jaw.

"That's because I haven't slept with anyone since Jane. Not anyone, except you. And before that, English," I growled low, "I didn't sleep with anyone else but Jane. I never cheated on her."

She opened her mouth, but I held my hand up. I didn't want to hear it. I was tired of hearing it from everyone else. I didn't need it from her, too.

I stepped away from her. I picked up her discarded dress, her heels, and then finally her purse.

"So, if you're so fucking convinced that I'm a horrible person, like your fucking husband, then take your shit," I said, tossing the bundle of clothes into her unsuspecting hands, "and get the fuck out of my apartment."

"Court, I…"

"I really don't want to hear it."

"Okay," she said softly.

She didn't move for a few seconds. As if she was debating on trying to reason with me anyway. But then she shuffled out of the bedroom, and a minute later, the elevator dinged.

I loosed a breath.

Fuck. Just…*fuck.*

PART III

NOT WHO I THOUGHT

17

ENGLISH

"Earth to English," Lark said. She waved a hand in front of my face. "Are you in there?"

I jolted out of my train of thought. "Yes, sorry."

I'd been thinking about Court kicking me out of his apartment. And how I'd been so wrong about him. So many fucking assumptions that had exploded in my face.

"Are you okay?"

"Yeah. Yep. Fine. Just tired. I haven't been sleeping well."

That was at least the truth. Ever since what happened with Court, I'd been sleeping like shit. It didn't help that the night we'd been together was the best night of sleep I'd had in months, maybe years. I'd never been a good sleeper. My stepmom had always said that I had too much going on in my head. My brain wouldn't shut down. Apparently, it'd only taken five hours of sex with Court Kensington to get my brain to shut up.

"You never sleep well," Lark said. "But worse than normal?"

"Yeah. I don't know." I twirled my fork through my pad thai. Lunch with Lark had been postponed last week. So, I hadn't seen her since she'd gotten back. She'd had too much work to catch up on. “I’m just glad you’re back. I can’t wait until November, when you have more time to be a human.”

Lark laughed. “Yeah. I get it. But I love campaign season. I honestly can’t even believe we’re in the middle of September. Where did the time go?”

“No idea.”

“Have you thought about what you’re going to do after the election is over?” Lark asked. “You won’t have to work with Court anymore. I can’t see you going back to LA.”

“No, I can’t either. Not after what happened with Josh,” I said, grinding my teeth together. “He’s been a total maniac since I did the interview.”

“I still can’t believe you did it.”

“I won’t tell him this, but it was to help the campaign. Some jackass pap took a picture of Court and me leaving the club that night, and I didn’t want it to hurt Leslie.”

Lark took a sip of her water. “I appreciate that. Though it’s a big sacrifice for a picture.”

“It was fine. The article barely said anything.”

“Enough to make Josh go crazy.”

“Well,” I muttered softly, “he doesn’t want a divorce.”

“Don’t think he gets a say in that after what he did.”

“True.” I ate a few bites of my food before speaking again, “He wants to see me when he’s in town next month. He’ll be here, promoting the last Bourne movie. He thinks we should try to go to counseling.”

Lark snorted derisively. “He thinks that counseling will fix what he did?”

I shrugged. “I don’t know, Lark. On one hand, I know it doesn’t fix anything. My dad is proof of that. But on the other hand...”

“You were together for five years.”

“Yes. I don’t want to be with him. I don’t even want to see

him." A small smile crossed my lips. "But I wouldn't mind seeing him grovel."

Lark howled with laughter. "I love you, Anna English."

I waved my hand at her. "So, I just have to get through November and then this divorce. I've been doing some extra work for Winnie here in New York."

"You have?"

"When her clients are in town or they have a breakdown, I'll go and handle it. It might be nice to have a permanent person here to do that for Poise. I could take on a few more clients. Figure it out."

"Or… you could start your own agency," Lark suggested.

I laughed. "Do you know how hard it is to start your own PR firm in New York City? Without an established name?"

"But you do have an established name."

"Not in New York. Just in LA. And still, I've had Poise behind me the whole time." I shook my head. "That's like a long-term, twenty-years-from-now goal. Not anytime soon."

"Just throwing it out there," Lark said.

"Anyway, you haven't told me how the Hamptons went last weekend."

Lark cringed. "Well, it was interesting. Natalie and Katherine came to a truce, but I think they still want to claw each other's faces off. It's weird to me that Penn just came home, married, without telling all of us."

"Yeah. I can't believe you didn't know."

"Me either. We've known each other our whole lives." She shrugged. "Not that I could have gone to the ceremony or anything with the campaign. But it's crazy. And now, Leslie is throwing a reception for them. You're coming next weekend, right?"

"Wouldn't miss it," I told her. "I got the invitation yesterday actually."

"A bit of short notice. But it's mostly for locals anyway," Lark said. "Well, it's mostly for Leslie. I doubt Penn and Natalie had much say in the matter."

"That sounds fun."

"Now that I think about it, I don't blame them for eloping. If I were marrying a Kensington, I'd want to elope, too."

I snorted. "Was there any fear of you marrying a Kensington?"

Lark shrugged and took another sip of her water. "Like, in high school maybe. But... probably not. That was a different Lark."

"Bad Lark," I said with a wink.

"Exactly. Anyway, I heard that your Labor Day was about as fun as mine."

"Oh, yeah?" I asked softly. Because... my Labor Day weekend had been a hell of a lot better than dealing with friendship drama. Until it had all hit a wall, going seventy miles per hour.

"Robert said that you went to his party with Court."

"Ah. Yeah, I did. Everyone else was gone. We were celebrating."

Lark leaned on her elbow. "That must have been awkward, considering he's your client."

I swallowed and glanced down at my half-eaten pad thai. "Yeah, well, he's Court."

"Well, he probably found some easy ass and ditched you anyway," Lark said with a wave of her hand. "His MO."

"Is it?" I asked carefully. "Is that the kind of guy he is?"

"Pretty much. Why? You've been working with him since May. Shouldn't you know?"

"I don't know. He just told me that he'd never cheated on Jane."

Lark laughed, and then it slowly evaporated when she saw I was serious. "Really? I didn't think he had that in him."

"Was he always sleeping around before Jane?"

"Yeah. For sure. He's not, like... a bad guy or anything. It's easy for him to attract women. They flock to Kensington men."

"Or just men with money."

Lark pointed her fork at me. "That, too."

"I just thought he was a playboy. Everything that I'd read about him when I did research for this job showed me to expect him to act just like any of my other rock star or movie star clients."

"But presumably... he hasn't?" Lark guessed.

I shook my head. "Nope."

"Well, that's good for you at least. You don't have to deal with his attitude as well as kicking women out of his bed."

I flinched at the phrasing. "You're right. It's just surprising."

"Those Kensington men are full of surprises. That's for sure." Lark pushed her bowl away. "Okay, I have to get back to work. So much left to do."

"Of course. I'm glad we got this lunch. Even if it was quick." I stood and pulled her in for a hug. "What are you wearing for the reception? I think we need to go shopping."

Lark cringed. "Ugh! I already promised my mother that I'd go shopping with her. You could come along."

"God forbid I interfere with your mother-daughter bonding."

"Stop," Lark said, making a face. "I can't."

"Hey, it's good for you. I'll find a dress on my own."

"Good luck. Wish we were going together," Lark said before waving good-bye and drifting out of the restaurant.

I was thinking about where exactly to go to find a dress for the reception when a text came in. I bit my lip, hoping it wasn't Josh begging to go to counseling again. I could only handle so much. But I was surprised that it was from Taylor.

Hey! It's been a while since we met up. I'm free tomorrow afternoon if you want to do lunch or something?

My eyes narrowed. What was the catch?

Since when do you want to meet for lunch?

Since now? I shouldn't have brushed you off like I did last time. It's hard, being far from home without anyone.

That sentiment at least I could understand. She was lonely. Or homesick. I was feeling a little homesick, too. And what would it hurt to give Taylor another chance?

All right. I'm free tomorrow. Where should we meet?

Taylor insisted on meeting at this edible cookie dough shop in SoHo that all of her friends raved about. I bought us both a scoop. Mine standard chocolate chip and hers loaded down with sugar cookies, vanilla icing, graham crackers, and sprinkles. We left the shop behind with our treats and headed east toward the nearby shops.

"This is amazing," Taylor said. "Why don't we have this in LA?"

"We probably do."

"Yeah, but not in the Valley."

"You're not wrong."

Taylor seemed subdued today compared to the first day of classes. She'd been trying too hard. Unsurprisingly, since she was a freshman. And already, she'd come into her own. She wore a plain white T-shirt under overalls and black statement Dr. Martens. Her black-to-blue-tipped hair was up in a messy bun on the top of her head. She sported little makeup and seemed to have this energy about her. As if she couldn't stand still. She had to keep moving, bouncing on the balls of her feet.

"You seem to be doing well. How are classes?" I asked.

She grinned up at me. "Pretty amazing. My poetry seminar is life-changing."

"Good. It sounds like you're in the right place then."

"I feel like it," she admitted.

"But you also feel homesick?"

She glanced up at me in surprise.

I just laughed. "Yeah. I get homesick, too. I love New York, but it's not California."

"Isn't that the truth?"

"No one ever understands how much I love California. It's in my blood."

Taylor nodded aggressively. "It really is."

"When do you get to go back?"

"Ugh! Not until Thanksgiving. Dad wouldn't buy me a ticket when I called him. He just told me to go hang out with you." She bit her lip. "Sorry."

"It's fine. I figured he'd talked you into it."

"I'm glad that we're doing it though."

"Me too," I said a bit suspiciously.

I felt like she wanted something. I'd sidled up to people in college to get what I wanted by being extra appreciative. But maybe it was my own bias. Taylor and I had nothing in common, except our father and his blue eyes.

After a few minutes of awkward silence, we tossed our finished cookie dough and headed into a boutique Taylor had suggested. It was all artsy madness inside. Not my style at all. But Taylor lit up.

"Bea talks about this place all the time," she gushed.

"And Bea is the friend who suggested the cookie dough?"

She nodded emphatically. "She's the best. Her parents used to bring her to New York a couple times a year. They live in Boston. She knows all the good places to shop."

Taylor reverently touched a long purple printed dress, carefully checking the price tag before hastily dropping it and moving on. I looked at the price. As expected, it was more than I'd ever paid for clothes before working at Poise. It had sucked, being at UCLA and Columbia without any money. Earning my place with scholarships and student loans and the force of my personality. I knew the feeling well.

"Why don't you try this on?"

Taylor shook her head. "Can't get my hopes up."

I took it off the rack and handed it to her. "Try it on."

She bit her lip. Her hands shook a little as she took it from me. "Okay."

Her hand grazed a leather jacket as she headed to the dressing room. I picked it up, checked the price tag with a shrug, and brought it with me.

Taylor came out a minute later, looking like a vision in the dress. It was something I'd never wear, but it looked great on her.

I passed her the jacket. Her eyes rounded.

"I'll literally die if I fall in love with that jacket," she said. Her fingers twitched as she reached for it, and then she pulled her hand back.

"Just try it on, Tay."

Taylor slung the jacket around her shoulders and stared at herself in the mirror. "Wow. It's perfect."

And it was. Edgy and fantastic with moto sleeves, spiked metal details, and perfect slashes across the material. It completed her outfit.

She shucked it off and passed it back to me without a word and changed, leaving the dress in the room.

"Next shop?" she asked wistfully.

I shook my head. Taylor and I were fresh. We were new. Trust was just forming. Our relationship like a baby bird trying to fly. I had money. And after the divorce was final, I'd have *a lot* of money. I could do this. Put her trust in my hands and see if we could fly together.

"I'm going to get them for you."

"What?" Taylor asked, her eyes slightly bloodshot and rounded. "Anna, you can't!"

"Sure I can. I'm your sister."

"Yeah... but..."

I waved her off and brought the dress and jacket to the counter. After I paid for them, I passed the black bag to her to carry.

"Thank you," she said softly. "You know, I'm sorry... about how I've always acted. I didn't know you... I just... assumed you were different than this."

"It's okay. I know all about that."

The words struck a chord. How was this any different than how I'd treated Court? If I could build a new relationship with my sister after all this time, maybe I could repair what I'd done with Court, too.

18

COURT

Work wasn't as abysmal as I'd thought it would be.

Everyone eased me back into it. No one expected me to try to take over the CEO position tomorrow. My office on the top floor was entirely ceremonial. I was pretty sure that I was doing basic work. And oddly enough finding that I enjoyed it.

Even if I hated the office and the desk and rug... and literally everything, except the library. I'd brought in a stack of books from home and replaced a group of legal books. It didn't have the same uniform effect, but it felt like the only part of the room that was really me. So, I didn't care.

Perhaps someone would question why *Pawn of Prophecy, The Eye of the World,* and *Mistborn* were next to an encyclopedia and accounting books. But oh well.

A knock sounded at my door. That had been happening constantly since I started working here. Not because anyone had anything really for me to do or anything to say, but just to "check up" on me. Whatever that meant. It was getting annoying.

"Come in," I ground out, pushing away from that stupid

desk.

The door creaked open, and Sam peeked his head in. "Hey, man."

I smiled. Well, this was better than another bullshit person interrupting to "help."

"Sam, come in. Shut the door behind you to keep out the vultures."

He laughed. "That bad?"

"You have no idea. Everyone is waiting for me to fail. Or to bail."

"But you're not going to, right?" he asked, sinking into a seat in front of my enormous desk.

"Would I have set up the huge publicity stunt around this if I intended to leave?"

Sam shrugged. "I wouldn't think so." His gaze shifted around the office, taking in the entire ostentatious thing. "This place is huge. It makes my office look like it's for kids."

"You're welcome to it."

"You don't like having the big office in the sky?"

"Not really," I admitted. "If they're going to make me do introductory work, wouldn't it make more sense to have me somewhere else?"

"But you said it yourself, it was a publicity stunt. Of course they wanted you in this swank office."

"Yeah... it's just my father's desk," I muttered.

"That's sentimental. I'm sure he would have wanted you to have it."

I frowned. "I doubt it."

Sometimes, I forgot that Sam was new to our group of friends. He fit in so seamlessly that it surprised me when he didn't know me as well as Camden. That he hadn't been there the night my father died. Or what had happened afterward.

"I'm sure he'd be proud of you," Sam insisted.

"He wasn't proud of either of his children a day in his life," I told him.

Sam sighed. "I'm sorry. I didn't know what your relationship was like."

"It's in the past," I said dismissively. "I don't like to think about it."

"I'm sure. Must have been traumatic."

I met Sam's searching gaze.

"Are you doing okay otherwise? You seem jittery."

Jittery. Sure, that was the way to describe it. Mostly, I felt like a fucking idiot. And as much as I didn't like to think about my dad, I didn't *want* to think about English. Just like everyone else, she hadn't wanted to see me as anything more than what was on the surface.

For a minute, I thought about telling Sam. Confessing to the entire thing. It would probably feel good to get it off my chest. I was only keeping it a secret because I didn't want English to get fired. Despite everything, I knew her job was important to her. She was damn good at it. And she shouldn't lose it just because we'd fucked a night or two. Especially since it clearly meant nothing to her.

But I couldn't tell Sam. I'd always been careful who I showed my entire self to. I was over being judged for who I was. Only Camden really held no judgments against me. Whether from mutual trust or he just had darker tastes than me... it didn't matter. Sam was too new. And he lived with Lark. I didn't want it to get back to her. Not unless English wanted to tell her.

"I'm fine," I finally muttered. "Just drained from all of this and Jane."

Sam nodded sympathetically. "That makes sense. Well, the poker game tonight should cheer you up."

"Me?" I asked, side-eyeing him. "You're the one who fucking cleans the table now. It's not even a fair game. I swear you count cards or some bullshit."

Sam laughed and crossed his arms. "I'll never reveal my

secrets."

"Whatever. Get back to work, you lazy lawyer."

"Ass," Sam said with a chuckle as he stood from his seat.

"I'm not spotting you another ten grand."

Sam grinned devilishly. "You might ask *me* to spot *you* tonight—after I wipe you out."

"I've created a monster."

"See you tonight," Sam said with a deep laugh before exiting.

Yeah. Tonight.

Sounded like therapy.

I showed up at Camden's early. Well, before Gavin or Sam were there. I'd decided that I needed to talk to him about English. At least he wouldn't judge me for it.

I strode into the living room before I realized my mistake. Katherine's voice was loud and angry.

"When are you going to get it through your thick skull, I have no interest in Penn Kensington?" she spat. "He's married."

"So are you. Doesn't stop you."

"You know what, Camden? Just when I think there is something human underneath your skin, you prove me wrong," she seethed. "Time and time again."

"That's right, Katherine. There is nothing human underneath my skin. This is the man you married. You knew what you were doing when you signed on that dotted line."

Katherine must have said something low that I couldn't hear, and then she stormed out of the back room. When she saw me, she just sneered.

"He's all yours."

"Always a pleasure, Katherine."

"Fuck off, Kensington," she snapped and then strode right

into the elevator.

What the hell was that all about? Did I even want to know?

I stepped into Camden's game room. I found him dressed in a three-piece suit and seated in a brother leather chair. He smoked a cigar and stared off darkly. He looked like every quintessential rich bastard who had ever shown up in film.

"Marital strife?" I asked with an arched eyebrow.

He responded by taking another long pull on his cigar.

"I suppose you knew the woman you decided to marry." I took a seat across from him. "She's a tad bit headstrong."

Camden's eyes flickered to mine. "A tad bit headstrong? That's how you would describe Katherine Van Pelt?"

A smile crooked my features. "Or the most headstrong woman I have ever met."

"*Person* you have ever met," he corrected.

"Eh. I've met you."

"Well, you didn't show up early to discuss my obstinate wife, I presume."

"I did not. Though we could continue if you'd like. Perhaps you could tell me why you decided to get her to marry you," I said with a grin, knowing he had no intention of ever explaining himself.

"Perhaps," he said with a wry look. "Though I think you are here about the woman you took to Robert Dawson's party. You know when I told you to go out and get pussy, I didn't mean a new complication."

"You know how I am," I said. "Always making things complicated."

"True enough." Camden assessed me. "Let me guess... it didn't feel like just fucking with English."

I shrugged noncommittally. "It didn't."

"It should have."

"Yeah, well, she made it seem like that's all it was. Said that we were just rebound and that we'd end poorly."

"She's right," Camden said evenly. "I mean... this is just a rebound. And if you don't think it will end badly for you, you're delusional, Kensington."

I hated when Camden was right. Especially when he agreed with English. It wasn't that I thought we were suddenly going to start dating and all would be well. But having her there had felt nice. It had felt different than before. Like she had seen beyond the bullshit mask I wore. Except that she hadn't. She'd seen me exactly how everyone else had. So, maybe I was just fooling myself.

"Fuck her all you want," Camden said. "But you know that's where it ends. If it's good sex, then have some good sex and draw a line in the sand."

"I think we're past that," I told him. "I might have thrown her clothes at her and told her to get the fuck out of my apartment after she insinuated that I cheated on Jane."

A laugh cracked Camden's dour demeanor. "Fuck, Court. You sure have a way with women."

"It's a gift."

"Want my advice?"

I frowned. "Not really."

"Tough shit. You're getting it anyway."

"Why am I not surprised?" I asked with a shake of my head.

"Anna English is in the middle of a divorce. She's about as fucked up as you are right now. What you need is someone... easy. Someone who will be a fun flirtation, who you can dabble with, but nothing serious. Find the hottest woman you can with little to no baggage and move on."

I nodded absentmindedly. Camden's suggestion made sense. English and I were both fucked up. I still hadn't escaped what Jane had done. And who the fuck knew when or even if she'd ever recover from Josh cheating on her? Thinking about anything more than a good fuck with her was emotional suicide. It'd be smarter to forget about her.

Camden didn't need a response. We knew each other well enough to know when the conversation was over.

We were in the middle of a game of pool when Gavin and Sam showed up for the poker night.

"Brought along a stray," Gavin boasted.

And then Robert Dawson appeared at the entrance as well.

I glanced at Camden. He didn't like surprises. But he didn't seem to be bothered by Robert's appearance. Which either meant that Gavin had run it by him or Camden had something else up his sleeve, like usual.

"Hey, man," I said, shaking Robert's hand. "Good to see you again."

"You too. I was honored to get the invite." Robert moved and took Camden's hand next.

Gavin reached for my hand. "So, your brother is having a wedding reception and no wedding. What the fuck is that about?"

"He eloped," I said with a shrug. "Penn kind of does whatever the fuck he wants. And gets away with it."

"Lucky bastard," Gavin muttered. "If I eloped, my family might literally kill me, raise me from the dead, and kill me again."

Sam chuckled. "Can your family raise people from the dead?"

"It's that Texas oil money," I said. "They can do anything."

"It's true," Gavin agreed.

We sat down at the table, and Camden began to shuffle the decks together. I poured drinks like a professional bartender before sliding into my seat at the end of the table, next to Robert. I side-eyed Sam as he shuffled poker chips like he was on the fucking World Series of Poker. I still couldn't believe how bad he'd hustled us the first time I'd all but dragged him along.

"So, Court, where did you meet your new girl?" Robert

asked, taking a sip of his old-fashioned.

Gavin perked up. "New girl?"

"What?" Sam chirped, his chips spilling in surprise.

I carefully glanced up at Camden, who looked unfazed, before turning to Gavin. "What do you mean?"

Robert seemed to read the room. "The woman you showed up with last week. Anna?"

"English?" Gavin gasped. "You're with English?"

"Wait, wait, wait," Sam said. He slapped his hand down on the table. "Since when?"

"I'm not with English," I told them all. "It's a simple misunderstanding. When we went to Robert's party together, I didn't want her to be uncomfortable. So, I didn't correct you when you said we were together." I shrugged, all nonchalant. "She's my publicist."

Robert's eyes widened. "Oh fuck, I had no idea."

Gavin sat back in his seat. "Fuck, that is way less interesting."

Sam just narrowed his eyes. He didn't believe me. And I could hardly blame him.

"Does that mean English is fair game?" Robert asked with a sly smile. "Because she's super hot."

Gavin snorted. "As if you'd have a chance with Anna English."

"No," Camden said abruptly, silencing the lot of them. "English isn't fair game."

He didn't meet my eyes. But I knew why he'd said it. And I was grateful. Even if I'd just decided to put the whole thing behind us.

"All right," Robert said after a minute. "Let's deal some cards then."

"Yes. Let's," I said.

It would be a good distraction from the rest of this conversation.

19

ENGLISH

I'd had every intention of talking to Court over the weekend. But Winnie had sent Max Henson, one of her A-list clients, my way, and I'd played babysitter the whole time. It had been bad before Max realized that I was married to Josh. Then, it had gone straight to miserable.

I still couldn't decide if it was worse that Max kept trying to convince me that Josh was a good guy and people just "made mistakes" or the number of times Max tried to get in my pants. Either way, I'd handled him. He hadn't botched his round of interviews for his movie. And he was off his merry way, back to LA, where he could be Winnie's problem again.

But now that Court was working, I saw him a lot less. I suddenly had free days like crazy. And I needed to talk to him.

I knew that, every Monday, he got off work at three and went with Camden to this traditional gentlemen's club. I'd assumed it was a strip club until I'd looked it up. Apparently, it was this super-snooty aristocratic social club that favored Ivy League educations and bank accounts in the nine- to ten-digit range.

The likelihood that I could get into this place was basically zero. But I'd shown up anyway in the hopes that they would send for him or some bullshit. Since I didn't want to interrupt his work and I didn't think just waltzing into his apartment was a good idea. All things considered.

But after a solid thirty-minute wait outside the gentlemen's club, it wasn't Court that appeared. It was Camden.

"English," he said with a hard, steady gaze and next to no kindness in his voice. "What are you doing here?"

"I'm here to see Court."

He arched an eyebrow. "He isn't here."

"He's been coming here every Monday for a month," I told him.

"I can assure you that Court has not nor has he ever come here on a Monday afternoon. He doesn't actually care about keeping up connections or appearances," he said stiffly.

"If he's not here, then where the hell is he every Monday? This is what's on his calendar."

Camden just stared at me. "How should I know?"

A bad feeling settled into the pit of my stomach. Why would Court lie about what he was doing? Was he seeing another woman? It would make sense based on his past actions. But he had said that he hadn't been with anyone else. He had no reason to lie about that. But still… I was uneasy.

"I don't know. You're his best friend."

"And you're his publicist."

I was. And I had somehow managed to lose my client.

"Well, thanks, Camden," I said, putting on my best publicist voice and smiling at him. "I appreciate your help."

"Was I helpful?"

"I know he's not here. That's more than I knew before."

Camden took a step forward. He was so domineering. A power unto himself. An asshole, but to get to the position that he was in, he likely had to be. "Be careful, English."

A shiver trailed down my back. It sounded more like a threat than anything. "Careful with what?"

He shrugged. "You tell me."

So... he knew.

Court had told him.

Was he saying that I should be careful with my heart because Court would break it? Or something more sinister?

"I don't know," I finally said. "But... I'll keep it in mind."

"You do that." He stepped back. "Now, you'll have to excuse me. You interrupted a meeting."

Then, he walked into the club without a backward glanced. Leaving me to feel chilled and uncomfortable. Camden Percy was slightly terrifying.

I strode away from the entrance to the gentlemen's club and paced the sidewalk. How the hell was I going to find out where Court was? And what would I find when I did? I couldn't stop imagining him with another woman, and despite it all, it made my stomach turn.

I scrolled through the calendar, checking over the last couple of Mondays. Nothing unusual. They all said they'd be here. He'd even said that. He'd lied to me, even when he claimed to hate lying. But... why?

Another thought hit me. When Court had started working at Kensington Corporation, I'd hired a full-time car service for him. Before, he'd been content to get around with cabs or on foot, but with the job, it looked good for him to have the car.

And that car service came with an app. Its main function was like Uber or Lyft. You could flag your service down, see where the car was parked, communicate with the driver, and the like. I had the app as well as Court so that I could call the car for him. I'd used the same thing with other clients on occasion and found it convenient.

Well, I hadn't thought about using it as a GPS before.

I pulled up the app, expecting to see the car parked on the

Upper East Side in front of an apartment building or something. But instead, it was parked on the Upper West near Central Park.

"Weird," I muttered to myself and then flagged a cab down to take me to the car.

It was a half-hour trek to get to the car's location on my phone. I was certain that it would move, and I'd have to follow it around through the city. But no. It was exactly where the app said it would be, parked harmlessly in front of a bagel shop.

I paid my cab and strode over to the car. I rapped on the window twice. The driver rolled his window down.

His eyes rounded in surprise. "You're... English, right?"

"That'd be me," I said with a smile. "I'm here for Court. Can you point me in the right direction?"

"Yeah. Sure." He stepped out of the vehicle and gestured in front of him. "One block up into Central Park, and then he's on the third field on the left."

The third field? What the hell?

He must have seen my confusion. "Do you want me to walk you?"

"No. That's quite all right. Thank you."

"No problem. Let me know if you need anything else."

"I will."

I headed across Central Park West toward the fields inside the park. I regretted my heels and lack of jacket as I hustled through the tree-lined trails. It opened up onto an array of fields—soccer, kick ball, lacrosse, baseball. They were all completely packed. A few games were going on, but mostly, it looked like practice.

The driver had said the third field. So, I headed that way and stopped before I reached the field. My eyes couldn't comprehend what I was seeing.

It was a lacrosse field with several dozen upper-elementary-school-aged kids running drills. They all wore matching red-

and-white T-shirts and shorts with helmets and gloves and sticks. Most of them were drenched in sweat but appeared to be both deep in concentration and having the time of their lives.

None of that was unusual.

What was out of place... was the coach.

I recognized him from a hundred yards off.

Court Kensington coached youth lacrosse.

My jaw dropped open at the sight of him. He looked hot as fuck out there in red shorts and a white T-shirt. A whistle dangled from his neck, and he had a stick in his hand, demonstrating some move that I had no hope of imagining its purpose. I'd never seen anyone play lacrosse. It was a rich white guy sport. But the way Court handled that stick made me wonder why I'd never given it a chance.

My mouth went dry. I was staring. Surely, he would be able to feel my eyes drilling into the back of his head.

But he never looked up. His full attention was on the team of boys learning the sport that he'd played all through college. In fact, it was the very sport that I'd made him donate a shit-ton of money to when we first started working together.

My eyes scanned the logo on their shirt. It was the same recreation team. He'd funded the team. And now, he coached them.

How had this happened? How had he kept this from me? *Why* had he kept this from me?

Surely, he could see how good this would look to the press.

And then I realized that was why he hadn't told me. He didn't want it in the press. It wasn't about him. It was about the kids and the love of the sport. Court Kensington had a heart.

I had completely misjudged him.

He wasn't who I'd thought he was at all.

I slowly backed away. As much as I wanted to watch him coach those boys, I knew he wanted this all to himself for a reason. And I wouldn't be the one to take this away from him.

20

ENGLISH

As I slipped into my black cocktail dress for Penn and Natalie's wedding reception tonight, my stomach twisted with doubt. I hadn't gone to see Court. We hadn't discussed what I'd seen. Or the assumptions I had made about him.

I kept wanting to do it. To tell him that I was wrong about what I'd said to him. Not that he'd given me an indication that he was in someway a different sort of person than he presented to anyone else. And it was unfair for him to place all the blame on me for not seeing past his facade. But I should have.

That was part of my job. To see my client for who they were and work toward a mutual, beneficial outcome. But I'd been blind to that. My research had all indicated that Court Kensington was a hellish playboy with no ambition and a streak of stupidity to which he never had consequences.

Now, I didn't know.

I'd spent the time apart, reconsidering the persona he'd crafted. I still had no idea *why* he let people believe that he was a grade A jackass who fucked anything that walked. But that clearly was not who he was. Or who he no longer was. One or the other. I wasn't sure which.

And so, I'd done my job. I'd worked with him the last week through text. Perfectly professional. All the while knowing it was leading to tonight, where I'd finally see him.

I wanted answers. And there was something stirring my chest. Maybe... hope. Hope that we could talk this out and figure out what to do from here.

Hope was a dangerous emotion.

It gave me anxiety.

But I still finished the waves in my hair and the smoky-eye makeup I'd perfected at a young age and called a cab to take me to The Plaza.

I was not at all surprised that Court and Penn's mother had insisted on a wedding reception at The Plaza. It seemed like something an Upper East Side mother would do. Something Lark's mom would do if she let her. Which seemed unlikely.

I'd gone to the Oscars, Emmys, Tonys, and a dozen various music award ceremonies, and I'd never felt like more of a fraud than as I stepped out on a red carpet for a fucking wedding reception. There were photographers waiting outside to take pictures of all the elite guests. And then there was me.

I handed my invitation over at the entrance and was ushered inside with the rest of the Upper East Side. I wasn't here to make sure some A-list celeb didn't forget their speech. I was here on my own merits. Somehow, it felt worse. More of a sham. There, I'd had a purpose. Here... I felt adrift.

As soon as I entered, I went in search of the Upper East Siders I did know. Preferably Lark. But I couldn't see to find her, and the room was packed. It seemed that they had invited every person they knew.

To my surprise, Whitley was the first person I recognized. Her petite, pixie frame was clad in a silver dress that only brought out her recently dyed dark red hair.

"Whit! What are you doing here?" I asked.

"English, you're here!" Whitley pulled me into a hug.

I immediately felt better with her at my side. I hadn't felt that out of it in a long time. This place sure knew how to drag a girl down.

"Yes. I got an invitation."

"No invite for me. But I met a new guy."

"A new guy this time? Swearing off girls for a while?"

Whitley bit her lip. "The last one got a little too clingy. I can't do clingy."

"And the new guy isn't clingy?"

"We'll see. This is only our second date. And there he is." She twiddled her fingers away from us.

I turned and found none other than Robert Dawson heading in our direction with a drink in each hand.

"Robert," I said in surprise.

"Hey, English," he said with that dashing debonair smile as he passed Whitley a drink.

"How do you two know each other?" Whitley asked, taking a large gulp of her fruity drink.

"I went to his Labor Day weekend party," I told her. "How do you two know each other?"

Whitley shrugged as if she knew everyone. "His mom was having work done, and he came to pick her up. Meet-cute."

"Wow," I said in surprise.

Robert just laughed. "I didn't even know that you were friends."

"We were in the same sorority at UCLA," Whitley said. "English is the best publicist in the business. The absolute best, most badass friend."

"And Whitley keeps everything interesting."

Whitley winked. "I try."

"She definitely does," Robert said, enamored with Whitley's enormous personality. Which was good because a lot of people couldn't handle her intensity. Plus, Whitley went through relationships as often as she changed her hair.

I plucked a glass of champagne off of a passing tray as I chatted with Whitley and Robert. I knew that I'd need something stronger for the rest of the evening. A little liquid courage. But my earlier anxiety had already loosened just by being in the presence of my friend.

We still hadn't seen Lark, but I saw Gavin and waved him over. He looked incredibly handsome in a tailored black tuxedo. His dark red hair combed back off of his face. He drew me in for a quick hug and then gestured to his date, a model-tall white girl with medium-brown hair slicked back into a severe bun and a nude dress. "This is Jada."

She took my hand for a weak shake. "Pleasure to meet you."

"You too," I said.

"Jada does runways for Dior," Gavin said hastily.

"Ah," I said. "That must be... fun?"

Jada shrugged. Unimpressed. "You said you were going to get me another drink."

"I am," Gavin said.

Though I could tell by the look on his face that he didn't like her attitude. Well, this one wouldn't last.

"Whatever," Jada said. She pulled her phone out and began to text, ignoring the lot of us.

Gavin gave me a sheepish look. But then his eyes shifted to Whitley, and he frowned and then looked away. It was fast enough that if I hadn't been paying attention, I might not have even noticed. Was Gavin into Whitley?

I had no way of knowing as he immediately turned to Robert, and the two began talking business, leaving us girls to our own devices. Jada was literally attached to hers.

It was about that time that the lights brightened. The DJ announced Penn and Natalie as the bride and groom. I stood on my tiptoes in my high heels to see over the crowd forming as the couple strode into the room.

"What do they look like?" Whitley asked.

She was a good head shorter than I was, and I could barely see anything.

"She's wearing white. He's in a tux."

"Is it a full gown?"

"See for yourself," I said just as a large circle opened up on the dance floor, giving us a perfect view of the couple as they began their first dance.

It was, in fact, not a full gown. But rather a demure A-line number that came to Natalie's knees. It was covered in lace, wrapping over both shoulders and securing around her neck. The dress was open to the middle of her back and then had an intricate row of seed pearl buttons. It managed to be both modern and classic without being over the top. Her shoes were nude Christian Louboutins that I'd enviously eyed in their store and put back. They had clearly spared no expense for this event.

With how gorgeous Natalie looked with her silver mane of hair pinned up into an intricate design and her makeup full and beautiful, it was hard to even notice Penn. Even though he was in a custom tuxedo that looked like he'd taken it right off of a movie set. He looked like James Bond, and he twirled his wife around the dance floor as if she were his Bond girl.

And for a second, he looked so like his brother that it was unnerving. I hadn't quite noticed that before.

Suddenly, I was searching out the other Kensington brother. Where exactly was Court?

I hadn't seen him in the crowd. And I'd been looking. I figured he must have been backstage with his family, but that didn't explain why he wasn't here now. It seemed that if Penn and Natalie had made it out, then he would have followed. I could see their mother standing nearby.

In fact, as the first song ended and another one started up, Leslie took the hand of a man standing to her left, and he escorted her onto the dance floor. But still, no Court.

"Have you seen Court?" I asked Gavin and Robert. "Surely, he's here for his brother."

Robert shook his head. "Haven't seen him."

"Which is strange," Gavin confessed. Then, his eyes roamed the room. "I thought he'd be here already."

"Maybe he's making an entrance," Whitley said.

"For his brother's wedding reception?" I asked incredulously.

"That actually sounds just like him," Gavin agreed.

I shook my head. That didn't sound like Court. If he wanted to piss his brother off, he had a lot of other ways to do it. And I knew that he didn't have any intention of pissing Penn off. He was happy that Penn was happy.

"Ooh," Gavin muttered under his breath. "Well, that makes a lot more sense."

"What does?"

Gavin pointed toward a far corner of the room. Court had just stepped through the entrance that Penn and Natalie had taken a few minutes earlier. And on his arm was a tall, beautiful brunette with her large breasts on display in a low-cut dress as red orange as a California poppy field.

"Poppy," I muttered in shock.

"Yeah. No wonder he was late," Gavin said with a laugh. "Poppy Arlington is as hot as they fucking come."

My stomach turned over. Court was *here* with Poppy Arlington. The same woman he'd purposely avoided at Robert's party. Who he'd sneered at because she was aggressive and desperate. What the fuck?

21

COURT

Poppy Arlington might objectively be one of the hottest women on the Upper East Side. But she was also objectively one of the most annoying. And I already regretted bringing her to the reception.

It had seemed like a good idea at the time.

Camden's advice had been to find the hottest girl without baggage and give it a whirl. I'd debated inviting someone else, but Poppy had been the easiest choice, and I'd gone with that.

"Court," she asked in that fake breathy voice she used, "are you sure you even want to go to the party?"

Her insinuation was clear. And it was even clearer as she leaned heavily against me.

"My own brother's wedding reception? Yes, I'm sure I want to go inside," I snapped.

She didn't flinch back or anything. Just stared up at me with wide, dark eyes and blinked slow.

"We should leave early," she said, her hand trailing to the front of my pants.

I grasped her wrist to halt her descent. "No."

She stuck her bottom lip out in a pout that probably

worked on most other guys in the city, but I just ignored it. I was too busy scanning the room. I hadn't seen English since Labor Day weekend. We'd texted, but it had been all work. Nothing to indicate that she'd thought about what I'd said. That she wanted to talk about it.

I shouldn't have been surprised. She'd made herself clear that night. This would end badly for us. And so, better to end it before that happened. Better to bring a date to the event and move on.

Move on. That was what Camden had said. As if I'd fallen for Anna English or something. Rather than just hate-fucked her on Robert's bathroom sink. And then fucked her into oblivion the whole night. It was great sex. But that wasn't reason enough to get attached to her. It wasn't like good sex couldn't be found elsewhere.

I just hadn't gone looking.

Not since Jane.

I cleared her name from my mind. *Move on. Move the fuck on, dude.*

I clenched my jaw as I maneuvered Poppy through the crowd. Not paying attention to her incessant chatter as I sought out my real quarry.

And then I found her.

Just like that, she appeared at the edge of the crowd as others moved in to fill the space of Penn and Natalie's first dance. She wore a sleek black dress that seductively hugged her. Nothing flashy like Poppy's low-cut top, but the dress lured me in like a siren's call. Her long blonde hair fanned out into loose waves over her shoulders. She looked powerful and tempting. And for a second, I forgot that I wasn't here for her. Not in that way.

Move on already.

Our eyes met across the distance. Her jaw clenched. Something fierce passed across her face. Something I wasn't sure I'd seen before. Anger, fear, disgust. It all passed through her in a split second and then disappeared just as fast. Then, she turned to the side and began to speak in earnest to Robert Dawson.

Was she here with him? He'd been interested in her. Not that many people would defy Camden, but it was possible.

"Can we dance?" Poppy asked, her voice a whine.

"Let's get drinks instead," I offered.

She grinned and flashed me a small, clear baggie in her purse. "Maybe something a little stronger."

I put my hand out to obscure it from view. "Don't just show that in public."

"Why not? No one here is going to care," she said dismissively.

I hadn't put in all this fucking work just for a little bit of cocaine to bring down the evening. "You can do it if you want but not near me. Fuck."

"Stop acting so self-righteous," she said with an eye roll. "Since when have you turned down a bump?"

It'd been a long time. It had always been easier just to say yes. But English's voice ran through my mind. *Imagine what would happen to all the work we'd put in.* What the fuck would be the point of me working for Kensington Corporation if I screwed it all up? I didn't need a bump that bad.

"Just do it later," I ground out. "Let's have a drink instead."

She shrugged a shoulder and followed me to the bar. I got her a Long Island iced tea and ordered myself a whiskey and Coke. Poppy finished her drink like a fish, as if it didn't have five shots in it. She immediately asked for another one, which I procured irritably, and then forced her to wander over to where Camden stood tensely with Katherine.

Honestly, I was a bit surprised that either of them had even come. Considering Katherine's history with my brother and her equally terrible history with Natalie. Not to mention, Camden's extreme dislike for Penn. Keeping up appearances was the name of their game.

"I'm going to go to the powder room," Poppy said, inelegantly patting her bag. "Don't move."

I just shook my head in frustration as she headed into the restroom.

Katherine sniffed her nose. "Is that the best you can do, Kensington?"

I narrowed my eyes. "As charming as ever, Katherine."

"Haven't you heard that she has a problem? She's been in rehab more times than I can count."

I had heard that. I'd thought it was exaggerated. Or that she'd be able to keep it together tonight.

"Not everyone can be as perfect as you, now can they?"

Katherine just smiled. "That is a fact."

Through all of this, Camden hadn't said a word. He just stared straight ahead blankly. He was my closest friend, and sometimes, he was such a closed book.

"And how awkward is this lovely wedding reception for the pair of you?" I asked with a cheeky smile.

But Katherine frowned and shot a tense look in Camden's direction.

Finally, Camden looked my way. "You tell me, Court. Should I have brought my wife to the wedding of the man she loves?"

Katherine froze. "I don't..."

"Is it cruel of me to force her to watch?"

"Probably," I said with a shrug.

"Camden," she said through gritted teeth as her cheeks heated.

But he wasn't looking at her. "You think she'd learn something from the experience."

Katherine was nearly trembling with barely suppressed rage and something like grief.

Her relationship with Penn had been fifteen years in the making. Even if she didn't love my brother like she once had, it had to be difficult to watch him marry someone else. Especially someone she detested. And for Camden to rub it in...

Fuck, he was a right bastard sometimes.

"And you think you'd learn," she finally said and then brushed past me as she strode away.

"Why do you do that, man?" I asked Camden.

His eyes followed his wife. A predator's gaze. "Katherine thinks that she can play games. That I, like everyone else in her life, will fall into one of her pretty traps. That she can wrap me around her little finger. But she's wrong. There is only black and white when it comes to Katherine. And one day, she'll learn which side of the line I fall on."

Poppy returned right after that, rubbing at her nose and looking a little more out of it by the second. "Can we dance now?"

"Sure," I muttered halfheartedly.

Camden smirked at me. "Have fun."

I flipped him off as I followed Poppy to the dance floor. The music had shifted from first and second dances to party music. Penn and Natalie were out there with their friends around them. My mother rubbed elbows with potential donors. Maybe once I got Poppy onto the dance floor, it'd be better. It seemed unlikely. But it was worth a shot.

The one good thing was that she knew how to dance. I didn't have to work with someone with no rhythm. But it sure as hell wasn't like dancing with English at Dawson's party. That had practically been foreplay. This was... just Poppy showing off for a crowd.

When I looked up again, English stood with a small group. Her eyes were on me. Or more precisely, Poppy. Her face was perfectly neutral. But English said so much in that look.

When the next song ended, I took a step away from the dance floor.

"Another one," Poppy said with a feral grin as she reached for me.

"Let's go talk to Gavin and Robert."

She sighed. "Seriously?"

"We can dance after. Look, this song sucks anyway."

She huffed but nodded. "Fine. I do like Robert."

It was a weak excuse. I really wanted to see English. I wanted to know exactly what she was thinking behind those mysterious blue eyes. Because she shouldn't feel anything but relief that I'd brought someone else.

Poppy and I headed across the room to where English stood with Robert, Gavin, and a girl that I didn't recognize but presumed to be Gavin's date.

"Kensington," Gavin said, grabbing my hand. "How the hell did you land Poppy Arlington?"

Poppy fluttered her eyelashes at Gavin and wrapped her hands around my bicep, leaning her head against my suit. "Just lucky, I guess."

The way she'd been acting all night, I didn't feel lucky. But I didn't disagree with her statement. Not as my gaze shifted to English.

"And you remember English?" I asked Poppy.

Poppy's brow furrowed. "You came to Robert's party."

"I did," English said.

"She's my publicist," I added even though I hadn't that night.

English pursed her lips. "I am."

"Wow. So, you, like, fix people's problems and handle their schedules and shit?"

"Pretty much," English said.

"She's being modest," Gavin said grandly. "She's the best in the business. She's even making Court look like—what did you say, Court?—the golden boy of the Upper East Side?"

Poppy laughed, low and breathy. "No one could be good enough for that. We all know you're the bad one."

She bit her lip as she stared up at me. I wanted to rip my arm out of her grasp, but I left her there.

"Thankfully, I *am* good enough for that," English bit out, her voice acerbic.

"Are you taking on new clients?" Poppy asked. "I could use someone like you to help with my image. Rehab is so tiresome."

"No, I'm not."

"Oh, I can pay," Poppy assured her.

English's eyes narrowed. "You can't afford me."

Poppy giggled as if she had never heard something so absurd. "Oh, I think I can. How much?"

"I didn't mean the money," she said, her voice dripping acid.

Poppy scrunched her face together. As if she couldn't think of another reason English wouldn't want to work with her. I had to keep my face blank or else I'd bust out laughing.

I changed the subject before Poppy could figure it out. "So, you showed up with Dawson?"

English looked startled. "What?"

I pointed between her and Robert, where they stood together. "You're here together."

"Whoa!" Robert said. "No way, bro."

It was my turn to look confused. "I thought..."

"Wrong," English snapped. "You thought wrong. Robert is here with *Whitley*. She just saw a client and went to say hello. I, on the other hand, showed up alone."

"Sucks," Poppy said. "Couldn't find a date?"

"Oh," was all that came out of my mouth.

English ignored Poppy's question and glared daggers at me. "Yeah. *Oh*."

"Can we go dance again, Court?" Poppy asked, already

bored with the conversation. She meandered back toward the dance floor without waiting for my response.

"Yeah, Court," English said, taking a step back, "go dance."

I opened my mouth to say something, but what the hell could I say? It wasn't my problem that I'd brought someone else and she'd shown up alone. She was the one who was married anyway. And I was perfectly single. She had no right to be upset. No fucking right.

"I think I will," I finally said.

"Good," English said. She smiled faintly at Gavin and Robert. "If you'll excuse me, I'm going to find the restroom."

Before I could say another word, she stalked away from me and out of sight.

Robert smacked my arm. "Why would you think I was here with English? I'm not stupid enough to go against Camden's word."

"Right," I said. "I just assumed."

"English is a bit intense anyway," Robert admitted. "Hot as fuck but really intense."

She really was. Intense in every aspect of her life. It'd been stupid of me to think she'd show up with someone else. My assumption had made me act like an idiot in front of her. But what else was new?

I wanted to go after her. But what would that solve? We'd slept together, and that was that. Chasing after her would just give her the wrong impression. It would look like I wanted this to work between us.

And I didn't.

I... didn't.

English was too complicated.

It'd be safer to follow Poppy out onto the dance floor. To forget that English and I had ever been anything more than client and publicist.

22

ENGLISH

Fuck Court Kensington.

He'd been strutting around the entire reception with a woman at his side he hardly tolerated, let alone liked. And then had the audacity to come at *me* about showing up with someone else. When I had come *alone*.

Why the hell had I gotten my hopes up? Why had I let myself be fooled that Court was somehow a different person?

He'd yelled at me for judging him and assuming he was a playboy. But then shown up with Poppy fucking Arlington on his arm. He might coach youth lacrosse in secret, but it didn't excuse the way he acted. One or two good deeds didn't cancel out years of asshole behavior.

The truth was, Court Kensington was a train wreck.

As much as all of my research had indicated from the get-go. Lark had said that he was a playboy. That he'd fucked around his entire life. Even his mother had feared hiring me because no woman resisted Court's charms.

She'd been right, of course, and it made it all the worse.

I slammed my hand into the restroom door and nearly

struck a girl in the face. "Sorry," I muttered and hastened inside.

I locked myself inside an empty stall. I needed a minute alone, away from this stupid fucking Upper East Side world that threatened to swallow me whole.

I took a few deep, healing breaths, using my jiu-jitsu training exercises to try to calm down. I wished I'd had enough space to go through the tai chi forms. But the breathing techniques would have to do.

The most obvious answer was to leave the reception. I wasn't a part of this world. Not in the same sense. I hadn't grown up here. I didn't have a trust fund to fall back on. I'd just worked my ass off.

But the other part of me said that I should stay and prove he couldn't get to me. Because he'd done this on purpose. He'd taken my spark of hope and lit it on fire, burning it all to cinders. And I didn't want anyone, not even Court Kensington, to think that they could force me out of a space.

When my heart finally stopped racing, I exited the restroom and found only one other person waiting at the sinks.

"Katherine," I said with a note of surprise.

"I barred the door. Someone is going to get mad soon," she said with a disinterested shrug. "But you and I should talk."

"Uh... should we? About what?"

"You and Court."

"What about me and Court?"

Katherine shot me a look. "To survive the Upper East Side, you have to be observant. Being married to Camden has only honed that skill. I saw your little exchange. The body language. Everything that wasn't said. You're together."

"We're not..."

"Then, you're just fucking?"

I cringed and deflated against the sink. "Is it that obvious?"

"To me." She frowned. "I have some experience with Kensington men."

"Oh, right. You and Penn were together."

She glanced away and then back. "We were. On and off." Katherine shrugged. She looked fierce and hard. But her fierceness was for me. Her hardness against the man who had hurt me. "I knew Court hadn't brought that dipshit Poppy for no reason. Even he wouldn't stoop that low. He clearly wanted to make you jealous. And it worked."

"I'm not jealous," I said at once.

Katherine looked incredulous. "So, you just spend a lot of time in the restroom for no reason?"

"No," I grumbled. Christ, *was* I jealous?

"Look, just take some advice from someone who knows. Don't fall for a Kensington."

"I haven't... I don't..."

But the more I thought about it. Maybe... I had.

I took responsibility for what had happened over Labor Day. I'd pushed him away. I'd let fear come between us. I'd assumed a lot about his character. Even if I wanted to strangle him right now, we'd had the start of something, and I'd smothered it. I'd projected my feelings about what was going on with Josh onto the situation. Colored it through the lens of my shattered heart until it all looked distorted.

But if I didn't care, would I be this upset?

I shouldn't give two shits that he'd shown up with Poppy. If it had just been sex, then it wouldn't matter.

But it did.

Oh god.

I took a step back. My hand went to my mouth.

I liked him.

Oh no. This was... no.

"Maybe it's too late for that," Katherine said, seeing my distress. "It usually is too late when it comes to a Kensington.

But if you want my advice, don't nurture it. Let him have his Poppy Arlington. Forget about him. Forget it all." She nearly choked on her words. "Otherwise, he'll just leave you for a nobody from nowhere. And you'll have to watch him parade around with his new wife as if the last fifteen years didn't matter."

Katherine's heartbreak cut deep.

I knew that pain. Knew the depth of betrayal that came from it.

That was the pain I'd had when Josh stomped on my heart and deigned to say I was overreacting.

I didn't know why Katherine let herself be vulnerable with me. But I wouldn't break the facade by telling her that I was actually the nobody from nowhere. She didn't really know that about me. Pretty much nobody did. Josh and Lark and Poise gave me social proof in these cutthroat industries. But I was no different than Natalie.

Which made it all the more problematic.

Because no fairy-tale ending waited for me and Court.

No wedding in Paris and a reception at The Plaza.

That was never going to happen.

I'd fooled myself into it once with Josh, and look at how well that had turned out.

No, Katherine was right. It didn't matter that I'd fallen for Court Kensington. That I… actually liked him. Because it was hopeless for a girl like me to end up with a guy like him. Not when I was clearly destined to end up just like my parents.

I needed to walk away. Just walk away from it all.

"Thanks," I finally got out. "Your insight is helpful."

She nodded once. I could see the thoughts swirling through her head. She was so cold and abrasive to so many people. But I could see the pain in that moment.

"What about Camden?" I managed to ask.

She lifted one shoulder. "He's Camden."

"Do you love him?"

Katherine met my gaze. "It really doesn't matter."

"Why?"

"Because he doesn't love me. He'll never love me."

Then, she unlocked the restroom door. A line had formed, just like in Robert's apartment. But Katherine disappeared through the door like a specter through walls. I wished that I'd had that ability.

I took another breath and then followed her out. I just needed to find Lark and let her know I was heading home. There was no reason to stay here and torture myself. No reason at all.

Lark and Sam held each other like a lifeline as they slow-danced. I had to meander around an array of couples before I reached them.

I tapped Sam's shoulder. "Mind if I cut in?"

Sam jolted and then saw it was me and laughed. "Sure thing, English." He winked at Lark. "I'll get us drinks."

Lark glowed as she looked at him. Then, she turned her attention back to me. "What's going on?"

"I didn't mean to ruin your dance. I just wanted to tell you that I was leaving."

"Leaving?" she asked in surprise. "But the reception just started."

"I know."

Lark took my arm and pulled me off the dance floor, stopping only when we were in a secluded area together. "Will you tell me what's going on? Is it Josh? I knew that a wedding reception would be hard for you. But I thought since there was no ceremony..."

"No," I said hastily. "It's not Josh."

Lark held my hand. "You can talk to me."

I opened my mouth and then closed it. I had no idea how to tell her this.

"English, I feel like something has been bothering you for weeks. You were the only one who was really there for me when all that stuff happened with Sam. I couldn't imagine going through that alone. Whatever it is, I don't want you to go through it alone either."

"I slept with Court," I blurted out.

Lark's jaw dropped. "What? When?"

I winced. "Which time?"

"Oh fuck," Lark said with wide eyes. "I never thought you and Court..."

"Me either."

"I mean, I suggested you for the job, knowing you were immune to douchebag behavior."

"I know. I know."

"How did this happen?"

I ran a hand back through my hair and sighed. "At first, it was because I was so upset about Josh. I was taking all my anger out on Court. And it just exploded between us. I thought it was all rebound..."

"But it's *not* just rebound?" she asked, her green eyes wide.

"Oh god, Lark, stop looking at me like that."

Lark ran a hand down her face. "I'm sorry. I'm in shock. Is this why you were asking me if he was a playboy the other day? Why you were acting so weird together at the primary?"

I nodded. "Yeah."

"And now, you... what? Do you like him?"

I winced again.

"Fuck," Lark whispered.

"I know. Look, I told him we were a bad idea. That I'd end up fired. That we couldn't do this. Plus, I was just some notch in his belt. That he was just a playboy and that he'd cheated on Jane. I just laid into him."

"But like... all of that is true?"

"Well, I guess he's not a playboy anymore? I don't know,

Lark. He said he didn't cheat on Jane, and I was the only person that he'd slept with since Jane."

"He's here with Poppy Arlington," Lark said, throwing her hand out. As if that proved that he was back to his manwhore ways.

"I know. Trust me. I don't know what to believe. All I know is that I hurt him by saying it, and then he brought Poppy to hurt me back. And it worked. I don't want to like him." I glanced down at the ground and shrugged. "I'm still married, for fuck's sake. This is the last thing I need."

Lark let out of a long breath. "Okay. Okay. It'll be all right. We can figure this out. You can hang with me and Sam. We don't have to worry about Court or Poppy or anything."

I shook my head. "No, I think I'm just going to go home."

"English..."

"It's for the better."

Lark sighed. "I can go with you. You shouldn't be alone. You've gone through a lot."

"You can't leave your oldest friend's wedding reception." I laughed softly and held my hand out. "Stay. Have a good time. I'll be fine."

"Are you sure?"

"Positive," I lied.

Lark dragged me in for a hug and promised to check up on me later. Then, I walked the perimeter of the room toward the exit. I took one last look over my shoulder and found Court dancing suggestively with Poppy. I cringed, hating that I felt anything at all, and then left the reception behind.

23

COURT

"Come to the restroom with me," Poppy said. Her arms dangled around my neck. Her eyes were wide, pupils blasted out until they were nearly indistinguishable from her dark irises.

"It's barely been an hour," I told her.

She tightened her lips, that euphoria heading straight into irritability. She was coming down from her high. "I just need a little more."

"Poppy..."

"If you won't go with me, then I'll go alone," she snapped.

"How much have you had today?"

Jesus, I was policing her. But it'd been a while since I was around someone whose drug use worried me. No wonder she'd been in and out of rehab so much.

"Who the fuck cares?" She ripped herself away from me. "I'll be back."

I ground my teeth in frustration. What a nightmare. Why had I listened to Camden? So much for choosing someone hot with no baggage. I was beginning to think that didn't exist.

A hand latched on to mine—hard. I whipped around to snap at Poppy, but it wasn't Poppy.

"Lark?" I asked in surprise.

She looked furious. Beyond furious. In fact, I didn't think I'd ever seen her look like this before. Like she might cut off my balls and force me to eat them for breakfast.

"We need to talk," she growled low.

"About what?"

She narrowed her eyes. "I think you know."

English.

She wanted to talk about English. So, that meant that Anna had finally told her what had happened between us. Great. Just what I wanted to deal with.

"I don't think so." I tried to extract my arm from hers, but she didn't release me.

"Oh no, this wasn't a suggestion."

"Lark, it's whatever. She made her point clear. To be honest, I don't want to rehash it with you."

"You fucking idiot," she snapped at me.

I jolted back. I hadn't heard Lark talk like that in... literal years. She was so professional. There was a reason she was my mother's deputy campaign manager. She knew how to get shit done. And now, she had her sights set on me.

"I'm not my brother," I huffed. "Your anger doesn't turn me into a sad puppy dog that makes me want to make it all better."

"Maybe it should! Can't you think about someone other than yourself for one minute?"

"When has that ever helped me before?"

She shook her head at me. "You're just proving her right. You are a train wreck. The playboy train wreck of the Upper East Side. And that is all you'll ever be."

I ground my teeth together. That wasn't even fucking true. I should just let her believe it. What the fuck did it matter to me? She was goading me. But it worked.

"Fine. You have until Poppy comes back," I said and then strode off the dance floor.

"What exactly are you doing with English, Court?" Lark asked, crossing her arms over her chest.

"Currently, I am doing nothing with her. As you can see, I brought a date."

"Yeah. On purpose, to hurt her!"

I narrowed my eyes. "You don't know my motives. She was the one who said that this wasn't happening. Neither of you can blame me for moving on."

"Is that what you think you're doing? Showing up here with Poppy Arlington and dancing like you're going to fuck her on the dance floor?" Lark glared at me. "I've put up with a lot of crap from Kensington men in my life, but honestly, this takes the cake."

"Really?" I asked in exasperation. "Me showing up with someone else when she said she wasn't interested."

"Do you know how to read between the lines at all? You think she wanted to see you with someone else? You think that saying she can't be with you is the same thing as she's not interested?"

"What else am I supposed to believe?"

Lark shook her head. "Put yourself in her shoes. She's getting a divorce. She's fragile. And she's worried about her career."

"I know all of that."

"Then, why are you being an idiot? I have no idea why she likes you."

I came up short. My eyes shifted to Lark's in surprise. "What? What do you mean, she likes me?"

"Why do you think she slept with you?" Lark asked.

"I've slept with plenty of women who didn't like me."

Lark held up her hand. "I don't need to know that."

"But English, I didn't think..."

"You're dense. Both of you. Why do you think she was upset in the first place? Why do you think she left?"

"She left?"

Something sparked in my chest. I didn't fucking know what it was. But I didn't want her to leave. I wanted her to tell me exactly what she was thinking. No more games. No more cat and mouse. Just the truth.

"Yes. She went home. Obviously, she didn't enjoy watching you with Poppy."

"Fuck," I whispered.

"Now, you're getting it."

I shook my head, shaking something loose. I'd been an idiot. I was mad at English for taking me at face value, but I'd taken her at it. She'd pushed me away because she liked me. She felt something for me that... scared her? It was unfathomable that someone like English would do that. It had never crossed my mind.

"I have to go after her."

"Erm... wait, what?" Lark asked. "Is that a good idea?"

"Fuck good ideas," I said abruptly. "I need to hear it from her."

"If this is just to pad your ego—"

"It's not," I said, cutting her off.

Lark looked at me, really looked at me. She tilted her head as if seeing something different in my expression than she ever had before. I wasn't showing her the Upper East Side playboy that I always wore. This was just me. And I needed to find English right now.

"Where is she?"

"She's at her apartment."

"I've never been."

Lark scoffed. "Seriously?"

I hadn't thought about how strange that was until this moment. We'd always met at my place. Everything, except her orgasms, had been about me. Fuck. I needed to talk to her. I couldn't wait until tomorrow.

"Tell me how to get there."

And to my surprise, she did.

"What are you going to do about Poppy?" Lark asked.

I shook my head. "We need to get her help. She's worse off than I thought. I swear she's gone to the restroom two or three times already. Can we send her back to rehab?"

"Jesus, Court," Lark said with a shake of her head. "I'll handle it."

"You sure?"

"Go! Before English changes her mind."

I laughed. I couldn't help it. I felt light for the first time in so long. "Thanks, Lark."

"For the kick in the ass?"

I winked at her. "For being a good friend."

Then, I left Lark to deal with Poppy and rushed out of The Plaza.

24

ENGLISH

My apartment still didn't feel like home. Even though I'd been living there for two months, it didn't quite belong to me. Likely because Josh had purchased it and we'd planned to live here together. A guilt gift. One I probably should have gotten rid of. I would have, if it wasn't perfect.

Still, it felt cold tonight.

Fall blew into the city, and the full glass windows overlooking Manhattan did nothing to trap the heat inside. But it was the empty space and the broken promises and the crushed dreams that made it so frigid.

I tugged off my black party dress and haphazardly threw it against my desk chair. I replaced it with my oldest, softest, comfiest black sweatpants and an oversize sweatshirt. My long hair went up onto the top of my head with a wayward scrunchie. And I settled onto the couch to watch some *Friends* and not think about the shit night I'd had.

I was halfway into the *pivot* episode when someone knocked on my door. I glanced up in confusion. No one had knocked on my door since I moved here, except when I ordered takeout. I really did not want to talk to a stranger right now.

With a huff of frustration, I paused the episode and went to answer the door. I pulled it open, prepared to tell whoever it was to leave, but standing on the threshold was Court Kensington. In a tuxedo. Looking sexy as hell.

"Court?"

"Hey, English."

"What... what are you doing here?" I forced myself to say. "How did you even know where I live?"

"Lark told me."

Lark. Ah. She must have said something to him. She was usually such a good friend. This confrontation was the last thing I needed tonight.

"I don't know what she said, but I really don't want to do this tonight."

"You just left," he accused.

"Well, yeah," I said with a shrug. "Why was I even there? I don't know Penn and Natalie. I'm just a publicist. I don't even know why I got an invite."

"But that wasn't why you left." He stuffed his hands in his pockets and looked up at me without guile.

I sighed. "It doesn't matter why I left."

"I think it does."

I reached out to close the door. "Just go back to your heiress, Court."

He put his hand out to stop it short. "Can we talk? Really talk."

"About what?" I said irritably. "I think I saw all that I needed. I don't need words wrapped in lies. I just want to get some sleep."

"You like me." He said it so matter-of-fact. As if there was no other option. Not a single other possibility.

I met that beautiful blue gaze and tried not to flinch. Hearing it out of his mouth made it all the worse. I was not supposed to fall for Court Kensington. A lamb wasn't supposed to fall for the wolf.

With a sigh, I let the door swing all the way open. "You might as well come inside."

I didn't wait for his reply. I just turned on my heel and strode into the kitchen. I'd just purchased a bottle of Hendrick's the day before with vermouth and olives. Thank god for yesterday English's quick thinking.

I poured the contents of the drinks into a shaker and vigorously shook them. Then, I carefully filled each martini glass nearly to the rim, leaving just enough room for olives.

"You look like you've done that before," Court observed.

"I started bartending when I was sixteen." I passed him the drink.

"How did that happen?"

"I grew up fast and realized early on that I could use that to my advantage to make a lot of money. If you think fixing your bullshit is hard, you should see me stop a bar fight without lifting my finger. It's a party trick."

Court furrowed his brow. "But I thought you grew up in Hollywood."

"I grew up in LA. Hollywood is for the birds."

He looked at me as if I were a puzzle that he couldn't quite put together and then took a sip of the martini. "You know I prefer vodka martinis."

"Go to hell, Kensington."

He smirked at me. "Why did you leave, English?"

"You know why I left."

"Because you didn't want to see me with Poppy."

"Because watching you throw another woman in my face felt less than stellar," I quipped.

"But you shouldn't care," he countered. "You were the one who said that this couldn't happen."

"It can't," I said unconvincingly.

"And yet..." He held his hand out, gesturing to the apartment. As if his very presence changed that.

"Just because I said that this couldn't happen... that I want to watch you with someone that you don't even like. Or watch your jealous stupidity about Robert." I shook my head. "I came there tonight, hoping I could talk to you and that we could mend what I'd fractured with my assumptions about your character. But then..."

"I proved you right," he finished.

I shrugged. "At least you proved that when you're hurt, you lash out. And I don't know what to do with that information, Court. Not after what happened to me."

"I didn't purposely lash out. I thought I should move on. That the easiest way to stop thinking about you was to be with someone else." He met my gaze, strong and steady. "Not only did it *not* work, but I had to deal with Poppy all night."

"You seemed perfectly okay with that from where I stood."

"I wanted you to think that."

I grumbled in exasperation. "That's exactly my point."

"So, maybe I did lash out." He drained the remainder of his martini and set it aside. Then, he stepped closer to me. "But if you didn't feel anything for me, then it wouldn't have even mattered."

"But I do," I whispered.

His eyes rounded. As if he couldn't believe that I'd admitted it. In some way, I couldn't believe I'd admitted it.

"I didn't know," I told him, biting my lip. "I thought that I was just mad because you brought Poppy. But it was more than that. I went to see you this week. I wanted to talk this through."

"What? When?" he asked with a furrowed brow.

"Monday."

He snapped his jaw shut. He knew what he'd been doing Monday.

"I knew that you worked until three and then met Camden at that gentlemen's club thing. So, I went there."

"You did?" he asked softly.

"Yes. Camden told me you weren't there."

"He did?"

"So then, I got worried. No," I corrected myself. "I got sick to my stomach. I thought you were lying to me. Hiding that you were seeing someone else."

"I wasn't seeing someone else," he said on a sigh.

"I know," I whispered. "I tracked down the car service while I was looking for you. He told me where to find you."

"Fuck," he muttered.

"I'm sorry that I know. As soon as I saw you out there, I realized you wanted to keep this to yourself. That you didn't want to coach for the publicity."

Court nodded. He looked as if he'd been caught red-handed, peeking in on Christmas presents early.

"It wasn't a secret," he finally said. "Not exactly. I just...I don't want to be Court Kensington when I'm out there. I just want to be me."

"And those two people can't be reconciled?"

"No," he said immediately.

"I don't get it."

"Look, for the longest time, I didn't give two shits what anyone thought about me. It was easier to let them have their own assumptions about who I was. I gained my reputation honestly, but that wasn't *me*. I don't know if that makes any sense."

"You aren't always the guy who gets arrested and fucks anything that walks?" I asked as I drained my drink.

He glanced at me, his eyes wide and concerned. As if he'd never explained this to someone else before. "That's the guy who always went along with everything else. I just let things happen. That was a part of me. And I started to get really careful about who I let see the whole me. Because every time that I did, it backfired. So, I stopped caring. But I cared what you thought of me. I thought you saw past that."

"Which was why you were so mad at me?"

I stepped back into the kitchen and shook us out more martinis. I needed one for this conversation. I'd never heard Court be so earnest.

"Yes. The truth is... I might have been a playboy. I might have been a train wreck. Christ, I might still be those things. I don't know. But something changed after the arrest... after Jane." He reached for the drink I'd offered him and took a large fortifying gulp. "I got a taste of what it was like to be used. I'd been doing this to women for years. And it felt like absolute shit for Jane to do it to me."

"Reality check."

"It pulled me up short. I'd thought what I had with Jane was real. I'd thought we were in love. But... it was a lie."

I winced at his words. They hit so close to home. Too close. Even if the situation with Josh was night and day compared to what had happened with Court and Jane. It felt so real. So familiar.

"I know what you mean," I muttered.

"I suspect you do."

"So, where does this leave us?"

"It means you like me," he said with a cocky grin.

"Oh god. Don't make me regret it, Court."

He set the martini glass down and then moved into my personal space. He tilted my chin up until I was looking at him. And I did look. He was mesmerizing. All strong lines and hard edges. Endless depths of blue ocean with that pinprick of black at the center. Long lashes that weren't even fair on a man. Full, lush lips that were perfectly kissable.

And something more. Recognition. He saw me. And for the first time... he was letting me see him, too. Not the Court Kensington he revealed to the public. The one that I'd read about. But the real person under that Upper East Side facade.

The youth lacrosse coach, the book nerd, the gentleman.

I didn't know what to make of him. He wasn't what I'd expected. Not by a long shot. And I'd had no intention of having feelings for him. Hell, for anyone. Josh had fucked me up beyond recognition. I'd already been dark and cynical and jaded, thanks to my bullshit parents. Josh had taken that to the next level.

And yet, when I looked up into those unfathomably blue eyes, I looked into a mirror. We'd both been forced to grow up fast. We'd both had to play our parts to fit in. We'd both been put through the wringer, and somehow, we had found it in ourselves to still *feel*.

After Josh, I'd never thought I'd feel again.

Court had ruined it all.

Or saved me.

Depending.

"I like you, too, Anna," he breathed an inch from my lips.

"You do?"

"Yes. I like your ambition and your wit and your insufferable need to always be right."

"I do not—"

He pressed a finger to my lips. "Like I said."

I snorted.

"I don't know where this leaves us," he admitted, trailing his fingers back into my hair. "But I know I want to try."

I breathed out at those words and nodded. He fitted his lips to mine, sealing it with a kiss.

PART IV

REALITY'S A BITCH

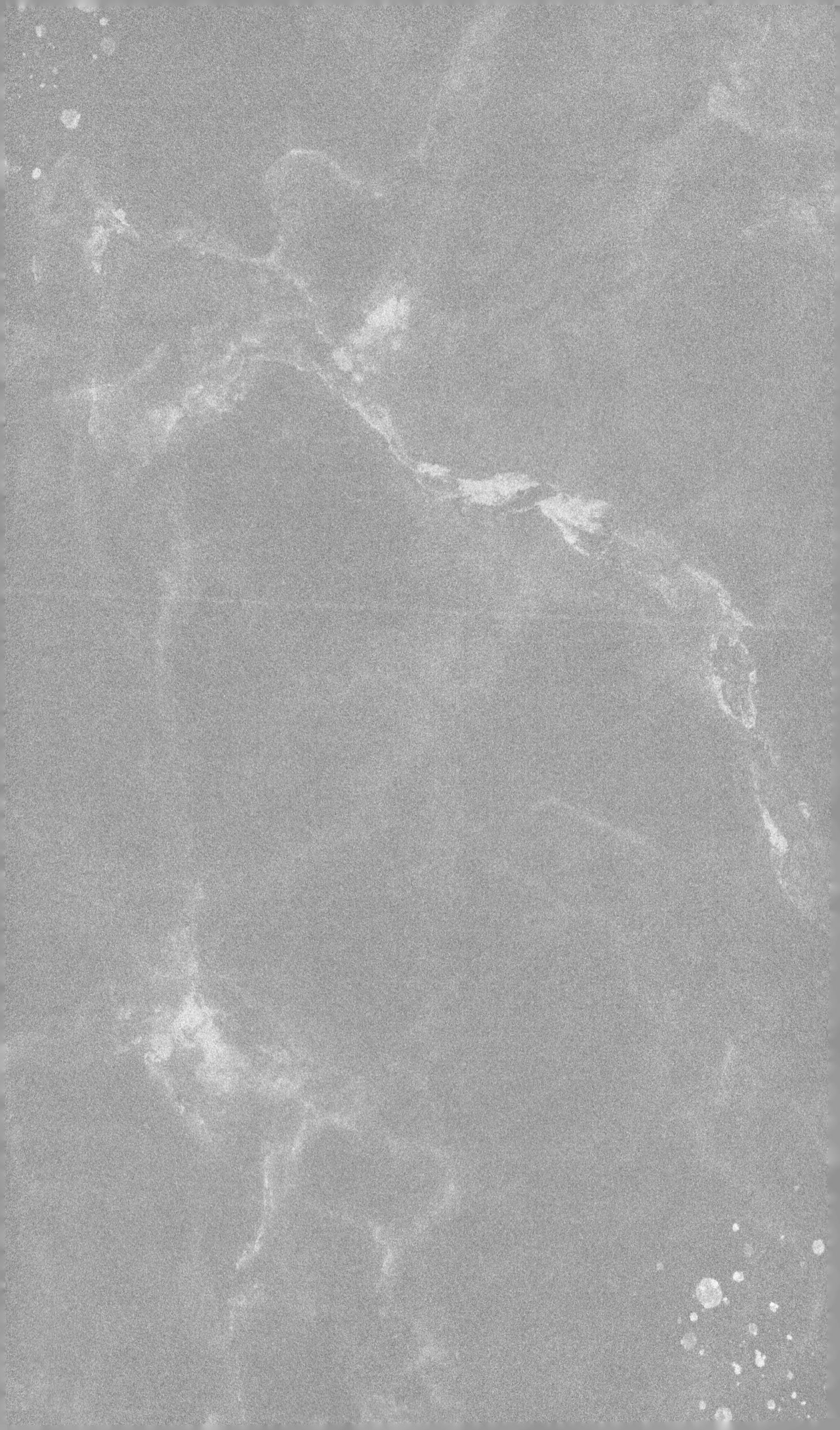

25

ENGLISH

The sidelines of the first youth lacrosse game of the year were a surprisingly loud event. The parents clearly knew the rules much better than I did. I had no idea what was happening. Court had tried to explain the mechanics of the game to me, but it just made little sense.

So, I watched him in his natural element and tried not to laugh when I overheard some of the moms going on about how hot the coach was. Couldn't blame them for that assessment. It was half the reason I braved the brisk October temperatures.

The referee blew the final whistle for the game. Court's team had lost terribly. They'd only had a few weeks of practice, and it was a brand-new team. So, it wasn't surprising, but it was disappointing.

After slapping hands with the other team, everyone huddled up around him. He swiped the red hat off of his head. He must have given some pep talk that energized them because they went from looking defeated to optimistic. They did a chant and then raced to their bags.

I stepped out of line with the parents and trotted forward

with a grin on my face. Court flopped the hat back down and met me at his bag.

"Good game, Coach," I said with a barely suppressed grin.

"Did you understand any of it this time?" he asked with his own smile.

"Ball goes into the mitt thing. You use the stick to try to get it into the net. They did not do enough into-the-net action."

He shook his head in dismay. "You catch the ball in the head of the lacrosse stick. The stick part is called the shaft. And yeah, scoring could have gone better."

I snorted. "Head and shaft. This sport was clearly created by a man."

"I can't with you."

"Oh, come on. Try to tell me it's not phallic."

He shrugged. "Fine. But isn't everything?"

"You can show me later."

"That I will." He gestured for me to stand to the side while he answered a few parent questions. He waited until his entire team had left with a parent, and then we walked off of the field.

Despite the wind, it was a beautiful day. The trees faded from vibrant green into gorgeous fiery red, burnt orange, and golden yellow. Leaves lined the walkways, crunching under our feet. And already, the sun lowered earlier on the horizon.

It was most people's favorite time of year. But as a California girl, I was not looking forward to my first year with seasons. And absolutely dreading the snow. Why couldn't it be seventy-five degrees everywhere?

"Bummed that you didn't win?"

He shrugged. "My competitive side says we should up practices to two or three times a week. That maybe I should recruit some other kids from better teams. I could probably convince the parents to switch."

"You're insane. You realize these are, like, ten-year-olds, right?"

"Yeah. It's just supposed to be fun, right?"

I laughed at his distressed face. "It will be fine. You're not doing it to win championships anyway. You're doing it to help kids with an outlet. Most of them wouldn't even be able to play lacrosse if it hadn't been for your donation. Between uniforms, masks, sticks, cleats, and all the fees. You've done a great thing."

"I still want them to win," he said, determined.

"I like this side of you. Why did you ever hide it from me?"

He grinned and slipped his arm around my waist. "Mostly, I didn't want it to be a publicity stunt. I thought you'd see it as one."

"I probably would have," I agreed.

"And now?"

"Now, we'll just use it if we have to."

He snorted. "You're a trip."

I wished I were joking. But if we had to use it, then we would. I just hoped that we stayed far enough ahead of everything that it wouldn't matter. We had a month left before his mother's campaign ended. I thought we could hold it together until then. So far, nothing more had come of Jane's trial announcement. But I knew December was going to be a rough month. At least it was after the election. We could deal with everything one at a time.

Court stowed his bag in the trunk of the awaiting car service and then held the back door open for me.

"Are you still okay with us driving to the river? I don't know if you want to meet Taylor... or do Oktoberfest with a bunch of New School college kids."

"I want to meet Taylor," he agreed easily. "After I change."

I laughed. "Obviously. Didn't think you'd want to head down there in your coaching uniform."

"That is a fact."

"But... you know, you don't have to come if you don't want to."

He turned to face me. "Why do I get the impression that you don't want me to meet your sister?"

"It's not that. Taylor and I only recently started to have a good relationship. It's kind of new, and I've never done this before." I bit my lip.

I wish I could get him to understand. My family wasn't like his family. Everyone had problems. Money didn't fix that. But I hadn't shared any of that with him. He didn't know that side of me.

"My family is just... different."

He put his hand on my knee. "I'm sure it will be fine."

I nodded, reassured by his easy demeanor. "I'm sure it will be."

He sat back in his seat until the car pulled over in front of his building. We headed upstairs at his apartment. I flipped through his collection of fantasy novels as I waited for him to shower and get dressed. He had hundreds of books in the back bedroom. I never would have guessed by looking at the living area. He really didn't want people to know who he was. All they'd see was the TV and video games and the wet bar. Perfect Upper East Side bachelor.

Court appeared in the doorway. His hair still wet from the shower, his shirt only half-buttoned, and he was still barefoot. He looked sexy as fucking hell.

"Trying to pick one to read?" he asked.

"Have you read them all?"

He shrugged. "Not this shelf."

He pointed at one measly shelf with about a dozen books on it.

"Wow. Tell me where to start."

"Easy. *The Eye of the World*. Jordan is a genius." He procured the book off the top shelf and handed it to me. "I have another copy at the office. You can have that one."

I held it up. "Lots of amazing women in this series?"

Something lit up inside him when I started asking about books. And I liked it.

"Actually, yes. Women are way more powerful than almost all the men in that series. They're the ones with the magic."

"I like the sound of it already."

"You would. You'll probably love Moiraine."

"And why is that?"

He chuckled. "She doesn't take anyone's shit."

I tucked the book into my purse. "You're right. I probably will like her."

We headed back out to the car, and I pointedly ignored him in favor of the first couple chapters.

"So, what's happening now?" he asked like a kid desperate for attention.

I threw a hair tie into the book as a bookmark. "I just started."

"Tell me when all the good stuff happens."

"You're obsessed."

"Yeah, well, it's my favorite series," he said with a shrug. "The other option is, you could tell me about your family. You know too much about mine. It might be nice to know a bit about yours."

I sighed and set the book aside. This was going to be fun. "Well, my parents divorced when I was ten. My dad was a serial cheater. He would disappear for weeks at a time and just leave me to fend for myself with my mom. Mom was..." I swallowed. How the hell did I explain my mom? I never talked about her. "We're estranged for a reason. I haven't talked to her in five years."

"I'm sorry."

I waved a hand at him. "Yeah. She was never a great mom to begin with. But when I started dating Josh, she wanted the money. I had to cut her out of my life to protect myself."

"Fuck, English." He sighed heavily. "Where does Taylor come into all of this?"

"My dad remarried a year after the divorce. He took me with him and his new wife—my stepmom, Ashley. She got pregnant a year later. Hence Taylor."

"He's still with your stepmom? Even though he cheated a lot?"

"They're still together. I think he cleaned up when he met Ashley. He could be a good husband for another woman but not my mom. And a good father for another daughter but not for me."

Court frowned. "His loss."

I laughed with a vulnerable pain in my voice. "Yeah. He poisoned Taylor against me for a long time because I was… wild in high school and college. He's trying to mend it all now, I guess. I just can't get over how he treated me when I needed him the most. And how he wants me to treat him now that I'm old enough to know better."

"Families are fucking complicated."

I managed a small smile. "Tell me about it."

Court didn't press me for more information. He just slung his arm around me and held me close the rest of the way south to the river.

The car service dropped us off in front of the pier where the Oktoberfest festivities were well underway. A woman in traditional dirndl dress checked our IDs at the front and slapped wristbands on us before letting us inside. I didn't want to ask how Taylor had gotten inside. I'd had a fake ID at sixteen, but it was hard to envision Taylor like that.

"Anna!" Taylor yelled dramatically as soon as she saw me.

Or maybe not. Maybe she was just like every teenager fresh out of high school.

"Hey, Taylor."

"And you brought your hot boyfriend!" she crowed.

I laughed but didn't contradict her. Court and I hadn't put a label on our relationship. It was easier that way. But it would be nice for an afternoon to think of him as my boyfriend.

"Taylor, this is Court. Court, my sister, Taylor."

He held out his hand. "Pleasure to meet you."

She giggled and shook his hand. "You too."

"I'm going to go get us beers," he said with a smile. "Do you need a refill?"

"Yes," Taylor gasped. "I am out."

I shook my head, but what could I say? I'd been much, much worse than this at her age. And I'd turned out just fine.

"Come meet Bea!" Taylor insisted. "She's the *best*."

I laughed and followed her. I'd heard a lot about Bea since school started. She sounded like the ultimate cool girl. Beautiful but laid-back. She liked football and video games. She wore only the coolest clothes that Taylor coveted. She was smart and funny. And if I didn't know better, I would say my sister was in love with her.

And as I watched her heart eyes as she finally found the infamous Bea, I realized maybe she *was*.

"Bea, this is my sister, Anna," Taylor said with a dopey smile.

Bea turned around, and she was everything I'd expected. Tall with dark hair and lots of makeup. Her clothes were purposely casual but high quality. Actually, everything about her seemed purposeful. She also looked high and not just drunk, like Taylor.

"Hey, Anna," Bea said. "I've heard a lot about you."

"Same. It's nice to put a name with a face."

"Definitely. I'm so jealous that Tay has family in the city. All of my family is up in Boston."

"Easier to get there than LA at least."

She smirked. "True."

Court appeared then with our drinks. "Sorry it took me a

minute. I had to fight my way through a stein-holding contest, which I didn't realize was a thing."

"Thanks," Taylor said, taking her beer. "So, what do you do? Are you like my sister? Do you fix people's problems?"

He laughed. "Uh, no. She fixes my problems generally. I work at a financial firm."

"Wall Street?" she asked, wrinkling her nose.

"Something like that."

"That sounds so boring."

I took a sip of German beer to keep from laughing.

"It is sometimes," he agreed. "That is what happens when you go to college to play lacrosse and just get a boring degree while you do it."

"Lacrosse?" she asked incredulously. "Isn't that a rich white dude sport?"

I nearly sprayed my beer all over him. "Taylor, how much have you had to drink?"

She laughed and then shrugged. "More than one?"

"Let her interrogate me," Court said, waving me off. "I don't mind."

"You work on Wall Street, and you play lacrosse. Next, you're going to tell me your grew up on the Upper East Side, and you went to Harvard." She drew out the word snootily, so it sounded like *Hah-vard*.

Court looked to me. "How much did you tell her?"

I snorted. "Nothing! You're just that easy to peg."

"Wait, really?" Taylor asked, wide-eyed. "That's hilarious."

Taylor and Court bantered back and forth for a while until she was pulled back into her group of friends. I had no hope of keeping up with their conversation.

Court just tugged me in closer. "She seems nice."

"To be honest, this is the nicest, chill-est I've ever seen her in my life. Maybe I should have gotten her drunk earlier."

"Bad influence."

"Pot, meet kettle."

"It's weird, hearing her call you Anna though. I thought you said no one called you that."

I took another sip of my beer. "I used to say only people who didn't know me. That included my family. But now, I don't mind when you call me that."

"Good, because I intend to call you that later," he said suggestively, leaning his mouth against the shell of my ear. "When I make you come."

I squirmed. "I might have to drag you out of here."

"I'm game. I think I've had my fill of Oktoberfest."

"You've convinced me."

As if I needed any convincing.

"Hey, Taylor, I think we're going to head back," I told her.

Taylor frowned as if she had suddenly sobered up at the prospect of us leaving. "What? It's so early."

"You stay and have fun. We can meet up again later."

"Come on. One more drink."

I shook my head. "I'll see you later. Text me when you get home safe."

"Okay, Mom," she said with a laugh. "Can I actually... talk to you for a minute?"

"Sure," I said cautiously.

She pulled me away from her friends and Court and over to a table against the water. She looked nervous and uncomfortable. I had a feeling I was not going to like whatever she was about to say.

"Do you think I could borrow some money?"

I raised my eyebrows. "What for?"

She anxiously chewed on her lip. "Does it matter?"

"How much are we talking?"

"Like five hundred bucks?"

I sighed out heavily through my nose. "What happened?"

"Nothing! It's for a friend."

"For a friend," I said hollowly.

I wanted to think there was a logical explanation as to why she was asking me for this amount of money. But in my line of work, I knew why they needed money. I knew who they needed to pay off. And I'd known before I'd gotten this gig. I'd seen transactions go down. I'd done my fair share of stupid shit.

"Yes. Seriously. It isn't for me."

"And why can't your 'friend' pay?"

She winced. "Please, Anna. I don't want her to get in a worse situation. I'm trying to help."

"Help would be therapy or calling a hotline, a school counselor, a rehab facility," I bit out.

"So, you won't help?" she asked bitterly.

"I didn't say that. I said that if your 'friend,' " I said in quotes, "doesn't get help, the money is going to do her no good."

"It's not for me!" she gasped out.

"Fine. I can give you the money. But that's it, Taylor. I don't want to know what drugs you're taking. I don't want to know how you got into this mess. I just want you to stop. Trust me when I say that I have been there and done that, and it's not worth it."

She drew back sharply. "You don't know the situation."

"It's always the same situation. I do this for a living. I make problems go away. But just because we hide them does not make them go away. Stick to weed. I'll buy you fucking alcohol if you want. But don't make me fix your problems for you again. I really don't want to have to tell Dad."

"Please don't," she whispered in horror.

"If you stop now, I won't."

"Thanks." She sounded hollowed out. "I'll get my friend to stop."

"Please be careful."

"I will. I really will."

I sighed as I walked away from my sister. I should do more, but I'd been in her exact shoes. I'd had no one to ask for the money. And it had taken me working my ass off to cover it. I should have made her work her ass off for it. But fuck.

"What was that about?" Court asked when I returned to him.

"Nothing."

He arched an eyebrow. "You sure?"

I glanced back at Taylor, who was already at Bea's side again.

"Yeah. She's just an idiot. I think it'll be fine."

I hoped. Still, I sent the money.

26

ENGLISH

Lacrosse games and campaign events filled the next two weeks to the brim. Until I was so busy that I didn't even have time to think about Taylor. Court had agreed to attend rallies with his mother, and I stayed close by to make sure it went off without a hitch. In public, we always appeared professional. But I looked forward to the hiding part of all this being over.

At least Lark was happy for me. As was Whitley, who I had confessed to over lunch, and Katherine, despite her insistence not to date a Kensington. She'd sent me an invitation to her annual Ears and Tails Halloween party, which benefited a local animal shelter. I tried not to overthink my costume to what I'd gathered was essentially a lingerie party. I needed to focus on the publicity I had lined up for Court going into the election. That was what was important.

Not Googling slutty costumes on the internet.

But it was way more fun.

I'd been dicking around in my home office, doing just that, when I heard the lock click over at the front door. What the hell? Who was coming into my house? No one else but me had a key. I hadn't even given Court one.

But fuck, the door handle turned. Someone was definitely entering my house.

I jumped up from my seat and dashed into the living room. My heart raced frantically, even as a cold calm settled over my body. I didn't need a gun or anything. I was well-trained weapon. I'd practiced martial arts for over a decade. My focus had been defense, but I would stop whoever sought to enter my sanctum.

The door flew open. I stood strong in a defensive position, prepared to attack whoever walked through that door.

And just as I moved forward to strike, I saw who it was. But I didn't pull my punch fast enough, and I hit my husband once, quick and fierce, straight into his windpipe.

"Josh?" I gasped.

He doubled over, clutching at his throat. "Jesus, English."

"Oh my god, are you okay?"

"Okay?" he wheezed. "You just throat-punched me."

"I thought you were an intruder. Why didn't you call or text? Why would you just barge in here?"

I hadn't even considered that Josh would still have a key. After today, I was changing the locks.

"Fuck, I'm going on *The Tonight Show* tonight. I'm going to sound like I have fucking laryngitis." He coughed a few times. "Can I have some water?"

I ground my teeth together. It was his own damn fault. He should have called me and not just entered my home unannounced. But I had just punched him, so I stiffly nodded my head once and let him inside the apartment he'd purchased but never seen.

Until we finalized the divorce, we owned the apartment jointly. Not that it meant he could come and go anytime he wanted.

I strode into the kitchen and pulled a glass out of a cupboard. It was brand-new, just like nearly everything in the apartment. I'd taken next to nothing from our place in LA. I hadn't wanted an even bigger reminder of Josh in my new apartment.

"I like what you've done with the place," he said hoarsely as I filled up the glass with water.

I had no interest in making small talk.

"Here." I passed the glass to him, careful that our hands didn't touch.

He took a sip and winced. Then another. I'd gotten him good.

Seeing him was... difficult.

I hadn't seen him since London. I'd flown out there to be with him on set for the last Bourne film. We'd made love in his flat in the city, and then the next day, I overheard two people talking about Josh and Celeste sleeping together. When I confronted Josh, he didn't even want to admit it. He only confessed to it when I said that I'd go to Celeste.

He'd barely groveled. Just claimed that he didn't love her. That it helped promote the movie. As if saying that to *me*, of all people, would make it okay.

I'd expected to feel fierce anger and disgust in his presence. That was all I'd felt the last time I saw him. But it had been months since I saw him. I'd expected him to look different. To be run-down by our impending divorce. Somehow, he still looked like Josh.

Cookie-cutter, perfect Josh with his surfer-boy blond hair, award-winning smile, and to-die-for blue eyes. He pulled off his peacoat, and underneath he wore designer jeans with a gray T-shirt. Simple but effective. That was his style. Who he was as a person. Or at least, I'd thought so.

My throat bobbed, and my stomach squeezed. My insides felt like my outsides, and my outsides felt like my insides. I was upside down. I didn't feel like the woman who had just been prepared to attack an intruder. I felt like the jaded woman who had met Josh at a party, assuming he was a goody-two-shoes that I'd have no interest in. Instead, he'd held my attention all night, been a complete gentleman, and insisted on taking me out for a proper date before trying to get in my pants. It had been revolutionary in my world. My sea of asshole suitors.

And then he'd turned out just like all the others.

Josh set the glass on the counter. "It's good to see you."

"What are you doing here?"

He blew out a short breath. "I'm on tour for Bourne. I'll be in New York for a couple days, running the circuit of talk shows. I had to see you. I miss you like crazy."

He reached out for me, but I stepped back.

"So, Celeste is with you."

"She's in the city. She's not with me. We're not together." He looked repentant when he said it.

I crossed my arms and nodded. I didn't know why I cared. But the thought of him starting a relationship with the person he'd cheated on me with made me want to set something on fire.

"You're the one I want, English." He stepped forward again and brushed his hand against my arm. His eyes zeroed in on my sweatshirt. "What are you wearing?"

I glanced down and froze. Fuck. I'd completely forgotten that I'd thrown on Court's Harvard Lacrosse sweatshirt this morning. I'd snagged it at his house the other day when I was cold.

"Uh, it's a client's," I said defensively.

"You're wearing your client's sweatshirt?" His eyes narrowed. "Is this the same client that I saw in the picture with you?"

"Yes. And not that I have to justify anything to you, but that was, as always, fake paparazzi bullshit."

"And the sweatshirt?"

"I was cold," I ground out.

He let his hand drop. "Are you together?"

"I am not having this conversation with you, Josh. You don't get to barge into my apartment, unannounced, and start making accusations."

"I thought we could make this work," Josh said. His eyes were wide. He'd really deluded himself into thinking it would happen. "I thought that once I finally saw you, you'd realize that we were making a horrible mistake. You're the one I want. You've always been it for me."

"You were it for me, too, Josh," I whispered. "But then you broke my trust."

"And you think trust can never be mended?" he demanded.

"I know it can't," I bit out.

"I'm not like your father. This isn't your parents' marriage. We can fix this. We can go to counseling. We can make it work." He was so earnest. So fucking earnest. "I love you, English."

My throat closed up. It'd be so easy to say yes. To just forgive and forget. To get back what I'd thought was forever. We'd move back to LA. We'd go to therapy. Life would move on. We'd get through it.

But... I deserved better than that.

I deserved so much better.

"I can never trust you again," I said softly. I hardly sounded like myself. I felt like I was breaking open all over again.

"Please, just give me a chance to prove myself to you."

I looked him directly in his eyes. "When someone shows you who they really are, believe them."

"This isn't really me," he said, gently massaging his throat. "The person who did those things... that isn't the real me."

"Oh, so someone else cheated on me? Your alter ego?"

"It was a publicity stunt. I told you that from the beginning.

I didn't even want to do it. But my publicist said it was the way to save the movie."

I froze in place. My head tilted slightly. But my entire world tilted with it.

"What did you just say?"

"It's like I told you in London. It was a publicity stunt."

"You said that, but you never told me that your publicist had told you to do it." I put my hand to my heart. "*Margery* told you to fuck Celeste to help the movie?"

He frowned. "I swore I told you that."

"No. You didn't," I bit out.

"This movie will make or break my career. We needed something to push it over the edge. We brainstormed ideas, and she said the easiest thing would be to *Mr. & Mrs. Smith* the movie."

I was still reeling.

Margery, my boss and the owner of Poise, had told my husband to sleep with another woman. Then, she had looked me in the eye when I went back to LA afterward. She'd treated me like family. All while stabbing me in the back.

"English, say something," Josh said.

"What do you want me to say? Margery betrayed me. You betrayed me. I do this for a living. I am very, very good at my job. We could have come up with a solution," I said, lethally calm. "Even if all of that wasn't true, you still fucked someone else."

"But I don't love her. I love you."

"No, you don't. You love yourself."

Josh took a step back. He looked me over as if expecting me to break for him. As if he thought that he'd somehow tamed the wild thing within me. But I wasn't tame. I'd just pretended to be housebroken. And the old me could come out to play at the drop of a hat. Don't kick a beehive.

"It's really over," Josh said. "You're really done."

"I was done the second you told me you'd slept with her."

He nodded, grimaced at the pain in his neck. "Fuck. I don't want it to be over."

"You should have thought about that before agreeing to sleep with your costar for money."

He opened his mouth, presumably to contradict me, but I held up my hand. Even as my heart broke all again, I silenced him. I didn't need this.

"Just go, Josh."

He looked like he might try to say something else. But at the end of the day, he was a coward. He nodded once at me and then left the apartment.

All the strength left my body, and I collapsed right there on the kitchen tiles. How had everything gone so horribly wrong?

I buried my head in my knees and tucked my arms tight around my legs. I rocked back and forth a few times. The last thing I wanted to do was cry. I refused to shed any more tears for Josh Hutch.

Whatever we'd gone through recently, I had loved him. I hadn't wanted a divorce. I'd thought we'd live happily ever after. And now, I was on the kitchen floor, trying not to cry.

Whatever his bullshit excuse, I found it hard to believe that Margery would do this. And at the same time, considering what I did for a living, it all made perfect sense. Except the part where she would burn one of her best employees to help one of her clients. But even then, I didn't know if she had a heart. If she'd care that it'd broken mine. She wanted her clients happy. She never cared who got hurt in the interim. Even if it was one of her own.

She'd carefully cultivated it so that it wouldn't seem like she'd done it, too. I hadn't taken Josh's comment about a publicity stunt at face value. Even working as a publicist the last five years, I'd been blind to the idea that someone would do this to me. When I had covered up enough scandals to know better.

I dabbed at my eyes and took a deep breath. I couldn't fall apart now. Not because of Josh. Not because of Margery. Not for *anyone.*

What I needed was answers. And I damn well was going to get them.

27

ENGLISH

Winnie answered the video chat almost immediately. Her long black waves were up in a neat bun at the crown of her head. Her dark eyes wide and glamorous with eyelash extensions for days and perfect winged eyeliner. Her beautiful British accent cut through the line as she smiled broadly. "English, what a treat to see your pretty face. I was just thinking about you. Our cross-country connection grows stronger every day."

But I wasn't smiling.

"Did you know about Josh?" I asked unceremoniously.

She furrowed her brow. "What about Josh?"

"Did you know?"

She was silent for a second. A heartbeat that felt like an eternity.

I didn't want Winnie to know. I didn't want my closest friend in this business to have played me and then made me do work for her in the city. It would be too much. But Margery had done it. I couldn't know if Winnie had.

"I don't know what you're asking," Winnie finally said. "Did I know about the affair? I knew when you told me. I did try to salvage the pictures, but once they went viral, there was little to be done."

I breathed a sigh of relief. There was no guile in Winnie's voice. Nothing on her face to indicate that she'd lied. We'd worked together long enough for me to be able to detect it. Plus, Winnie didn't bullshit. I'd seen her lie her ass off, but when someone genuinely wanted the truth, she always gave it. Aloof and indifferent. She was a hard ass but loyal. I'd been banking on that, but it also terrified me.

"Margery told Josh to sleep with Celeste."

Winnie breathed in harshly. "She did?"

"Yes, Josh just showed up at my apartment. He confessed it while we were arguing."

"Could he have been lying?"

I shook my head. "No. Not in that moment. He'd told me in London it was a publicity stunt, but I didn't believe him."

"Bollocks."

"Yeah. I had to know if you were involved. I didn't want to think..."

She held up a hand. "You don't have to explain yourself. I would have done the same thing. Margery is a pain in the arse, but I'd never thought she'd hurt one of her own. This is an all-time low."

"It is. I'm about to a call her next."

"I wish you were here, so we could do this together."

"Me too. Wish me luck, Win."

"You don't need it. I'm always here for you. Whatever you need."

I smiled warmly at her and then ended the video chat. Now, the fun part.

I swallowed hard. Thank fuck Winnie hadn't been involved. But that meant that Margery had gone behind everyone's back on this. Usually, we made big decisions together. She worked with all of us in tandem. It made us all stronger.

But this was unconscionable.

I dialed Margery's number. Her face appeared on the screen. She was seated at her desk. Her burgundy hair down and wavy with cunning eyes and pursed dark lips. She was a force in the industry. And she'd plucked me out of oblivion. She saw my worth. She'd given me a chance.

And now, she'd burned that bridge.

"Hello, English. Ready to come home to sunny LA? It's a balmy eighty-three degrees, and only half of California is on fire today."

She was so apathetic. As if California forest fires didn't matter as long as they stayed out of the city.

"Margery," I said curtly. "And no, I don't think I'm coming back to LA."

"Ah, so you've made your decision to remain in New York? Are you sure you want to decide that before you endure your first winter? Have you ever lived through snow?"

I ground my teeth. I didn't want this small talk. I couldn't handle the bullshit chitchat.

"You told Josh to sleep with Celeste," I blurted out.

Margery leaned back in her dark office chair. "Did I?"

"Don't play games with me. Josh is in New York. He just told me that you convinced him to sleep with Celeste to help the movie."

"And you believe him?"

"He told me from the start that it was a publicity stunt. I just hadn't realized you were the one to plan the stunt."

Margery shrugged her shoulders. "Well, cat's out of the bag. You understand how the business is run, don't you?"

"I know that you could have talked to me. We could have figured out something else. And instead, you threw me under the bus."

Margery laughed. She didn't even look sorry. "I did no such thing. Put blame where blame is due."

"Oh, I am. Josh will pay handsomely for his mistake. But so will you."

"I didn't force him to fuck her, English. It's not my fault that he did it," Margery said with her diplomatic smile.

"You put the gun in his hand. You're still responsible if he shoots someone."

"In this case, the gun is his dick, and the shot was inside of Celeste Gammon," she said crudely. "He wanted the movie to boost his career. He said that he'd do anything. We went through suggestions. We both agreed that Celeste was the easiest route. That's business, love. Nothing more. Nothing less."

I swallowed bile at her words. At this institution that I was a part of. This was what I was good at. I loved my job. But I couldn't stomach this.

"I was one of your own. You treated me like a daughter," I gasped out.

Margery smiled at me fondly. "I think of you like one."

And it was the tipping point.

Because I would not let one more parental figure treat me like shit.

"I quit."

Margery's eyes widened. "English, think about what you're doing."

"It's just business, Margery," I intoned back at her.

"You're making a huge mistake."

"No," I said evenly. "You made a huge mistake when you unilaterally decided to end my marriage. And then had the audacity to say I was like a daughter to you."

"What will you do? Where will you go? You can't work at another PR firm. You signed a non-compete."

I narrowed my eyes. "No judge in the country would hold that non-compete up in court."

"Then, I'll see you in court," Margery said, her eyes narrowing. "I made you, English. I own you. You'll find doors aren't quite so open to you without Poise behind you."

"No one owns me anymore, Margery," I bit out and then hung up without letting her get in another word edgewise.

My hands trembled as I stared down at my phone in shock. I'd done it. I'd quit.

Oh fuck, I'd *quit*.

What the fuck was I going to do now?

The trembling went from my hands to my entire body. Anxiety spiked through me. Terror hit me. I had no plan. No idea what I was going to do.

I needed to get out of this apartment. I needed... Court.

It took me a minute before I remembered that he was at work. I'd been avoiding his work. Letting him have that space alone. Especially because there were cameras everywhere and I'd been worried someone would see us.

But now, what did it matter?

I grabbed my purse and hustled out of my apartment. I dived into the first cab and drove downtown to the Kensington Corporation building. I paid and then hastened inside. The elevator dropped me off on the top floor. Court didn't have a secretary or anything since he was still acclimating to the work. So, there was no one to stop me from barging into his office.

Court's head popped up when he saw me. His brows furrowed. "English?"

I pushed the door closed behind me. My body still shook uncontrollably. My anxiety had gone into full-on panic attack in the car. I felt out of control. I knew exactly why this was coming on, but I felt helpless to stop it. Nothing could fix this.

Court didn't wait for my response. He jumped out of his chair and came to my side. "Are you okay? What happened? You look like sick."

He moved me across the room and pushed me into the

chair in front of his desk. Then, he bent down in front of me and took my hands.

"English, breathe. Just breathe. In through your nose. Hold it for a count of four. And then out through your mouth. Try it with me. Match my breathing."

I focused in on him. The lifeline through the waves of panic.

Breathe in, two, three, four.

Hold, two, three, four.

Breathe out, two, three, four.

Repeat.

And again.

I didn't know how long we sat there as he directed me through breathing exercises. But he never wavered, and he never moved. He just stared fixedly at me. He rubbed his thumbs over my knuckles. He spoke in the calmest voice I'd ever heard from him.

And then slowly, my shoulders loosened. The panic began to ebb. My voice returned.

Court reached forward and brushed a tear off of my cheek. "There we go. There you are."

"How did you know how to do that?" I whispered.

"I started getting panic attacks after my dad died," he told me. His eyes were still intent on mine. His thumb still rubbed soothing circles into my hand. "I tried to drown out the pain with alcohol, but it didn't work. I started meditating. It doesn't always work to stop them when I'm in a full-blown one. But it can usually hold it back if I know I'm on the verge."

"Wow," I said. "I didn't know that about you."

He laughed gently. "No one knows that."

I swallowed. "Josh came by the apartment today."

"What?" Court asked, his voice dropping. "Why?"

"He thought we'd get back together. I might have throat-punched him."

A laugh burst out of Court. "Damn, English. You're savage."

"It was an accident, but it felt good."

"So... panicking about Josh?"

I shook my head. "No. He told me that sleeping with Celeste was a publicity stunt. And that Margery—my boss, Margery—had been the one to suggest it."

"Fuck," he hissed.

"I called Margery to confront her, and then I quit Poise."

"Jesus. I mean, I think you did the right thing, but fuck. What a bitch. Why would she do that behind your back?"

I shrugged helplessly.

"Okay. Okay," he said and then rose to his considerable height. "I'm pretty much done with my work for today. I'm going to take off early and get you home."

"You don't have to do that."

He looked at me as if I'd grown a second head. "You showed up here in the midst of a panic attack and then told me you just had a confrontation with your soon-to-be ex-husband and *quit your job*. I think that calls me to take you home and take care of you."

"Court..."

"I'm thinking sweatpants, a *Harry Potter* marathon, and takeout."

I laughed softly. "That... sounds nice."

"Good. Let me send in this last report, and then we'll go."

"Court," I whispered as he stepped back to his computer.

He looked up at me expectantly.

"Thank you."

He smiled at me. Not a smile I'd ever seen from him before. It wasn't teasing or laughing or like he was ready to devour me. It was... something else. Something I couldn't put my finger on. But it made butterflies flap away in my stomach. And I decided I liked it very much.

28

COURT

Color finally came back into English's cheeks by the time I got her back to her apartment. I'd never seen her look so pale and terrified. It was unnerving. Part of me wanted to go find Josh Hutch and beat the shit out of him for hurting her. The other part thought about flying to LA and doing it to her damn boss. Not a single part of me wanted to stand still. Even though I knew that was what she wanted… what she needed.

I arranged the Chinese takeout on the coffee table and streamed the first *Harry Potter* movie while she went to change. She came back out of her bedroom a few minutes later in black sweats and my Harvard Lacrosse sweatshirt.

"So, *that's* where that went," I said with a laugh.

She tugged on the sweatshirt and then grinned. "Yeah. I was accidentally wearing it when Josh showed up."

"Did he notice?"

She sank into the couch. "Yeah."

"And?"

"And what?" she asked, wide-eyed.

"Does he know we're together?"

She tilted her head. "Are we together?"

"You're the one who is just getting out of a marriage. Whatever this is, it's up to you."

"Okay," she said.

"But I think we are," I added. "Together."

She smiled up at me, and it took a lot of self-control not just take her to the bedroom and remind her how much of mine she was.

But she didn't agree or disagree with the assessment otherwise. So, I let it go. It didn't matter to me whether or not we were something. As long as she was here. The rest we could wade through when the time came.

"Josh guessed that we're together. I didn't really say anything one way or another. He wasn't happy to see it."

"Good," I said vengefully.

She snorted, reaching for the Chinese food. "You're such a dude sometimes."

"Hey, he hurt you. I can be happy to see his downfall," I said as I plopped down onto the couch next to her and dug into the noodles.

She just laughed at me and picked at her rice. She ate like a bird. I watched her sigh over her food and barely touch it as we watched the first movie.

I'd just turned on the second when she tilted her head back onto the couch and stared at the ceiling.

"I quit my job," she muttered.

"Yeah. How are you feeling about that?"

I pressed the pause button on the TV. I'd been waiting for her to be ready to talk again.

"Shitty," she said.

"Even after what she did?"

"Yeah. Margery found me. She helped build my career. She

was like a parental figure to me." She laughed sardonically. "The only good one in my life."

"And then she fucked you over."

"Yep," she said, popping the end of the word. "Just like everyone else. All the time."

"Well, what's the plan now?" I asked.

She shook her head. "There is no plan. I was confident on the phone. Acted like I'd be able to take her down, but really, Court"—she finally met my gaze—"who the hell am I?"

"You're one of the most successful publicists in the industry."

"I'm not even a publicist. You know, technically, I don't even work for you anymore. The contract was through Poise."

I grinned. "Well, that makes us a little easier."

"Yeah," she said softly, "it does."

She silently chewed on her bottom lip. I knew that I was supposed to be sympathetic that she'd only quit her job because of what she'd found out. But I thought English was way ahead of the company she'd been working for. She didn't need Poise. They needed her.

"What am I even going to do? I have a non-compete. I know Margery is going to try to blacklist me from getting another job. And it's not like I can start my own company."

"Why not?" I asked.

She huffed and rolled her eyes. "I have five years of experience. Plus, I'm just breaking into the New York scene."

I shrugged. "So? Five years to become one of the best. That's impressive as hell. And you have me for the New York scene. You have all of us."

She frowned as she looked at me. She thought I'd been joking, but now that she was looking at me, she could tell I was serious.

"You actually think I could do it?"

"No," I said evenly. "I *know* that you could do it. Look what you did for me in six months, English. Fuck."

"Yeah, but... you're different."

"I'm different in that I'm more difficult than your usual clients. In fact, I remember you telling me that I was the worst client you've ever had. So, if you can fix my problems, the sky's the limit, right?"

"Yeah. I did say that," she said softly as if finally considering it as a real option. "But... I don't know. I wouldn't even know where to start. I'd need my own agency and a name and an office space. I'd need to contact my old clients. I'd need capital." She sighed and shook her head. "That I don't really have. Not until the divorce is finalized." Then, she glanced around her apartment. "Well, maybe I could sell this place. I don't know if I even could. I'm probably not supposed to make any big purchases or sales yet."

"Don't worry about the money."

"What? Why wouldn't I worry about the money?" she asked, her blue eyes returning to mine.

"I can help."

"No way," she said immediately.

"It's just money, Anna," I said tightly. "What am I going to do with it?"

"Court, you just got in trouble for giving Jane money. I could never ask you to help me with this."

I shrugged. "You didn't ask. I offered."

She vigorously shook her head again. "It would look terrible. Not only did you just get arrested for this, but you were also my client the last six months. We were discreet for a reason. This would be a big splashy red sign in the middle of my divorce. Not to mention, public perception is everything. And right now, they're on my side with Josh. It would hurt my integrity." She sighed heavily and then reached for my hand. "But I appreciate the offer. Even if I can't take it."

"Well, it's on always on the table."

"I'll find another way to get the money. I'm sure that I can get a loan," she said, a crease forming between her brows.

I could see all the steps she needed to make circle through her brain all at once.

"Hey."

Her eyes refocused. "I don't know if I can do this."

I grabbed her hand and tugged her into my lap. She straddled me and put her arms around my neck.

"You can do it. I know you can. But you don't have to figure it all out tonight. It's been a busy day."

"True," she agreed and then bent down to kiss me. "Thanks for being there for me today."

"Always. Plus, you told me you throat-punched Josh. I'm pretty sure today was great for me."

She pushed my shoulder. "You're never going to let me live that down, are you?"

"Definitely no."

"Well, he's on *The Tonight Show* today, and I think he's going to say he has laryngitis."

"*Because my ex-wife throat-punched me when I broke into her apartment* doesn't have a nice ring to it?"

She snorted. "Oh my god, could you even imagine?"

"It'd be hilarious."

She leaned forward and pressed her lips to mine. I was greedy with my time with her. I wanted more. I wanted faster. I wanted harder. But she was fragile right now. She didn't need me pushing her facedown into the couch and fucking her like I wanted to do. She needed me to care for her. And I could do that.

I gently tugged her hair out of the topknot and let the long strands cascade down her back. Then, I brushed them back off of her face and ran my fingers through the tresses. She purred like a kitten, which did nothing for the erection that was already forming.

My hands slipped under the sweatshirt that she'd stolen from me. I ran my fingers and down her back before exploratively skimming her ribs. She squirmed against me, grinding her heat into me. I reflexively tightened my hands, and she stopped moving.

She bit her lip. "Sorry."

"Why are you apologizing?"

"You were being sweet, and then I..." She grinned devilishly.

"You what?"

"I was dry-humping you on the couch like a teenager."

I pressed her down more firmly against my cock. "Again, why are you apologizing?"

"Oh, should I keep going?"

"Fuck yes, you should," I said immediately.

She giggled, one hand going to her mouth to cover her devious smile. "Today has been a day," she said softly. "Can I tell you something?"

Her pussy pressed harder against me, and my brain functions were beginning to shut down. "Anything."

"Remember when you first went down on me?"

My ears perked up. "How could I forget having you pinned against that wall with your leg over my shoulder?"

She flushed all over. "Well... that was the first time I'd ever come from oral."

I froze in surprise, and then a pleased smile crossed my face. Satisfied. "Oh, really?"

She nodded.

"How is that possible?" I asked, dumbfounded.

"I don't know. A lot of selfish jerks?"

"But you were married," I blurted out.

"Yeah. Well, Josh kind of... I don't know... he wanted to rush to the main event."

"What a douche! I bet he made you give him blow jobs."

She wrinkled her nose. "I hated them, but... yeah."

"Douche. Fucking douche."

She laughed. "What? And you've never just gotten yours?"

I shrugged. "Yeah. Sure. But not with a woman I intended to marry."

"And how many women have you intended to marry, Court?"

"Touché," I said with a head tilt. "Probably just Jane."

"Really?" she asked, her eyes wide.

I glanced away. This was not the conversation I wanted to be having when my dick was hard as a rock and she was sitting on top of me.

"Anyway, it doesn't matter. Jane is in prison."

"Right," she said easily. "Josh doesn't matter either. They're both liars."

Then, she leaned forward and claimed my lips with a possessiveness I'd never felt from her. Seeing Josh had really made it final. Over and done. I could feel it in the way her lips pressed against mine and the lightness to her limbs and the aggressiveness of her demeanor. She didn't just want to be fucked. She wanted *me*.

"I think we should try for another orgasm while I go down on you," I told her, guiding her back toward the couch.

She shook her head, holding on to me to stay upright. "Actually, I thought... we could try something else."

Then, she slipped to her knees in front of me.

"You just said you hated them," I said. Even though the thought of turning her down when she was expectantly sitting there would be pure torture. I'd done it that first night, but I hadn't realized what I was giving up. That she might not offer again.

"I hated being forced to give one," she said. "It always felt, like, guilt. But... I want to make you feel good. The way you make me feel good."

"I'm not saying no, but you can stop at any time, Anna," I said, reaching forward and cupping her cheek. I brushed my lips to hers.

She groaned deep in the back of her throat, and fuck, my cock responded accordingly. I wanted to shove it straight down the back of her throat. But I knew I couldn't do that. I was usually in control here. She was such a control freak in every aspect of her life that I loved when she gave it up to me. I'd guide her here if she wanted, but this was whatever she wanted.

I shucked off my sweats and boxers, dropping them to the side before pulling my shirt over my head. English reached forward and gripped my cock in her slender hand. She experimentally stroked up and down, up and down. As if she were getting acquainted with me. My cock jerked in response, aching for more of her.

She moved her body between my legs and then lowered her mouth onto the tip of my cock.

"Oh fuck," I groaned as her hot, wet mouth encircled me.

She hummed in response. She opened wider and bobbed her head lower, taking more of me into her mouth. I didn't think she could get me all in there. Not unless she had no gag reflex. But with her hand working me, it didn't even fucking matter.

I collected all of her hair into my hands, holding it out of her way. I wrapped it around one hand like a rope. As she dragged her way back up my cock, I had to remind myself not to use her hair to shove her back down. Self-restraint was not my forte.

"Anna, oh god," I said encouragingly. "Keep going."

She moved back down, taking me just a little further.

"That's right. Fuck."

From my view, I could see her straight back and her ass in the air while she was on her knees before me. Just the thought of taking her from behind again made me jerk up into her mouth.

She coughed, and her eyes flickered up to mine in surprise.

"You just feel so fucking good," I groaned.

She flickered her tongue out against the tip of my cock and met my gaze again. "Show me how you like it."

I arched an eyebrow. "Are you sure about that?"

"I've been sure about everything with you, Court. I trust you."

That was a high praise. I took it that Anna English trusted very few people. And even fewer since what had happened with Josh.

"Tap me if you need to stop."

"I won't need to."

"Fuck," I muttered. "Put your mouth back on my cock, Anna."

She shuddered between my legs, her body squirming. But she did as I'd said. Then, I used her hair like the rope I'd wanted to use, pushing her face down against me and thrusting at the same time. She opened her mouth wider. Her fingers dug into my thighs. But she didn't stop me. She didn't tap out.

Her lips and her mouth and everything about her felt so fucking good. I should stop. I should pull back before I was done, but here she was, giving me exactly what I wanted. And she was getting off on it. Like I was the one going down on *her*.

So, there was no way of stopping. Not as I fucked her mouth. Not after she'd begged me to.

"Close," I ground out. "God, you feel good."

And then my climax hit mercilessly, pouring out of me and deep down the back of her throat. She gagged once around me and then pulled back to swallow reflexively.

"Holy fuck." My eyes were closed, and I leaned back against the couch, panting. "Holy fuck."

"Yeah," she said softly. Tears glistened under her eyes, and she swiped at them.

"Are you okay?" I asked automatically. I hadn't wanted to hurt her.

She responded by stripping out of her sweats and thong. She dropped the sweats but handed me her underwear. They were soaking wet.

"Fuck," I said, my dick responding already. What the fuck was going on? I usually needed more rebound time than that. But I was already getting hard again. As if just the thought of her getting wet while giving me a blow job was too irresistible. "Come here."

She stripped out of my lacrosse sweatshirt and climbed back on top of me. This time, there was no fabric between us. No dry-humping.

She hovered over my cock, just barely grazing it with her wetness.

"Condom?" I forced myself to ask.

"I'm on the pill."

"Are you sure?"

She responded by spreading her legs wider on the couch and sliding her pussy onto my cock. My hands went to her hips, and I hissed through my teeth. Good fucking god, she felt so fucking incredible. It was impossible. Just fucking impossible that anyone could feel this good.

She seated herself fully, and then with a smirk, she said, "I'm sure."

"You're so... wet," I said as my finger slipped down between us to graze her clit.

She jerked like I'd hit her.

"Sensitive?" I asked, making slow circles.

"Jesus, I'm so close, and all I did was blow you."

I laughed as she bucked under my hand. "Now, you get how I feel every time I go down on you."

"Fuck, Court," she said, her eyes snapping closed.

Then, she began to move, lifting off of me and driving back down. Slow and steady and not at all the pace I wanted. So, I reluctantly stopped playing with her clit and gripped her hips in my sturdy hands, slamming her back down on my cock.

"Oh!" she gasped out. "So deep."

"Good," I said, doing it again and again.

She was so primed from the blow job that it only took a few thrusts before she was coming all over my cock. She yelled out, "Oh fuck, god, fuck yes, god yes, fuck," and held me still inside of her.

When she was done and she looked back at me with glazed, satisfied eyes, I picked her up and carried her into the bedroom. I laid her out on the bed and spread her legs wide, wide, wider and then dragged her ass forward until it was nearly off the bed. Then, I entered her in one long thrust. Perfect height for my taking.

She gripped the comforter with both hands as I fucked her hard and deep.

Perhaps it should have been gentle after the day she'd had. Maybe it should have been a soft lovemaking. But this was what I liked... and this was what she responded to. That didn't seem to change just because I'd finally admitted we were together.

If anything, this felt more secure.

More real.

More us.

29

ENGLISH

Starting my own company sounded impossible. When Lark had suggested it a few months ago, I'd laughed at her. Called it ludicrous. But when Court had suggested it, somehow, it hadn't sounded quite so crazy.

I was actually contemplating it. Not just contemplating it, but I was also figuring out how to put it in action. Planning for it, looking into office space, and designing what I'd want my own company to look like. The twenty-year long-term goal had just become the right-now, get-the-fuck-to-work *job*.

Which meant, while Court was busy at work each day, I had so much extra stuff to do. So much to do and so little time to do it. Especially since I needed to figure out what to do about Court... like yesterday. He wasn't my client anymore. Which was good, considering how unethical it was that we were fucking... and how little I wanted that to stop.

Together.

He'd said we were together.

Fuck, I didn't know what to think about that. Was it too soon? Should I care if it was?

I didn't know. All I knew was that I didn't want to overthink it, and I was too damn busy to stress it.

I'd just gotten off the phone with Carmin, a business real estate agent Court had recommended. She'd promised to get together a list of possible locations for the new office, and we could tour them this weekend if all went as planned.

I checked that off my list and was about to move on to the next item that I had to tackle when my phone started ringing.

"Anna English," I answered automatically.

"Anna, hello. This is Mayor Kensington's office."

"Oh, hi. How can I help you?" I asked, straightening in my seat.

"The mayor wants to schedule a meeting with you this afternoon. She's at the campaign office at four thirty. Does that work for you?"

"Yes," I said before even checking my schedule. I'd rearrange if I had to. "That works. Did she say what we're discussing?"

"She did not," he said amicably. "I'll mark you down. Thanks, Anna."

I hung up the phone with a frown. Just what I needed to take up my afternoon, a meeting with Court's mother.

I flopped backward, sighing heavily. It was overdue, to be honest. I had to tell her that I'd quit the agency. I would honor the next two weeks up until the election, as per my commitment, but I couldn't after that. She'd have to find someone else. It wasn't a conversation I was looking forward to. Hence why it had been at the bottom of my to-do list.

Still, I changed into a suit, braved the rapidly decreasing fall temperatures with my winter coat even though Court made fun of me for it, and headed to the mayor's campaign office.

With the temperature change, the traffic was brutal. I was used to it coming from LA, but it was still a pain in the ass. Especially as my nerves hit me fresh. I usually varied heavily between extreme self-doubt and unwavering confidence. As long as the confidence hit when I needed it to, I could fool anyone into believing the self-doubt never existed.

The cab finally pulled up in front of the mayor's campaign office, and I headed inside about twenty minutes early. Thank fuck I'd left well in advance.

I pulled off my jacket as soon as I stepped inside, slung it over my arm, and went in search of Lark. Her assistant was seated at her desk and smiled brightly at me.

"Hey, English," she said cheerfully.

"Hey, is Lark in?"

"Sure thing. Go ahead."

"Thanks, Aspen."

I passed her assistant and strode into the room to find Lark piled under mounds of paperwork up to her ears. With empty coffee cups littering every free surface.

"Is Lark under there somewhere?" I asked with a laugh.

Lark popped her head up. "English, hey! I didn't know you were coming by." She checked the time. "Did we have plans? I swear I didn't forget. It's just been crazy, and you know... it's less than two weeks until the election."

I held up my hand. "We didn't have plans. Breathe."

"Thank god," she said with a sigh.

"I have a meeting with Leslie."

"What about?"

I bit my lip. "Probably because I quit Poise."

Lark's eyes bulged. "You did what?"

I explained to her what had gone down between Josh and Margery and how I'd left Poise behind for good.

"What are you going to do?" she gasped frantically.

"Uncertain. Court kind of suggested I should start my own company."

"Wait, we're giving Court credit? I said that months ago!"

I laughed. "You did. I give you credit."

"Are you going to do it?"

"I'm looking into it at least. I have to talk to Leslie first. My contract for Court was through Poise. So, technically... we don't work together anymore."

Lark clapped her hands together in excitement. "Does this mean what I think it means?"

I shook my head and then nodded and then shrugged. "I don't know what you think it means."

"That you and Court are an item."

"Well... he said we were together. But I didn't say anything back. I don't know exactly."

"Oh my god," Lark gasped and jumped up. She dragged me into a hug. "I'm so happy for you. I know, after Josh, things were so bad, but Court seems to make you happy."

"You don't think it's too soon?" I whispered my fear out loud.

"Does it feel too soon?"

"Sometimes," I admitted. "It's only been three months, and Josh and I were together for five years. But... I like being with him."

"Then, I don't think it's too soon. Someone else might say that because they don't know you. But I know that you wouldn't rush into anything unless it felt right. I'm surprised it's Court," she said with another laugh, "but also glad it is. He's changed because of you. And you seem so much happier."

I flushed at the words. I'd always thought I was happy with Josh, that things were perfect. But maybe I'd just had such fucked up expectations that I'd dismissed his behavior too easily. I'd thought he was perfect when really he just wasn't quite as douchey as the guys I was used to. Until he was.

"It's kind of a relief to say it out loud. And to not have to hide it anymore. I didn't like lying."

"I know what you mean," Lark said seriously. "It only gets easier from here."

I held up my hand. "Fingers crossed."

"Let's get dinner after your meeting. Or coffee!"

"Do you *need* more coffee?" I asked, gesturing to her desk.

"What kind of question is that? Everyone needs more coffee."

I shook my head. "All right. Coffee Grounds after!"

I smiled at my friend and then headed back into the main office space. Leslie's office was at the very end of the hall. I'd met her there when I came out to interview for the position. We'd mostly communicated through email about Court's progress since then. For some reason, it felt even more daunting, walking toward her office now than it had before.

I knocked twice and heard someone inside say, "Come in."

I turned the knob and entered. Leslie was seated at a large desk. It was immaculate in comparison to Lark's mayhem. This was her second office, but I knew her main office at City Hall was equally perfect.

"Ah, Anna. Good. Right on time," Leslie said. "Shut the door and take a seat."

I shut the door behind me, closing me in with Court's mother. I hadn't felt this anxious about a meeting in a long time. But this wasn't a normal meet-the-parents endeavor. And I didn't know how it was going to go.

I knew that Leslie Kensington was volatile with her sons. I'd seen it firsthand. But I also knew that she loved them and prized them even if she was a total hard-ass. I still didn't know how she'd react when she found out about me and Court.

Still, I took a deep breath and sat.

Leslie finished typing out what appeared to be an email and then turned to face me again. "So, I just had a call from your PR firm. Apparently, you quit?"

"Yes," I said softly. Then, I cleared my throat and reached for my publicist vote. "Yes. I received some disturbing news about the firm and made the decision to sever ties."

"Care to share the news? Margery made it seem like..." Leslie waved her hand about. "Well, that you weren't entirely with it."

I gritted my teeth. So, it had begun. The slander against my good name.

"Well, I found out from my ex-husband that she'd convinced him to sleep with his costar to help promote the movie. And instead of telling me or talking to me about it, she went behind my back. I just found out about it, and when she finally admitted to it, I decided I didn't need that kind of person in my life. Let alone as a role model."

Leslie steepled her fingers in front of her mouth. "Hmm."

"I understand that I probably should have come to talk to you about it right away. I know that it impacts our contract. That we had two weeks left before the election. But things have been tumultuous, and that is my fault. I take responsibility."

Leslie was silent a minute. She looked me over, assessing me. As if she could see straight through me. Then, she nodded. "Well, no matter."

I nearly choked. "What?"

"I don't care who you work for. I agreed to terminate the contract with Poise under the circumstances," Leslie said evenly. "It will be much easier to work with you directly."

"I don't understand," I said softly. "I thought you would be upset."

"Upset? Why? When I hired you, Lark said you were the best in the business. That proved true. It's all the better that I can bring you in-house and not have to share you with a company in LA," Leslie said like the strategic businesswoman she was.

"Oh," I gasped. "You want to hire me in-house?"

"Yes, of course. You're an excellent publicist, Anna. Or do you prefer English? I've heard others call you that."

"Yes, English," I muttered, still in a state of shock.

"So, we can discuss salary. I was thinking the same as what we'd agreed on with Poise, but of course, they're no longer taking a cut. You'd be making more. But I'm willing to negotiate before someone else snaps you up."

I was reeling. To work for Leslie full-time. I wouldn't have to start my own company. I could just work under her umbrella. I could deal with the things she needed and make even *more* money than I had been making. Enough to sustain the life I'd grown accustomed to living.

But also, she would be expecting me to work for Court. To keep working with Court. He'd be my client and responsibility again. Just as we were beginning to become something.

"I appreciate the opportunity," I said carefully. "But I'm going to have to decline."

Leslie raised her eyebrows. "Really? Do you want to move back to LA? Has another firm already reached out to you?"

"No," I said. "But... I can't work for Court anymore."

Leslie sighed heavily. As if she had heard this so many other times before. "What did he do this time?"

I laughed softly and shook my head. "Nothing. He's actually... wonderful. And I know that you won't approve, but I would rather pursue a relationship with him than take this job."

Leslie's mouth dropped open. "Well, I can still be surprised."

"This isn't how I wanted to tell you," I said quickly. "It's brand-new and..."

Then, she leaned back and held her hand up. "You don't have to explain. I'm glad that you're staying in Court's life. He's better for it."

"Oh," I whispered. My cheeks heated. "Really? I thought you'd be mad. Since you didn't want to hire someone like me because you were worried I'd fall under his spell... and then I did."

Leslie shook her head. "No. He fell under *your* spell. And that's a different story."

I opened and closed my mouth. "But..."

"You got him to work for the company. You got him to stop drinking excessively. Not only is he showing up to campaign events, but he's also sober *and* giving speeches. I don't know if I've ever seen him sober at a campaign event," she said crisply. "I wanted someone who could handle him. Someone who wasn't so pretty that they'd fall all over themselves over him. I didn't realize that it could even happen in reverse. And I'm grateful. Whatever the circumstances."

I really had no idea what to say to that. I never thought that I'd put Court under my spell. But the way she described it, it felt so certain. I'd seen it as my job to make him a better person. I hadn't realized that us falling for each other was what would help him all along.

"What does that mean for us for the future?" I finally sputtered out.

Leslie smiled. "I suppose we can find someone else for Court, if you think it's necessary." She tilted her head. "I'm starting to expect that it won't be though."

I left Leslie's office in a daze. I'd been expecting to be put through the wringer, and instead, I'd found that she didn't even mind that I was dating her son. That was not the Leslie Kensington I had been expecting. Even Lark was shocked. After how Leslie had reacted to Penn dating Natalie, she'd sworn that Leslie would freak out. Though we were both glad she hadn't.

I skipped going to my apartment to change and went straight to Court's penthouse instead. He had just come out of the shower when I entered his place and changed into running pants and T-shirt.

Court startled when he saw me. “English, I didn’t know you were coming over.”

“I just talked to your mom.”

“Oh, yeah?”

“Margery called her about me quitting. She offered me a job to work as your publicist for the company.”

“That’s great,” he said evenly.

Not the answer I’d been expecting.

“Well, I turned her down,” I said giddily. “I mean, since we’re you know... something. Together.”

“You turned her down?”

“Yeah. Conflict of interest.”

He looked so far away in that moment. As if he couldn’t fathom it.

“Unless... I shouldn’t have done that? I mean, I was already looking at starting my own business. But we both agreed that with the transformation you’ve made, you probably don’t even need a full-time publicist anymore.”

“Oh, good. No more babysitter for me.”

I frowned at his comment as he went to the wet bar and poured himself some whiskey.

“Everything okay at work today?” I asked.

He took a long sip of his drink. “It was fine. Just... draining.”

“Oh, okay. I thought you’d be more excited.”

He downed the rest of the whiskey in one long shot and then set it down heavily. Something shifted in his shoulders. Something eased as if the tension had never been there. And then when he turned back around to face me, it was gone. As if a phantom had passed through his body and out the other side.

“I am excited,” he said with that smile again. “This means you’re all mine, right?”

I bit my lip and nodded. “I suppose that I am.”

He strode back toward me, wrapped an arm tight around

my waist, and kissed the breath out of me. It was a needy kiss. As if he were trying to suck my soul right out of my body.

I came away breathless. “That was some kiss.”

His hands traveled over my ass and hoisted me up with my legs around his waist. “You’d better get used to it.”

30

ENGLISH

"Just come out of the bedroom and show me your damn costume already," Court all but growled from the living room.

I'd been teasing him all week about the Halloween costume I'd gotten for Katherine's party. She'd insisted that, this year, we have a group costume, and so all my careful planning had been thrown out the window. I knew the group idea would be better, especially for pictures.

"Katherine is going to be here any minute. I need more than a few minutes with this costume," he called again.

I giggled a little at his impatience. Yes, I'd been a big cock-tease about it, but it was more fun that way. I was just glad that whatever had come over him last week hadn't returned. He'd been back to being his regular Court self.

Then, with a bit of theatrics, I opened the bedroom door and stepped out to face Court. But it was his costume that made me stop. He was dressed as Don Draper just as I'd thought in the St. Regis all those weeks ago. He wore a sexy gray suit with a little white pocket square, shiny black oxfords, and a fedora.

"Wow," I swooned.

Court's eyes rounded. "Wow is right. Holy fuck, English. I don't think I can let you leave in that."

I put a hand on my hip. "And who says you control where I go and where I don't, Draper?"

He laughed. "No one. But I'm considering keeping you inside and fucking you all night if that's any consolation."

"Well, achievement unlocked," I said with a wink.

He twirled his finger in place to ask me to spin, and so I did for him. I let him get a good look at the way my legs looked forever long in my mile-high, strappy black Jimmy Choos. His eyes traveled up to the cheeky black lace underwear with the matching garter and fully blinged-out black push-up bra. My hair was blown out, and I rocked a smoky eye like it was my job. But the best part of the entire thing... was the black fallen angel wings at my back. Alone, I just looked like a dark angel, but when I met up with my girls, we'd look like a collection of Victoria's Secret Angels preparing for the runway.

He whistled low. "The teasing was worth it. Can we stay home now?"

I giggled and shook my head. "This party is important to Katherine."

"I might get handsy," he warned me in advance.

"I'd find this acceptable," I said mischievously.

Court circled my waist and drew me in for a sensual kiss that made me reconsider his offer.

"Okay, okay," I said breathlessly. "You might actually win if we don't stop now."

"Then, don't stop."

I hastily stepped around him and went back for the small clutch that went with my outfit. I checked my phone and saw I had a missed call from Taylor. It was from a couple of minutes ago, but she hadn't left a message. If it was important, she'd have left a message. I stuffed the phone into my clutch and followed Court downstairs to meet the Percy limo.

Thankfully, it was already waiting for us, so I could just skitter across the sidewalk and get inside without needing my jacket, which I had no intention of carrying around tonight.

Gavin whistled as I stepped into the limousine. "Our angels are complete!"

Katherine looked me over and then nodded. "Dark is fitting."

I grinned at her and then took a seat with Court next to me. Katherine along with Whitley and her date, Robert, sat along the back wall. Sam and Gavin were next, dressed in "costumes" that appeared to just be suits. Next to Gavin were more of Katherine and Lark's crew—Lewis with his girlfriend, Addie, and then Rowe with his boyfriend, Nicholas. We had to have been the last stop because the limo was packed full.

It seemed that the only people missing were Lark, who was busy on campaign, and Camden, Penn, and Natalie. And after the interaction between them all at Penn's wedding reception… maybe this was better.

The limo pulled up in front of Club Marquee, which had the full red-carpet treatment for the attendees. Katherine's Halloween party was the biggest event of the season. She'd sold out the massive club months in advance and raised millions for an animal charity. I was surprised to find out that she had a particular charity that she always worked with, but also, it made sense, considering this was the Upper East Side.

This felt so familiar to me though. Even if this was the Upper East Side and I was the outsider, I'd been to enough premieres and award ceremonies to know the drill. I'd been in this world for six months, and I still couldn't get over the fact that I was part of this and not just on the sidelines.

And this event felt even more unbelievable.

It was my first event with Court.

Not just as his publicist, but as… *his*. No hiding in the shadows tonight. This was our debut. And I had a feeling that he wouldn't be able to keep his hands off me. Not when I was in this outfit.

Katherine was herding everyone out in order, saving the three of us for last. We wanted to make an appearance, of course.

Court firmly kissed me once on the mouth. "I'll wait for you after Katherine steals your attention."

I laughed and kissed him again. "Can't wait."

He disappeared, exiting behind Nicholas. I pulled my phone out, intent on sending him a sexy picture when I saw I had a text from Taylor.

Anna, I need to talk to you. Call me right now.

I huffed. I hadn't heard from Taylor in weeks. She hadn't called or texted or met up with me since she asked me for money. And tonight of all nights, she wanted to try to reach me. Not even a, *Hi, how's it going?* Just a, *Call me right now.*

I can't talk right now. Busy. I'll call you tomorrow.

I snapped the shot for Court, sent it to his phone, and returned my phone to my clutch.

"Ready?" Katherine asked us.

I nodded.

Whitley grinned like a fool. "Fuck yes, Katherine."

Then, Katherine stepped out of the limo. I could hear the intake of breath at her appearance. She was clad in red lingerie with red Louboutins and bright red angel wings. Her dark hair fanned all around her. Her muscles were toned to perfection, as if she had been killing it in the gym lately. She looked like a goddess. And tonight was her night.

Whitley went next, ironically clad in virginal white. The

light to Katherine's devil red. The light to my darkness as I followed.

Katherine stood with her hands on her hips before the photographers clicking away, flashes blazing. Whitley moved to one side, and I stepped up on the other. A mirrored set. Katherine red with her dark hair. Whitley white with her current red dye job. And me black with my platinum-blonde hair.

Applause came from the awaiting crowd as they took us in. I picked out Court nearby. He looked hungry. And it made me giddy. This was real life. It was hard to believe that we'd made it to this moment. That we were here.

We followed Katherine around for a few minutes as she answered questions about the charity and posed for pictures. Then, she waved her hand at the photographers and bustled toward the entrance.

Court snatched me up before I made it inside. "You're a natural."

I swatted at him as he dived in to claim my lips. "I just followed Katherine's lead."

"Psh," he said, disbelieving.

My gaze swept behind him to the cameras flashing at us. "Well, I guess we're out now, aren't we?"

"That was kind of the plan, wasn't it?"

"Yes. I'm glad we're not hiding anymore."

"Me too. Because if I'd had to watch one guy hit on you tonight in that outfit, my fist would have found his jaw."

I rolled my eyes and pulled him inside after our friends. "You're outrageous."

"On occasion."

Club Marquee was an enormous multi-floored club with balconies and all sorts of private booths. Katherine already stood in her place of honor in a booth next to the DJ. I didn't know how she'd gotten there so quickly when the dance floor was packed with women in lingerie dancing suggestively against men in suits.

Court took my hand in his and veered us through the maze of people until we reached the booth. We stepped past the bouncer and found it full of all of our friends. Penn and Natalie had apparently decided to make an appearance. Seemed ballsy, considering how precarious their relationship with Katherine was. Even Camden stood off to the side, surveying the room like it was his job.

"I'm shocked they're all here," I told Court.

He shrugged. "Welcome to the Upper East Side. Once you're in, there's no escape."

"Sounds ominous."

"Can be."

Court grabbed us both drinks, and I sipped on my gin and tonic. Whitley appeared a minute later.

"Going to need her, Court," she said with a wink. "She needs to lose her halo."

Court gestured before him. "By all means."

I laughed as Whitley dragged me away, and we started grinding to the music. Katherine eventually agreed to join us. I was just missing Lark. I could not wait for that damn campaign to be over. Not just for me, but also for her sanity.

"So, how are things with you and Robert?" I asked Whitley.

She grinned. "I mean, I think I'm generally a bad girlfriend, but he likes it. It's so strange."

"He likes that you're a bad girlfriend?"

"Yeah… like all the things that normally happen to me that drives other guys away, he's kind of into."

"Like what?" Katherine asked.

"Well, like getting calls and texts from my exes. I'm not into them anymore, but I still keep up with some of them."

"You also ruin some of their lives," I pointed out.

"They had it coming!" she said, gesturing wildly. "But

anyway, he doesn't seem to care that I like my space. That I don't want to come home to some clingy person after working all day in surgery. He doesn't seem to care that I'm bisexual. I mean, I like women, but that doesn't mean I want to hook up with one with him."

"That seems reasonable," I said.

"You'd think!" Whitley said. "I don't know. He's very accommodating. It's weird and strangely nice."

"Sounds like a keeper," Katherine said softly.

"We'll see. If we make it past three months, it might be something."

"You've never dated anyone longer than three months?" Katherine asked.

"Oh, I have," Whitley said. "But… the three-month mark is how I know whether I can handle their bullshit."

"And whether they can handle yours?" I finished for her.

She snorted. "Something like that."

For some reason, my gaze dragged over to Gavin, who hadn't brought a date. When we'd asked him about it in the limo, he'd said he planned to pick someone out at the party. All bravado. But just as I'd suspected, he was watching Whitley. I wondered why he didn't make a move. It seemed very un-Gavin-like.

But as soon as he caught me watching, he returned his attention to whatever Robert had been saying and ignored Whitley entirely. Bizarre.

"No," Katherine whispered under her breath. She had stopped dancing.

"What?" Whitley and I asked at the same time.

I followed her gaze and found Fiona had just entered the booth. She was dressed like a Playboy bunny, complete with ears and a tail, just like the invitation had requested. And I knew she was also the last person that Katherine had wanted to see at her event.

Fiona had been Camden's side piece before Katherine and Camden entered their arranged marriage. As far as I knew, he'd cut off ties with her after the wedding, but he'd stumbled upon Katherine and Penn alone together, and that had all changed. He started showing up to events with her again.

Then, the night of the raid at the gambling ring that had started this entire thing with me and Court, Camden had apparently abandoned Fiona to help get Katherine to safety. Their relationship hadn't been… perfect since then, but I hadn't seen Fiona around either. She was a menace.

"Tell her to leave," I said.

Katherine shook her head just once. "I can't."

"I didn't know that was still happening," Whitley said gently.

"It's whatever," Katherine said dismissively. But she hadn't taken her eyes off of the woman.

"Why is that okay?" I asked her.

Katherine lifted one shoulder. "Because she's nothing. And if I send her home, then she wins."

"No, she doesn't. She wins if you let her stay," Whitley said. "I'll send her home if you don't."

"No," Katherine said harshly. "Trust me. It's not worth it."

And my heart broke for Katherine in that moment. I didn't think that I'd have it in me. Having Natalie and Fiona in the same place, in *her* space. Sometimes, I didn't understand the Upper East Side at all.

31

COURT

"What the fuck is Fiona doing here?" I asked Camden.

He looked at me. "Why do you think she's here?"

"I thought you'd moved on from her. Why do you even like her?"

"What makes you think that I like her?"

And he was serious. This woman he'd been sleeping with on and off for years, and supposedly, he had no real feelings for her.

Camden was my best friend. I didn't judge him. He didn't judge me. But that didn't mean that I always understood him.

"Don't go to see her, man," I said instead.

He smirked. "Why ever not?"

"Oh, I don't know. Your wife maybe?"

"Katherine doesn't care."

I snorted. "Like hell."

Camden's eyes darkened, but he remained silent. Just staring at his little Playboy bunny standing on the edge of the booth.

"Why don't you just tell Katherine how you feel?"

"And how do I feel?" Camden asked.

"You love her."

Camden didn't even meet my gaze. "Is that what you think?"

"I can't think of another reason why you'd marry her."

"It's an arranged marriage," he said flatly, finally looking at me. "A contract. A business transaction. That's it, Court. Feel free to delude yourself with romantic platitudes in your own life, but don't attribute them to mine."

"Fine," I bit back.

"And anyway, if Katherine cared one way or another, then she'd send Fiona away. Let's wait and see if she does."

His eyes shifted to his wife where she stood with Whitley and English. She watched Fiona like a hawk. There was nothing in her expression. She was carefully blank. Then, after a minute, she turned her back on Fiona and the whole situation.

"See?" Camden said as if that proved his point.

But I didn't think that it did.

Not that he seemed to care as he patted my shoulder and then strode away from me, straight to Fiona.

"Idiot," I muttered under my breath.

Sam raised his eyebrows. He must have caught the tail end of that conversation. "Well, the Upper East Side is sure showing its true colors tonight, huh?"

I laughed. Leave it to Sam to cut straight to the point. "You have no idea."

"Am I supposed to understand what's happening between Katherine and Camden?"

"Not the slightest. I still don't get it."

"Good. But I'm happy for you at least," he said with a smile. "You and English actually work together. It's a miracle."

"A bit. Though I guess I should thank you, too. You were the one who made me stop fighting her on everything back in the Hamptons."

Sam shrugged. "Hey, I just told you to stop acting like a dipshit."

"Worked out."

"It did. I'm going to grab another drink," Sam said. "Want anything?"

"Nah, I'm good." I held up my still-half-full dirty martini.

Sam nodded and then headed to the bar.

I was just about to go steal English away from the girls when my brother appeared in front of me.

I arched an eyebrow. "Penn."

To my surprise, he stuck his hand out. We shook, and it was amicable. No posturing of any kind. This wasn't the same person who had ditched me when I first started back at the company. There might even be repentance in the blue eyes that matched mine.

"So, you're still with the company, *and* you're dating English," Penn said. "That's all new."

"Yeah. That's right."

"She seems to be good for you."

"We work," I told him. "Mother even offered her a job with the company, and she turned it down. She wasn't even mad that we were together."

Penn's eyes darkened. They shifted back to Natalie. "Guess she only made that mistake once."

"Thanks for taking the brunt of it."

Penn just shook his head. "I don't know how to say it," he said with a sigh. "But I acted like a dick the last time we were together. I thought you were just fucking around, but you've really done a one-eighty."

I mockingly put my hand to my chest. "Is that almost an apology?"

He snorted. "Yes. And don't make me regret it."

I laughed and held my drink up to his. He clinked his against mine, and we both took a swallow.

"How did it even happen?" Penn asked. "I thought everything you were doing was all bullshit."

"It was," I told him honestly. "But for one, English believed in me. And two, somehow, I just stopped pretending. And I realized this was just me."

"Huh. I didn't think that you had it in you."

"Me either," I admitted.

Penn looked around with a worried expression on his face. As if he were just seeing the room for what was going on.

"Is Camden going home with Fiona?" he asked.

I shrugged. "Uncertain."

"Jesus, Katherine must be sick."

He was staring over at her as if he was going to march over there. But I just shook my head. Not a good idea.

"She looks fine to me."

"Maybe I should go talk to her," Penn said.

I put my hand out to stop him. "Uh, no. You do realize that even though Katherine is your oldest friend, you also fucked her for, like, a decade, right?"

"I..."

"It's better for everyone if you don't. You'll make it worse."

His face hardened. "Yeah. You're probably right. I should just go find Natalie and not get involved."

"See, you can learn, too," I said with a laugh.

"Plus, it looks like you have incoming anyway," Penn said, nodding his head.

I turned and saw English storming across the booth toward me, like an avenging angel. Sam was close on her heels, speaking hastily as if to calm her down. What the hell?

But at the same time, I could see it in her face. I could see that she knew. That it had all come out somehow. Even though I'd been so careful.

A cool feeling of dread settled in my stomach.

"What the fuck did you do?" English spat at me.

I swallowed. "I, uh… what do you mean?"

"You went to see Jane!" she accused me. "You saw Jane, and you were photographed with her!"

Fuck.

32

ENGLISH

How could he?

My blood boiled. My hands were clenched into fists. I thought about throwing one into his perfect face. This was the most idiotic thing that I could think of him doing. It was so fucking stupid that I hadn't even considered it. Hadn't thought for a second that he would do something to put everything in jeopardy.

The minute Sam had come over to me to say that Lark had been trying to call me, I had known something was wrong. He'd handed me the phone, and she'd relayed that images had been leaked, that it was being reported already, viral. Words that made me want to vomit.

And the next: betrayal.

He'd gone, and he hadn't told me. On purpose.

Why? Why the lies? How could he claim he hated lying and then go see his ex-girlfriend in prison without telling me?

I stood before him, shaking with barely suppressed rage. And he just looked like a child who had been caught with his hand in the cookie jar.

"Say something," I demanded.

He sighed. “What do you want me to say?”

“Anything, Court. Is it true?”

“Yes,” he said finally.

Penn sighed next to him, nodded his head at me once, and then ducked out of our conversation. I didn’t blame him.

“There are pictures. Lark has seen them. She was trying to get ahold of me, but I haven’t checked my phone all night. She finally went to Sam, who found me. And now, it’s everywhere.” My voice broke. “Everywhere.”

“I didn’t know.”

“You didn’t care!” I barked back at him.

“I thought I was careful.”

I laughed at him. “How exactly could you be careful in this instance?”

“I just didn’t think that I was followed or that anyone saw me.”

“Great. So, at least we know you’re not an expert in sneaking around any more than my husband,” I bit back at him.

He flinched. “It’s not like that.”

“Really? Feels exactly the same, oddly enough.”

“Anna…”

“Don’t,” I growled. “Why didn’t you tell me? Why hide it? Why lie? Fuck, why did you even go in the first place?”

He removed his fedora and ran a hand back through his hair, mussing the ’60s style. “I just wanted to know the truth.”

“From a con artist?” I asked with wide, disbelieving eyes. “You thought someone who literally lied about who she was and stole millions from banks across the world was going to give you a straight answer?”

“I hadn’t seen her since the arrest. I just… wanted to know why.”

I shook my head in frustration. “You want to know why? Why? Are you serious? Because you were an easy mark. That’s why.”

Court winced. He clearly didn't like that I'd reduced his entire year-and-a-half relationship down to this. But that was the truth. He should have been able to handle it by now.

"She did it because she's a con artist. She did it because she needed social proof. I'm not even a fucking con artist, Court, and I could tell you that Josh gave me social proof in Hollywood. I could see instantly how Jane, who was lying about her life, would need it. And she got it from you!"

"Yes, but..."

"But what?" I demanded. "None of this explains why you lied."

"What did you want me to say, English? I needed to go see my ex-girlfriend to get closure? That I was nearly certain none of it had meant anything to her, but I wanted to know for sure. And guess what. I was right. None of it meant anything to her."

My heart throbbed for him. The pain that must have caused.

But it didn't excuse going to see her five days before the election. It didn't excuse hiding it. It didn't excuse anything.

"That must have been hard to hear. But you could have told me that. I told you when Josh showed up in my apartment. I turned my husband away, who I had been with for five years, and the first thing I did was come to see you."

"I know but..."

I laughed. I couldn't help it. The manic laugh that erupted out of my chest. "I don't want your *buts*. I don't want your Upper East Side Court Kensington bullshit explanation for why you should get out of this. I once said that I'm not sorry for being the only person holding you accountable for your actions. That doesn't stop today." I swallowed back my own pain at the words. And the heartbreak in them. "You could have told me. You chose not to. And worse than all of that, Court, you just ruined everything."

"Come on, it won't be that bad," he said optimistically.

"I spent the last six months making you the golden boy of the Upper East Side. I did everything in my power to distance you from Jane and the person you had been before, who gave her money. Now, five days before the election, you decided to go see Jane in prison. What the fuck do you think the headlines say?"

He didn't answer. His face had gone pale.

"Collusion. That you're helping her defense. That you were in on it all along. That you got away with it because of who your mother is." I shook with anger. "Your mother's reelection is in five days. Jane's trial is in a month. This could not be worse timing."

"Okay, I fucked up," he said finally. "I just had to see her."

"Do you still love her?" I asked, forcing the words past my teeth.

I didn't want to know the answer. In some ways, it was unfair of me to ask. I still had feelings for Josh despite his bull-shit. It would take time for them to go away. But we'd been married. We'd had a life together.

And suddenly, I was seeing the truth. How he'd been more worried about her well-being when she hadn't taken the plea deal. He'd been stressed that she didn't have the right represen-tation. He'd wanted to help. The way he'd reacted when I suggested that he'd cheated on Jane. It was the only time I'd seen him so pissed off. He'd thrown me out because of it. And then the other day... I'd jokingly asked if he'd ever wanted to marry someone. He'd come back with one name—Jane.

I took a step back.

My stomach twisted.

He still loved her.

Was that... was that possible?

"Does it matter, English?" he begged me. "She's in jail. She's not going anywhere. And whatever we had wasn't even *real*."

"It was real to you," I whispered.

Fuck, I'd fucked up.

My trust was so fragile. It always had been. Ever since my dad had cheated on my mom and married someone else without a backward glance. Ever since my mother had been more interested in oxycontin than raising her child. The world wasn't kind, and it wasn't fair. I'd been used and abused and cheated on. I'd felt my heart be torn out of my chest and smashed into pieces. And somehow—*somehow*—I'd deluded myself into thinking that Court Kensington, of all people, wouldn't do the same.

"English, this is real to me," he said. "You and me."

I took another step backward. "I can't do this."

"What? No. We can fix this. That's... that's what you do. You fix things."

"I don't know how to fix this, Court. Not the campaign or the pictures or us."

"Please don't say that. It was one stupid mistake," he begged.

"Yeah," I whispered, "that's what Josh said, too."

"I am *not* Josh."

"And yet, I can't trust you either." I swallowed hard, hating the words coming out of my mouth. "I'm just going to go."

I turned and headed back to where I'd left my clutch with Katherine's and Whitley's bags. Court followed close behind me.

"English, you can't do this. You can't just leave. We should talk."

"I'm done talking, Court. If we keep talking, I'll say something else I regret," I snapped back at him.

"At least let me drive you home."

I stood up with my phone, prepared to pull up Uber. "No, I'll take an Uber."

He sighed heavily. "English... Anna..."

"Jesus," I muttered when my phone lit up.

"What?"

I had nineteen missed calls, twice as many texts, and five voice mails. I clicked the call list—fifteen calls from Taylor, three from Lark, and one from an unknown number.

"Oh god," I said, my stomach dropping to the floor.

I'd thought Taylor was just being her normal teenage self. I hadn't thought that she really needed to talk.

I clicked to the voice mails and listened to the first from Taylor.

"Anna, please pick up your phone. I keep calling, and you won't answer. Bea is in trouble. She owes this guy five grand, and I have no fucking clue where we're going to get the money. I hate asking you for it, but can you spot it for me? I'll pay you back. I swear. Just call me back."

The line ended.

And the voice mail said, "Next message."

Taylor was crying. No, sobbing. "I haven't heard from you. I don't know what's going on. Bea wants me to go with her to talk to the guy. She thinks we can work out a deal or something. I'd rather just give him the money. Please, please, please, Anna. I'd never ask if it wasn't important."

"Oh god," I whispered as fear hit me fresh.

"Next message."

"I still haven't heard from you. I'm trying one last time. I texted you the address just in case. Meet me there with the money if you get it in time. I'm so sorry for how I acted before. You were right. You were so right."

The line ended.

"Next message."

And Lark's voice came through the line. "English, pick up your phone. There're images of Court..."

I ended the message before I could hear the rest. I didn't care about that right now.

My stomach flip-flopped as I moved on to the final message.

"Anna English, this is Officer Peake with the New York Police Department. You were the last call from the phone of one Taylor English. She was shot twice in a drug-related fight in lower Manhattan. Please call us back at this number as soon as you get this."

My heart stopped at those words.

I didn't breathe.

"Taylor's been shot," I whispered in horror.

PART V

AND THEY ALL COME TUMBLING DOWN

33

ENGLISH

I stood outside of Bellevue Hospital Center. I'd ditched my wings at the club, and Court's jacket covered my lingerie-clad body. It wasn't enough, but it'd have to be for now. There was no way I was going to go home to change. Not with Taylor in critical condition.

Those were Officer Peake's words. Critical condition. Shot once in the thigh. The other barely grazed her hip.

I'd run out of Club Marquee as fast as my Jimmy Choos allowed. I hadn't even cared that Court had followed me. I couldn't think about our argument or the implications of the pictures or what would happen to the campaign. Not after Taylor.

We skidded inside, getting strange and stranger looks from the people around us, including the hospital staff. We weren't the only ones dressed up. I just... probably looked like a hooker.

"I just received a call. My sister was shot and brought to this hospital. Her name is Taylor English."

The woman checked her computer. "Yes, I see her here. She's been moved into surgery."

"Surgery?" I gasped. "What for?"

"The bullet went into her thigh and hit an artery. She's lost a lot of blood. The doctors and support staff are working diligently right now. I can move you into the waiting area, and then when the doctor has any information, he can come directly to you."

I felt sick. This couldn't be happening.

Court stepped forward. "That would be great. Thank you."

The woman nodded with a sad smile. She pushed a button that buzzed us through to the back and then directed us to a separate, much more secluded space. "A doctor will be out to speak with you as soon as they can."

"Thank you," I whispered.

The waiting area was practically deserted. There was a woman alone in the back corner, but otherwise, it was just me and Court. I sank into a seat at the front. My feet were anxiously tap, tap, tapping away. All the adrenaline that had coursed through my body when I got that phone call was still hyping up my system.

Court plopped down next to me. "It's going to be okay."

I held my hand up. "Don't talk to me."

He sighed. "Okay."

"And you don't know if she'll be okay. We don't know anything."

"Yes, but..."

I glared at him. "Don't."

He fell silent.

We both did.

All I could do was stare at the doors and wait. I tried to call my dad. Tonight was the only time that I was thankful for the three-hour time difference. Because even though it was already one in the morning here, it was only ten at night in LA. He answered right away, begged for more news, *any* news, and promised that he and Ashley would be out on the first flight that they could get.

"My dad and stepmom are coming," I said and sat back down.

"Good," he said softly.

And then we returned to silence.

And waiting.

And feeling like I was going to vomit.

I didn't know how long we'd been sitting there. It could have been minutes or hours or days. It felt endless.

But then a doctor appeared. Court and I both stood. The woman in the corner stood, too. We all waited, breathless, hoping it was us and not the other. Feeling bad that we even thought it.

"Anna English?" the doctor asked.

"That's me," I said, rushing forward with relief.

"Your sister has just finished surgery. We were able to repair the damage to her femoral artery, but she lost a lot of blood. We had to give her a transfusion. She's currently stable."

"Oh, thank god," I gasped out. My legs buckled underneath me, and I fought to stay upright.

"Her friend is still in surgery though," he said softly.

"Her friend," I said stupidly, not comprehending. Then, it hit me. "Bea?"

"Yes. Taylor was wheeled in with Beatrice Reynolds. We've reached out to her family, but we've had no luck so far. If you know how to reach them, it would be really helpful."

I blinked. "I don't. They're college friends. We're in LA. I think Bea... uh, Beatrice is from Boston."

"Okay," he said with a sigh. "Well, I thought we'd ask."

"Is Bea going to be okay?"

The doctor frowned. There was a *no* on his face. Written all over his expression. A terrifying look that said everything he didn't. "She's still in surgery. We'll know more in the next couple of hours."

I nodded mutely, terrified. *It could have been Taylor.* The words ran like a mantra through my mind.

"Can I see my sister now?"

"Yes. She's resting, but you can go in to be with her."

"Thank you so much," I said, choking on the words.

A nurse came and brought Court and me to Taylor's room. I stepped inside first to find my beautiful little sister hooked up to an IV. She was dressed in a nightgown and looked as pale as death. The covers were pulled up to her chest, but it couldn't disguise the state of her left leg. It looked huge and bulbous under the covers, as if it had been wrapped around and around and around until it looked like the game Hot Potato and I was meant to unwrap it to find candy.

My feet carried me farther into the room. I sank into the seat next to Taylor and gently took her hand into mine. I didn't know what to do or what to say.

Court stood nearby, just inside the room, as if he didn't know whether to be in or out. As if he were guarding the door. But I didn't care. I didn't want to think about him, not now. I just wanted to be here with Taylor.

It wasn't until an hour later that I realized Court must have made some calls. Lark rushed into the room. Her red hair was curly and frazzled. Her eyes were smudged with purple half-moons under them, and she looked worried.

"English," she said, coming to my side and pulling me into a hug. "Oh my goodness, I don't even know what to say. How is she doing? How are *you* doing? Has she woken up?"

I shook my head. "No, she's still asleep. The nurses say that she's sedated for the pain. They don't think she'll be up for a couple hours. Her friend just went into another surgery. I don't know what's happening with her."

Lark squeezed me tighter. "It's okay. You don't have to know everything." Then, she drew back. "I brought you clothes. Court said you were still in your Halloween costume."

I glanced down at myself. The red lingerie and Court's oversize '60s suit coat. I hadn't even realized.

"Thank you," I said, taking the clothes.

I entered the small bathroom and changed out of the costume and heels. Lark had brought me a pair of yoga pants, a black T-shirt, and a sweatshirt along with socks and sneakers. I realized half-consciously that this was all stuff I'd left at Court's. I'd never given anyone a key to my new place. It felt like an oversight now.

"Feel more human?" Lark asked when I stepped out of the bathroom.

"Sure," I said with a shrug.

"Do you want to talk? I didn't know if..."

"No," I said quickly. "Not really."

"Court seems... upset."

"You saw the pictures."

Lark nodded. "I did."

"I don't want to talk about it. I just... I just want him to go. Can you tell him to go?"

Lark bit her lip. "If that's what you want. But I think you should talk to him."

"No. I already talked to him. I just want to be here for my sister."

"I don't know if he's going to leave you here alone."

"Please, please, Lark. I can't do it tonight." I helplessly stared down at Taylor. "She was *shot*. Her friend might not make it through the night. I can't deal with Court , too."

"Okay," Lark said softly, rubbing my back. "It's okay. I can ask Court to leave. Or at least to stay out of your way."

"Thank you." I breathed a sigh of relief.

"Of course."

Lark disappeared then, leaving me alone with Taylor once more. I couldn't hear what she said to Court. I didn't want to know. I just wanted to be alone.

Early the next morning, Taylor woke up. Groggy and clearly in a lot of pain. A nurse bustled in. He checked her vitals and pain levels, gave her some more painkillers, and then headed back the way he'd come.

"Anna?" Taylor said, blinking a few times. "How long was I out?"

"Most of the night."

"Fuck."

"Yeah." I chewed on my fingernail. A habit I'd given up in college. "I got all your messages and voice mails. Just a little too late."

"I'm sorry," she immediately blurted out. "I should have come to you as soon as I found out how much money Bea owed that guy. It just all..." She shuddered.

"Hey, it's okay. Whatever happened, happened. You're going to be okay. Your leg will take a while to heal, but the doctor said that you should make a full recovery."

"And Bea?" Taylor asked, her voice thick with emotion.

I swallowed. "I don't know much. They won't say anything until her parents arrive. I know she was in and out of surgery last night. They're still working on her."

"Jesus," Taylor said. She slammed her eyes shut. "I can't fucking believe this."

"Do you want to tell me what happened?"

Taylor frowned and then shook her head.

"I'm afraid you're going to have to tell the police. They called me last night. That's how I knew where you'd been taken. I think they're going to want to file a report."

"Okay... but not right now."

"Okay. Dad and Ashley are flying out this afternoon. It was the soonest they could get a flight."

"You told Dad?" she gasped and then winced.

"You'd been shot! You were in surgery. What did you expect?"

Taylor nodded, chastened. "Yeah. Of course. You're right."

A soft knock came from the door. I frowned and then yawned as the realization that I hadn't slept all night hit me. I stiffly dragged myself out of the chair and went to the door. When I opened it, Court waited on the other side.

"Hi," he said softly.

"What are you doing here?" I asked, stepping out of the room and closing it behind me.

"I brought you breakfast." He held up a bag stamped with the logo from my favorite bagel place. "I wasn't sure that you'd eaten anything."

"I haven't," I said. "I haven't really left the room."

But I didn't move forward to take the bag.

"Has Taylor woken up?"

I nodded. "She just did. She's in a lot of pain and worried about Bea and about my dad flying in."

"Did she tell you what happened?"

"No. Not anything more than what I'd gathered from her texts and voice mails. I'm not pushing her. She needs time." My eyes told him I needed time too.

"Look, I know that you're mad," he said. "I don't want to push you either."

"I'm not mad. I'm disappointed."

He winced at the words.

"I'm disappointed because you could have come to me, you could have trusted me, you could have thought about the future. But you didn't. All you thought about was yourself. And

I'm just tired of dealing with men who only think about themselves."

He opened his mouth like he was going to argue and then closed it. He had to know I was right.

"And this," I said, "is too little, too late, Court. I needed to trust you for the hardest things. For all the times we weren't together. While I appreciate you coming to the hospital last night, it doesn't excuse or change what happened." I took a step back, my hand on the doorknob. "So, I'm going to go back to be with my sister. You should... go figure out how to salvage your mother's campaign."

"Is this the end?" he asked hoarsely. "Because I don't want to give up on us. I won't."

"I don't know. I can't think about it right now. I need to be with Taylor."

He swallowed hard. As if the very thought made him sick. Then, he passed me the bagel. "At least take the food."

I sighed and took it out of his hand. I stayed where I was and watched him walk back down the hallway. It wasn't until he was out of sight that I leaned my head against the door and squeezed my eyes shut to keep the tears at bay.

34

COURT

Walking away from English was… fucking horrible.

It'd been bad enough that Lark sent me away the night before. It had been the last fucking thing I wanted to do.

But I'd thought it would be better in the morning. Nope. It'd been worse.

Worse because she had a point.

I'd been an idiot.

I'd thought that I had to see Jane. I just… had to.

With the way that I was feeling for English, I needed to talk to Jane. I needed to know if it had all been real. Why she had picked me. *Why?*

In the end, it hadn't even mattered. Jane had been… Jane. She was exactly the same as she had always been. Even six months in jail, in an ugly orange jumpsuit. She acted as if she had a hundred and fifty million dollars in the bank, but it just wasn't liquid enough for her. That she'd be out in a pinch. That was why she'd pled not guilty. Why she had pushed for a quicker trial. She honestly had deluded herself into believing that she hadn't done anything wrong.

I'd left more pissed off than relieved.

And I'd meant to tell English. I kept meaning to tell her. But at first, it felt ridiculous. Like... it was over with Jane. It would always be. She was in jail. She'd tried to ruin my life. She'd stolen tens of thousands of dollars from me.

Then, the longer I didn't say anything, the more it felt like it was too late. I would have had to say it at first... or not at all.

So, I had gone with not at all.

Now, I felt like a coward and an idiot.

I'd ruined everything. Just when it was getting started.

I spent the rest of the day trying to figure out how to fucking fix this. And I hated the answer. Hated it. But not as much as hurting English. Not as much as that look on her face when she'd asked me if I still loved Jane.

And so that was how I stood on the sidelines of my youth lacrosse match the next day with the fucking media in attendance. I'd promised an interview afterward. My mother was even here.

I'd been shocked that she hadn't screamed at me the second I entered her office. But I'd shown up with a solution. Even if it went against every reason that I had started coaching to begin with. I'd wanted one thing that was mine. Well, if I hadn't fucked it up, then I wouldn't be here.

And we lost the game. Again.

Still, I told each and every one of those kids how great they had done. Pumped them up in a way my father never had. Nor had any of the intense competitive coaches I'd had growing up. I spoke to one kid individually about a particular play, and then they were free.

I played the part. I answered interview questions. I deflected the bullshit about Jane. I smiled and took pictures with my mother. Became the person that English had set me up as. The election was Tuesday. If it wasn't enough to squash what I'd done, then I didn't know what else I could do.

"You did good," my mother said as we walked away from the last reporter.

"Did I?"

"Yes," she said. She sounded shockingly sympathetic.

"But I fucked it all up."

She sighed. "Yes, you did. But you're trying to fix it. And you're doing it authentically."

"Since when has that ever mattered to you?"

"Since when have you ever tried to genuinely fix something?" She arched a perfectly manicured eyebrow.

"Fair," I finally admitted.

"She's good for you," my mother said. "English, that is."

"I thought so, too. She's mad about Jane and not talking to me."

"Can you blame her?"

I glanced over at my mother and shook my head. I didn't blame her. I'd known what I was doing. If it hadn't been wrong, then I wouldn't have hidden it from her. I was no better than her stupid fucking husband in that regard.

My mother brought me to a stop right in front of her awaiting black car. "You've had both an incredibly privileged upbringing and a rather tragic one. I wasn't the best mother. Your father was never the best father. I know that he was hard on you. He was mean and judgmental and thought the worst of nearly everyone. He let his vices get the better of him, and you were closest to him. You took the brunt of that."

I had.

But no one had ever acknowledged that.

"I was supposed to take over the company. Everything rode on my shoulders."

"In a way that Penn never really understood," she said with a nod. "And afterward, I wasn't there. I'd lost my husband and the governor's race in one fell swoop. It felt like all of *my* dreams were ending. I left you to your own devices. And... I'm sorry."

"You're sorry," I muttered. I'd never, ever heard that from her.

"Yes. I see now where you could have been all along. And that I did nothing to help you get there. So, you might have screwed up. But you're owning up to it. You're going to have to do that with English, too."

I nodded. "You're right."

She smiled once. A warm, genuine smile that took me off guard. "I love you, Court."

I pulled back in surprise. I didn't remember the last time my mother had said that to me. "I love you, too."

"I'm off to win an election. Wish me luck."

I laughed softly. "You don't need it."

"Right you are," she said and then disappeared into her limo.

I had no idea what to say. That might have been the most... normal conversation I'd ever had with my mother. As if we'd finally made up for all the horrible things we'd done to each other. One foot in front of the other. It had seemed impossible only six months ago. Another thing that English was responsible for.

And now, I needed to try to fix our relationship like I'd worked it out with my mother. For some reason, I didn't think it would be quite as easy.

The car service dropped me off in front of the hospital, and I beelined for Taylor's room. I'd stopped on the way to get flowers and clutched them in my hand now with all the confidence and bluster I'd ever needed in my life.

I was almost to Taylor's room when I saw a figure walking

toward me from the other end of the hallway. I could tell immediately that it was English. Her steady gait, the way she clutched her hands in front of her as if to hold herself together, the wave of energy she gave off that said she was the most powerful person in the room. She'd always had that energy. Even when it wasn't remotely true. But she'd earned that confidence, and no one could take it from her. It just *was* her.

She saw me then, and her lips pulled down. A sight I'd seen many times before. Before we were something. And now, I hated it. This was the after. I didn't want to elicit that response.

"Hey," I said, reaching the door before her and stopping.

"Thank you for the flowers. You can go," she said curtly. Her eyes glanced anxiously toward the closed door.

"They're for Taylor."

"I assumed," she said, biting her lip as if to keep herself from saying anything else.

"I... just wanted to see her."

"And talk to me," she finished.

"Yes. Of course."

She shuddered at the words and crossed her arms over her chest.

When she didn't say anything, I barreled forward. "I told my mother about the lacrosse games."

Her eyes blinked back up at me. "That was smart of you."

"We just had a press release at the fields. The parents were into it. I'd thought they'd hate it as much as I did. But I guess everyone wants to see their child on TV. My mother came. She approved."

"Great," she said hollowly. "I hope it's enough for her."

She said nothing about me. And she hadn't uncrossed her arms.

I opened my mouth to try to say something else. To apologize, to fucking fix this somehow. But that was her job. I was the train wreck, and she fixed me. I'd thought I was just getting the hang of trying to fix her. But I didn't even know where to begin to fix us.

I closed my mouth just as the door to Taylor's room was wrenched open. Both of us jumped as if a gunshot had gone off. But it was just a giant of a man standing in the door. He glanced between us. Me standing there, holding the flowers, and English looking wary and uncomfortable.

"Hey, Bug," the man said. "Why don't you go back inside with your sister? She's asking for you."

"Okay, Dad," she said in what sounded like surprise. She stepped toward the door.

"Take the flowers. Taylor will like them."

English reached out and removed the flowers from my hands. "Thank you," she said and then walked past her dad and into the room.

Leaving me alone with her father. He was a large, imposing man with dark brown hair peppered with silver and bright blue eyes that I'd recognize anywhere. They were the exact same shade as English's. He wore a faded Dodgers T-shirt and Levi's. He wasn't what I'd expected. English had said that she hadn't grown up in the nice side of LA. But I still hadn't been able to conjure that she had grown up with a normal life when she was so extraordinary now.

"Son, I think we should have a talk," he said, closing the door behind his daughters and gesturing down the hallway.

"All right," I said evenly.

We walked a few feet away from Taylor's room, and then he stopped as if deciding that was sufficient.

"I'm Joe. Joe English," he said, holding his hand out for me.

I took it and shook, startled by the power in his grip. "Court."

"Yes, I know a little about you. Bug told me that you two were going through a rough patch."

A rough patch. Was that what she'd called it? Or... were those his words?

"Yes, sir," I said, manners appearing out of thin air. "We are."

"Now, I don't know all the details. Frankly, I don't need to know them all. But I do know my daughter. I know that she's strong-willed like her mom. She's hardheaded like me. And she doesn't trust very easily. She got that all on her own by being burned over and over again by the people who claimed to care about her."

"Yes, but—"

"I wasn't finished," he said, holding up his hand. "Her trust is fragile. And once you break it, you just have to give her time to figure it out on her own."

"I understand," I said hoarsely.

"I don't think you do. If you push her, she'll buckle down. And then there's no coming back from that."

I stared up at him, understanding finally blooming. He was talking about himself. He'd broken English's trust by cheating on her mom, by leaving them. And when he'd tried to put it back together, it had just hardened up into bulletproof glass. Even now, he couldn't get through it. Years and years later. What chance would I have?

"Oh," was all I got out.

"Just give her some space."

"For how long?" I croaked out.

"As long as it takes," he said with a sad smile and turned and walked back down the hallway.

I was left standing there, feeling powerless. I'd ruined something again. The most important thing in my life. And there might never be a way to mend what I'd broken.

35

ENGLISH

The day of the election, Taylor was finally discharged from the hospital. It felt surreal that I was going to be wheeling her out of the hospital today instead of helping Lark with last-minute Election Day stuff. To know that I was going to be on an airplane back to LA instead of at the victory party. Or what I hoped was a victory party. It was still too early to tell.

"Can I just see Bea once before we go?" Taylor asked for what had to be the hundredth time.

I felt guilty, continually saying no. But not only did the doctors and psychiatrists and nurses think it was a bad idea for both of their recovery, but also, the police frankly thought it was a bad idea. It had come out that the drug lord they'd been buying from was the same person the police had been trying to track down for six months. He apparently had a nasty habit of killing young impressionable women. Taylor and Bea were the luckier of most of his victims.

And if all of that wasn't enough, Bea's parents refused to allow Taylor access to Bea. They'd told us all next to nothing about her condition since they'd flown in from Boston. Just that the gunshot wound had gone into her abdomen and grazed her liver. We gathered that she was still in critical condition and that it would be several weeks before she could do much of anything. But at least she had made it through the long night of surgeries. Though the hardest part might still be ahead of her.

"I don't think that's a good idea, kiddo," my stepmom, Ashley, said from her shoulder. "Bea's parents still think it's best that she's left alone to recover."

Taylor looked wounded by the statement. "Right. Her parents."

"But we're finally going home," Ashley said. She affectionately ruffled her daughter's hair. "Won't it be good to get back to the sunshine? It's so cold in New York."

"It sure as hell will be better," my dad said next to me. "I remember why I never came to New York."

I just laughed softly at them all. This might have been the longest my dad had ever spent out of the state of California.

He always argued, "Why bother going anywhere else when California has it all?"

"Let's go home," I said. Even though I was uncertain what that meant for me anymore.

We wheeled Taylor out of the hospital, laden down with instructions for her recovery and paperwork to transfer her to an LA-based doctor. I blinked against the blinding sunlight. I hadn't seen it in days and felt a bit like a zombie myself.

I'd given my dad and stepmom the keys to my apartment, so they could go back and sleep the days they were there. They'd brought me a change of clothes and the good shampoo and conditioner. So, I felt more human, but I'd refused to leave Taylor's side. Even when she'd complained that she was "fine." But I was the one who had gotten those terrifying voice mails. I couldn't imagine leaving her now. When I could have prevented it all to begin with.

Six hours later, our flight touched down at LAX. My body was telling me it was time for dinner, but the sun was telling a different story. Time zones were weird.

I yawned dramatically and took my phone off Airplane mode as we waited for a wheelchair for Taylor. I'd splurged on first class, so we were all comfortably seated, but I hadn't been able to sleep. I'd always been a bad sleeper, but ever since Taylor had been shot, I couldn't get more than two or three hours in at a time. I kept waking up from nightmares, gasping for breath. No amount of tai chi had been able to calm me down.

A string of texts appeared on the screen, but it was the news alert that simultaneously had my stomach swooping and a smile appearing on my face.

Mayor Kensington Clinches Reelection Win 51–48 Against Opponent Quinn.

I breathed out in relief. She'd done it. She'd won. All that hard work had paid off. Court's blunder at the finish line hadn't completely tripped them up. Though it had been a very narrow margin of victory. Likely that extra one percent going to the third-party candidate had certainly helped.

I leaned back in my seat in relief. I'd gone to New York to help the mayor win reelection by getting her son to fall into line. I'd done it. Mostly.

And now... it was over.

It was all over.

We settled Taylor back into my old room on the first floor since she couldn't get upstairs to hers. My room had long since been a guest room that essentially collected odds and ends. The bed had been pushed into a far corner to make room for an elliptical and sewing machine. Right now, all of Ashley's current business venture products were scattered across the space. Though she promised to move everything upstairs.

Taylor used her crutches, which she was still trying to figure out how to best maneuver with through the pain, to get into the empty bed. I carried my carry-on up the stairs and placed it into Taylor's room. Nothing had changed since she moved out. It still looked like a young artist's dream with sketches and poems plastering the blue walls. Paint and clay and notebooks filled every available space. Her bedspread was a map of the constellations.

It felt weird to stay here. I hadn't stayed here for more than a night since my dad kicked me out at seventeen. My dad had kicked me out at sixteen, but it hadn't stuck. The second time, it had, and I'd moved in with my boyfriend. A boyfriend I'd promptly broken up with after graduation. How I'd ever gone to UCLA and made something of myself was a real mystery.

But I wasn't here for a walk down memory lane. I was here for Taylor. At least for a little while as she got settled, started with her new doctor, and got into physical therapy. My dad had gotten her a medical exemption for the semester at The New School. I just hoped she'd be able to go back to school after all of this. I couldn't imagine wanting to return to New York.

That was a conversation for later. Much later.

Since my dad had to get back to work and Ashley had recently gotten a part-time job working at a daycare, I promised to take Taylor to her appointments when no one else was around. It was monotonous. And Taylor was unsurprisingly in a shit mood about it. She was still upset that she hadn't been allowed to see Bea. Seeing as there was nothing I could do about that, she seemed to take it out on me more.

I didn't really care. I was used to clients taking out their issues on me. It just sounded like background noise. And anyway, none of them had been shot. So, I cut her some slack.

Even if being back at home was super strange, being back in

LA felt... wonderful. It felt like *home*. The constant weather. The horrid commuter traffic. Even the smell was different than New York.

Taylor had gone to bed early. I sat up late on the couch with my computer in my lap. I was still plotting out my business. Deciding if I even wanted to do it. I had to push back my appointments with the real estate agent. I didn't even know if I was going to open the business... let alone open in New York.

Suddenly, I heard someone coming down the steps. Everyone in my house went to bed early and woke early. Since I was still sleeping like absolute shit, I did neither. And I was surprised that anyone was awake.

My dad appeared in those same shorts he'd always worn and a plain gray T-shirt. "Hey, Bug."

"Dad," I said with a nod of my head.

"Want a beer?"

I arched an eyebrow. "This late?"

"Eh, never hurt anyone."

"Sure. I'll have one."

He went into the kitchen and came out with two Heinekens. He passed one to me, and I silently sipped the beer. I didn't drink a lot of beer. But it used to be the only thing I could afford. It brought me back to being seventeen with a dirtbag boyfriend or being a groupie in the back of a rock star's bus or going to frat parties. Lots of frat parties.

"You know, I appreciate what you've done for Taylor," he said after a minute.

"I don't mind at all."

"But when are you moving on?"

I blinked up at him. "What?"

"It's time for you to go."

"Are you kicking me out?" I stammered out. "Again?"

"No, it's not like before."

"Then, what? You don't want me here?" I couldn't keep the sad, broken thing inside of me from unraveling.

"That's not it either. You have a life. And you can't just hide here."

I swallowed hard. "So, you want me to leave?"

"I want you to *live*."

I shook my head and closed my computer. I took another long sip of my drink. "I am living. I just need to take a break from everything that went wrong."

"I know you told me some of what happened. I confess not to understand most of it. But what I did get out of it is that there's a boy back in New York City who loves you," my dad said.

I sputtered, spewing some of my beer. I swiped my hand over the top of the computer to clean up some of the mess. My eyes were wide when I looked back at my dad. "What? He... he does not."

My dad smiled down at me. A real smile. Not the half-assed thing he normally gave me. "He does. Whether you want to see it or not."

My stomach knotted at those words. I'd known Court six months. He couldn't... he didn't... he'd never even indicated. How could my dad even know that?

"It doesn't matter," he continued. "What matters is that you can't give up your life. It's a good one."

He almost sounded... proud.

"I thought you hated it," I gasped out. "I thought you despised me working in Hollywood as a publicist. That you thought it was trash work."

"I didn't despise it. I don't understand it, but I realize its importance. That you're good at it. The only thing I hated was that... you never needed me. But I did that to myself. When you needed me when you were little, I wasn't there. I shouldn't be surprised to find you grew up independent and that you didn't need anyone." He gently touched my shoulder. "You got out of here. You made something of yourself. I'm proud of you, Bug."

I swallowed back tears. "Thanks, Dad."

"Now, get out of my house."

I laughed and swiped at my eyes. "I'm not ready to leave just yet, if that's okay. But maybe I'll call up a friend and get out of your hair for a while?"

He patted my shoulder twice and stood. "That's fine with me. As long as you know that this isn't permanent. I like having you home. Just not as a hidey-hole. You can come and visit more if you want."

"I'd like that."

He smiled at me and finished his beer. "All right. I should get back to bed. Ashley is going to wonder where I went."

"Night, Dad."

"Night, Bug."

I watched him walk away, wondering why it had taken so long for us to have that conversation. Stubbornness sure ran in the family.

Before I could let myself dwell on what he'd said about Court, I picked up the phone and called Winnie. I needed to get out of here.

36

ENGLISH

"When I said that I wanted to meet up, I was thinking coffee," I told Winnie two days later as I stood at the entrance to The Beverly Hills Hotel on Sunset Boulevard.

"Welcome back to Hollywood," Winnie said.

She slid her arm through mine and walked me up the front steps. I'd been inside the iconic hotel more times than I could count. It was a favorite of my clients. Plus... it was the place that Josh and I had met. Which used to give me a thrill every time that I stepped inside the classic pink building, but today, my stomach just turned as the happy memory was now twinged with sadness.

"What is this event even for?"

I'd had to head into the city and get a new dress since I'd brought nothing remotely high fashion back with me from New York. I was in love with the red bustier dress I'd purchased. It gave me ample cleavage while hugging my frame and accentuating my assets. I'd paired it with a new set of Jimmy Choos.

"Who knows? Who cares? Gregory is meeting us inside."

I groaned. "I thought you were off-again with Gregory?"

"Yes, but you've been gone forever, English," Winnie said, waving her hand. Her British accent tight around my name. "We're back on. Have been for a few months. The event rented out all the bungalows, and he's secured one for us."

Gregory was a director, producer, composer, and all-around entitled dude-bro prick. He thought the world revolved around his pretentious ass. I was not pleased to hear that Winnie was back with him. She could do so much better. Even if... I was going to take advantage of his generous hospitality.

"So, tell me about New York," Winnie said as we stepped into the main ballroom already bedecked with celebrities. "Was it snowing?"

"No, not yet."

"Did you choose an agency to work with up there?" Winnie grabbed two flutes of champagne and passed me one.

"Actually, no. Currently unemployed."

Winnie wrinkled her nose. "But why?"

"Well, Kensington Corporation offered to take me on full-time. But I said no."

"Isn't that what you wanted though?"

"At the time... I was sleeping with Court."

Winnie froze. Her large brown eyes rounded. She reached out and grasped my arm. "English! You?"

I laughed at her expression. Winnie had always been the naughty one. She thought nothing of fucking her clients. She was able to keep her heart separate from her vagina.

"Yes. Me, of all people."

"Well then, good for you!"

"But... we're not together right now."

Winnie sighed. "Broke your heart? Left you hanging?"

"Something like that." I shrugged, ending the conversation I didn't want to be having. "I've actually been considering starting my own agency."

"Then, do it," Winnie said like it was that easy.

"I don't even know if I'm going back to New York at this point."

"We'll open it here in LA."

"We?" I asked, raising my brows.

"What? You think I'm going to let you have all the fun?" She gripped my wrist and pulled me closer.

"We have the non-compete still."

Winnie waved her hand, unconcerned. "Those things are never held up in court. And *anyway*, if Margery can do it to *you*, she can do it to me. And I don't want to be under her fire. So, if you're starting your own company, count me in."

I put my hand to my heart. I was touched. I couldn't believe Winnie would go out on a leap of faith with me like that.

"All right," I said, nodding my head. "Let's do it."

"What were you thinking of calling it? Maybe Class? Because we actually have it."

I laughed at her slight. "I'm thinking E&B."

Winnie grinned. "English & Bardwaj PR. I approve."

A few minutes later, we ran into Gregory. He was tall and skinny and pale, built like a reed. He wore a ten-thousand-dollar suit and a smile like a fox. His dark hair was thinning and receding. His fingers twitched as if desperate for a keyboard. He was a bit of a genius. But in the way that he had been told too many times and truly believed it. He had this nasty habit of insulting everyone in his presence and always tried to make you think it just might be a compliment.

I had no idea why Winnie put up with him.

"Anna English," Gregory said in surprise. "It's been a while since I've seen a disgraced woman in public with her husband."

I arched an eyebrow. "Excuse me?"

He pointed his long, bony finger over my shoulder. I whirled around to find Josh standing at a window with a blonde actress that I recognized but couldn't remember her name. My stomach flipped. Of course he was here. He'd had to show up at the one place I was. And, that place had to be where we'd first met.

I hadn't seen him since I throat-punched him in my apartment in New York. I hadn't wanted to see him in LA. I definitely didn't want to see him flirting with someone else. Regardless of our current divorce situation.

"Thanks for that, Gregory," I ground out.

"Of course, English. Whatever they're feeding you in New York looks great on your hips."

I bit back a reply about his receding hairline, and instead, I shot a pleading look at Winnie. Seriously, how could she stand him?

"I'm going to get some fresh air," I said with an eye roll.

"I'll come find you in a minute," Winnie called.

I waved her off and then slipped through the side door that led out to the veranda and the pool beyond that. I breathed in the autumn LA air, which smelled faintly of smog, dashed dreams, and year-round summer. It didn't smell at all like New York when I'd left. It'd had this faint smell like winter was about to descend and blanket the world in its never-ending cold. Here, I could wear a strapless dress in the middle of November. There, layers were my friend. LA I'd missed so badly all the time. And now, was I missing New York?

I turned around to head back inside and just deal with Gregory's behavior. But standing in the entrance was Josh. He stared at me as if seeing a ghost.

"English?" he whispered hesitantly.

"Hi, Josh."

"What are you doing in LA?"

"Well," I said, leaning back against the railing, "my sister was shot in New York."

His eyes bulged, and he stepped fully out onto the veranda. "Taylor? Holy shit! Is she okay?"

"Went through her thigh and one grazed her hip. Hit the

femoral artery, and she had to have surgery to stop the blood. But... she's lucky. She was discharged within a week, and we were able to bring her home. Her friend is still in the hospital. And apparently, the guy who did this... has killed most of his victims."

"Jesus Christ," Josh said. "That's horrible. I'm so sorry. Is there anything I can do?"

I shook my head. "No, there's really nothing anyone can do. It's been... horrible."

He tentatively stepped forward, as if afraid I would throat-punch him again. He rested a hand on my arm. "I'm really, truly so sorry to hear that. Taylor is a good kid. She doesn't deserve that. And I just... I hate that you're going through it alone."

I nodded. I hated that I was going through it alone, too. It was so much to carry on my shoulders. And suddenly, tears hit me fresh. Josh and I had been together so long. I'd always been able to be myself with him. To tell him everything. Now, I couldn't stop the tears.

Without hesitating, he pulled me into his arms. "Shh, it's okay. It's okay, English."

I cried into his shoulder. My tears soaking through his rather expensive suit coat. Likely totally fucking my makeup. But he didn't say anything. He didn't stop me. He just rubbed my back and held me.

After a few minutes, I hiccuped and pulled back. I wiped under my eyes with my fingers. "God, I probably look like such a mess."

"No, you don't," he whispered softly. His eyes so wide and caring.

I pulled a compact out of my purse and adjusted my makeup. My cheeks were red and puffy, and my eyes looked like, well, like I'd been crying. But it wasn't as bad as I'd thought it'd be.

His hand was still on my shoulder, steadying me. "You

know, I'll always be here for you, English. If you need someone to talk to or just cry on, I can be there."

"Thank you." I swallowed back the last wave of tears and sniffed once. "I appreciate it."

His hand was *still* on my shoulder. Rubbing slow circles into my skin. "Do you have a sense of déjà vu?"

"A little," I whispered.

It did feel the same.

We'd met on a night just like this one. Except that I'd been so out of my element and he'd been pure confidence. I'd never thought that I could fall for someone like him. And within hours, I'd handed over my entire heart, hook, line, and sinker.

He stepped in closer. His arms came around my shoulders. "I want it to be like it was. I wish we could go back to that night and start over."

I did, too. A small part of me really wanted that.

A part of me even wanted *this* right here. For my husband to have been here for me through all of it.

It would be so easy to just play the night over again. To get lost in conversation with him for hours on end. To let him call me after and woo me into a date. We'd go to a fancy restaurant. He'd insist on ordering, but I'd order for myself anyway because that was who I was. We'd dance in the lobby of the bar to no music, and he'd drive me home and kiss me at the door.

We'd make up. Go to counseling. Forget what had happened. And live happily ever after.

I could see the entire future in his eyes as he waited for my response. Waited for me to agree with him.

But as much as that would be wonderful, it wasn't even what I wanted anymore. He wasn't what I wanted.

So, I stepped back, away from his comforting arms. "But we can't go back."

He sighed heavily. "Maybe we can."

"No," I said with a shake of my head. "No, we can't."

"Is it still about what happened in London? It would never happen again."

"I know," I said. Because a part of me did know. Losing me had changed his mind. Made him realize his mistake. He wouldn't do it again. Not to me. "But it doesn't matter. I'm not the same person I was before you cheated on me, Josh. I can't go back to being that innocent and wide-eyed with wonder over you. I put my entire trust in you. I gave you my whole heart. And that girl just… doesn't exist anymore."

"I understand," he said sadly. "But I still love you."

I swallowed and nodded. He stepped forward then and pressed a kiss to my forehead. I closed my eyes as his scent enveloped me.

"Good-bye, English."

Then, he walked away, and I let him.

And I wished then that there were a blue-eyed Manhattan playboy with a penchant for fantasy novels and a love for lacrosse here tonight instead. I wished I could cry on his shoulder about Taylor… and have him tell me it would all be okay.

But I did none of those things.

I just went back to the party to see Winnie and live this new life.

37

COURT

The stick cracked into the cue ball and smacked hard into the red three ball, and I pocketed it in the top-left corner.

"Phew," I muttered, leaning back against the pool table and forcing a smile. "Thought I'd miss that one."

Camden had just lit a new joint and passed it to me. "I think you're going to miss them all."

"Ass."

I waved off the joint even though I probably needed it. My anxiety had been through the roof since English left. It had been ten, going on eleven, brutal days without her. Not a call, not a text, not even an active notification that she was online. It was as if the world had screeched to a stop.

"Suit yourself," Camden said as he took a hit of the joint. "Make your next shot."

I stared down at the pool table and saw essentially no clean shots. I was fucked. Camden was a better pool player than me anyway. I usually lucked into a lot of my success. As per usual, apparently.

I lined up my next shot. Camden chuckled softly behind me. Yeah, I was going to miss it. We both knew it.

"I don't think you understand how geometry works," Camden said when I whiffed the ball.

"Fuck," I grumbled.

Camden smirked at me as he took his own pool stick and effortlessly made his next three shots without looking up. It really was pointless to play with him.

"Did I ever tell you that I found out who had leaked that image of you with Jane?" Camden asked as he nailed the next shot. He glanced up at me. His face was surprisingly indifferent, but I could see something else simmering underneath there. That darkness that lurked just beneath the surface.

"No, you never mentioned that. How did you even find that out?"

He shrugged. "I have sources."

"Well?"

"Do you know Margery Wells?"

"No."

"I think you do."

I stilled. "Is that... English's old boss?"

"Indeed."

"What a bitch!" I gasped out. "She got ahold of pictures of me and released them just to fuck with English."

"Actually, I believe that she had you followed."

"Jesus Christ. How did you find any of this out?"

Camden shrugged once more and then pocketed another ball. "Like I said, sources."

I'd never get a straight answer out of him. Camden was a powerful man, who ran one of the largest hotel companies in the world. He was not easily discouraged from getting what he wanted.

"Also, no one fucks with me or my own," Camden said, lethally quiet as he easily won the game, pocketing the final ball. He straightened and smirked at me in his victory.

But I just put my hand to my chest. "Aw, I'm touched."

"Fuck off, Kensington," Camden ground out.

I laughed and stepped forward to pull the balls out of the holes and rerack for another game. I was going to lose. But at least I was losing to a friend.

I finished the rack and stepped back. "Winner breaks."

It was then that Katherine Van Pelt stepped into the room, looking like a hundred pounds of femme fatale. She wore a slinky red dress and matching cherry-red lipstick. Her hair was down in waves, and she wore black fuck-me heels. I'd never go for Katherine. With the feud between my brother and my best friend, I'd have to be an idiot, but I wasn't blind.

I whistled at her as she strutted inside. "Going out?"

She dramatically rolled her eyes. "Yes," she said curtly. "Big plans."

Camden's expression was neutral. No one should be able to look at her in that dress and be neutral. Let alone her husband. Who I was certain wanted to at least bang her.

"Do you have a reason for interrupting us?" Camden asked. He leaned back against the pool table, crossed one ankle over the other, and brought the joint to his mouth.

She pursed her lips. "As if you're so busy."

"We just finished a game," I cut in before they could go at each other's throats.

"The game never finishes," Camden quipped. More directed at Katherine than anything to do with billiards.

"I'm well aware," she said dryly. "I'm here for the idiot Kensington actually. I heard you in here. I assume you don't read celebrity gossip or else you wouldn't be doing this bullshit."

I arched an eyebrow. "Celebrity gossip?"

"Do you *want* English to get back together with her husband?" Katherine asked pointedly. "He's hot as fuck after all. A movie star. The latest Jason Bourne. He has a mansion in LA with a swimming pool the size of your penthouse. He doesn't match your net worth, but well, he's *earned* his money."

"What do you mean, she's getting back with Josh?"

I was suddenly very attentive. I'd spent the last ten days trying to give her the space that she needed. There was no fucking *way* that she had forgiven Josh in that time. It wasn't even fucking possible. The last time he'd been in town, she'd throat-punched him and sent him on his merry way.

"I mean, this."

She pulled out her cell phone and passed it to me. On the screen was a picture of English and Josh hugging. She had her arms wrapped around his neck. Her face was pressed tight into his shoulder, and he held her close. Like they had always been just like this.

The article read:

Reconciled? Josh Hutch Reunites with Wife at The Beverly Hills Hotel.

After a messy breakup, talks of divorce, and dating rumors, our latest Jason Bourne is caught with wife out at Universal's party with Director...

I stopped reading.

"What the fuck is this trash?" I demanded, tossing the phone back to her.

"It looks like someone went home and decided to get back with her husband. While you're dicking around here, playing pool and getting high."

"She is not getting back together with Josh."

"Are you sure?"

"What the fuck?" I repeated with a shake of my head. "She wouldn't. Not after what he did."

"Are you sure?" Katherine repeated.

"English says those tabloids are all lies," I bit out.

"Are you going to stake your relationship on that?"

I ground my teeth together. "No. Fuck. Of course fucking not."

Katherine smiled. She looked triumphant. I was sure she was going to take credit for this if it worked out. Though I still had my doubts. Had she been gone long enough for her to not still hate me? Was it long enough for her not to dig her feet in like her dad had said she would? I wouldn't know that… couldn't know that until I saw her.

I turned to Camden as if to apologize for leaving, but he just waved me off. "Go."

I handed him the pool stick. "Thanks, man." I patted Katherine's shoulder as I passed. "And you, too."

She shrugged one shoulder. "Apparently, my job is to remind men how stupid they are."

"Mission accomplished," I told her.

Then, I hustled out of their apartment, prepared to fight for the woman I loved.

38

ENGLISH

"This all appears to be in order," Mr. Jenkins said. He was a partner at Jenkins, Jones, and Jameson LLC, one of the top-rated law firms in LA.

And Winnie and I were paying him a pretty penny for this meeting.

He shuffled the paperwork around. We still had a lot to do before English & Bardwaj would get off the ground, but we wanted to cross our t's and dot our i's before we got started.

"Mostly, we're concerned about the non-compete," Winnie said primly.

"Yes. Is it likely that Margery will sue us through Poise because of that document?" I asked.

"It's possible," he said finally. "Even likely. I've had clients who left popular PR firms in the past, and she's attempted to go after them. A lot of firms believe that this protects them from building up agents and then having them walk out with all their clients. But it's really a tool to keep talented agents like yourselves saddled to one agency for life and prohibiting you to work."

"So, you believe we'll still have to go to court?" I asked. "Even though, legally, it's bullshit."

He laughed. "To put it plainly, yes. But she won't win. Most of my clients settle out of court, or the non-compete is thrown out the window. Legally, she can't keep you from working."

"And how do we ensure that she doesn't win?" Winnie asked, leaning forward.

"I'll go through the process with you and everything that I suggest you do for your business setup so that it's as seamless as possible."

"Excellent," I said. I pulled out my legal pad and prepared to take Margery down.

A few hours later, Winnie and I stepped out of Mr. Jenkins's office and back out into the California sunshine. It was a gorgeous eighty-one degrees in the middle of November, and I immediately stripped out of my blazer as we walked into the parking lot.

"This is actually going to work," Winnie said in triumph.

"I think so."

"I'm so excited. I can't wait to see her face when she finds out we've started our own firm."

"I hope I never see her face again, to be honest."

Winnie tipped her phone at me. "Touché."

"Okay, I have to head home. I need to take Taylor to a PT appointment soon."

"How is she doing?" Winnie asked sympathetically.

"Well, it's her first PT appointment. Mostly an assessment. She's still in a lot of pain, and they don't want to take it too fast, but you know, we'll see."

"And mentally?"

I breathed out heavily. "Worse than her leg, I think."

Winnie nodded. "I'd suspect so."

"She blames herself for what happened with her and her friend. And it doesn't help that her friend's parents won't even update us on her progress." I sighed heavily. "I don't know. I think the mental side might take longer than the physical."

"Doesn't it always?" Winnie said with a sigh. "Well, good luck. Let me know if you need anything. I can pitch in."

"Thanks," I said with a smile and then walked over to my awaiting Mercedes.

It was nice to drive again. In New York, I never drove anywhere. There was no need. But I'd grown up, driving everywhere in LA. Sometimes, we just *drove* for fun to get out of the city and out of the traffic. It'd been six months since I was behind the wheel, and I suddenly didn't want to give it up just yet to head home.

So, I drove.

I drove with the windows rolled down and my hair whipping around my face.

I drove like I was sixteen again, just figuring out how to live.

I drove, not even knowing where I was going until I was there.

I pulled into the old, familiar neighborhood. It looked smaller than I remembered. Grungier. As if the world had grown up around it, but this place had just sunken deeper and deeper and deeper. Growing into the ground instead of up out of it.

There were still three blocks ahead of me when I began to bring the car to a crawl. It wasn't the kind of neighborhood to leave a brand-new Mercedes idling. Not if I wanted to find it where I'd left it when I came back. But I couldn't exactly park it in the driveway either.

I didn't even know if I wanted to see my mom.

It had been nearly five years.

I could remember the day in its entirety as if it were a

movie I'd watched over and over and over again. She'd begged me to come see her. To meet her at the house, so she could "fawn over" me. I'd gotten the job at Poise about six months before. Josh and I had only been dating three months. She pretended to be proud. Her little girl off to conquer the world.

But it was a pretense. I could see it in her eyes. It was the same look she'd given me as a kid when she thought she'd come in to some new money to pay for her problem.

And at first, it wasn't her fault. When I was a toddler, only three or four years old, she'd gotten into a horrific car accident on her way to pick me up from daycare. They'd had to remove the doors to get her out of the car. I'd seen pictures of it. It was beyond comprehension that she'd lived.

What they hadn't accounted for... was that she'd live with the chronic pain of the accident.

Like any good doctor, he wanted to manage the pain. But at that time, there wasn't enough information about opioids. Or the information was a lie. And what had started out as managing pain turned into full-blown addiction within a couple years.

No matter how many times we tried to get her to stop, to treat the pain with marijuana or go to a rehab facility, the drug had her in its grasp.

And that day that I went to see her, she saw *me* as the dollar signs.

I'd put up with her bullshit as a kid. Hated myself for it in my teens. Thought I'd finally escaped in college and law school. And realized in that moment when she asked me for money to further her addiction that I'd never escape.

When I said no, she railed against me. Screamed in my face. Called me every horrible name I'd ever imagined. And then she threw some-

thing at me. Her favorite coffee mug. I cried out as it hit me in the jaw and then shattered on the linoleum floor.

She tried to run after me as I raced to my car with tears streaming down my face.

"Baby, baby, I didn't mean it," she cried. "I just need the money. You know I need the money. What will I do without it?"

I looked at her then. Hopeless, ragged, refusing help after she just struck me, her only child, and knew then it was over. "That's all you care about. The money. The drugs. If you won't get help, then I can't help you."

She spat more vitriol at me, even as I sped away and promised myself that I'd never come back.

Yet here I was. A block from her house. I could see her driveway from where I sat in the car.

I eased the car forward until I slowly moved in front of the tiny two-bedroom that I'd called home all those years ago. The front curtains were pulled back. I could see my mother standing in the kitchen, taking a drink out of the refrigerator. She popped the top on the can, opened a pill bottle nearby, and swallowed the pills and the drink together.

I frowned. Of course she had.

I followed my mom as she walked into the living room and handed the drink to a man seated on the same sofa she'd had when I was a kid.

I didn't know who he was. How could I? But I knew the type. After my dad had left, there had been a string of guys she dated. It got to the point where my dad didn't want me to stay in the house with them. My every other weekend with my mom became only when he really needed someone to watch me. I should have given my dad more credit for that. I hadn't understood when I was young.

I knew what would happen if I knocked on that door.

The same old.

My mom looked happy now. But she wouldn't be happy to see me. Because I wasn't going to give her money. I wasn't going to go back into that toxicity. And if she was still popping pills, then had anything really changed?

I swallowed back my own sadness and then pushed the pedal to take me away from the sight before me. I'd seen what I needed to see. I'd made the right decision five years ago when I cut her out of my life.

And maybe I needed to cut my dad some more slack.

I drove back to my dad's house in a daze. My mom always had that effect on me. I just needed to get inside and change, and then I could take Taylor to PT. Thinking about her would be a good way to not think about my own life.

I parked the Mercedes behind my dad's truck and trudged up to the front. With a yawn, I pulled opened the front door. I stepped inside, prepared to call for Taylor.

But I stopped with one foot inside.

My dad and stepmom were both standing in the living room. Taylor leaned into her crutches and had apparently just stopped talking as I entered. They were all clustered around the couch.

Where Court Kensington sat like a fish out of water.

39

ENGLISH

"Court?" I asked with wide eyes.

I couldn't believe he was in my dad's house… in LA… in the fucking Valley. What kind of alternate universe was I living in?

He stood hastily, dusting off his jeans. "Anna," he said softly.

"What are you doing here?"

"I came here for you," he said so sincerely that I thought I might fall over.

He'd come all the way to LA for me.

My dad cleared his throat. "Well, don't mind us. Maybe we can finish that talk later, Court. You two should take some quality time and talk."

"That's a great idea," Taylor said, grinning like a fool. It was the first time I'd really seen her smile since the incident. "Go to the beach!"

"Taylor, honey, just let them decide what they want to do," Ashley said. "Why don't we get ready for your PT appointment?"

"Oh, I was going to take her," I said.

Ashley waved me off. "No need. I can handle it."

My dad just nodded his head at me and then followed Ashley and Taylor out of the room.

"The beach might be nice," Court said. "Since it was thirty degrees when I left New York."

"I just... can't believe you're in my dad's living room."

"To be honest, it was not easy to find."

"How?" I muttered. "How did this even happen?"

"Taylor actually. She gave me her number when we were at Oktoberfest. I was supposed to send her book recommendations. Instead, she helped me get to you."

"Little weasel," I muttered under my breath.

"So... beach?"

I nodded. "All right, but I need to change first."

"No problem. I'll wait here. Your stepmom was just regaling me with stories of your childhood."

I groaned. "Great."

I hastened upstairs and changed into jean shorts and a tank top, pulled my hair up into a high pony, and added a coat of pink lipstick just because. Why the hell not? I took a deep breath and then went back downstairs.

Court was still standing in my dad's living room. It was utterly surreal.

"Ready?" I asked.

"Sure."

We walked back out to my Mercedes. He didn't offer to drive, which I thought was a relief. A lot of men got weird about that sort of thing. But I definitely had more driving experience than Court... and it was my city.

We drove away. I turned on the radio and let the Top 100 station drown out the silence on the drive down to Santa Monica. Parking was as awful as ever. Maybe worse because it was so beautiful out today, but I finally nabbed a spot not too far away from the pier.

We stepped out of the car and headed toward the pier. I

didn't know what to say. I'd left him behind in New York. I hadn't even had enough time to think about what the fuck I wanted to do. If I could forgive and forget him lying to me. Or why he'd done it in the first place. It all just hung between us as we walked.

"Sooo..." I prompted a few minutes later.

"Yeah, so..." he said. He glanced up at me. "I missed you."

I swallowed. "I missed you, too."

"It's been almost two weeks. It felt like a fucking lifetime."

"God, two weeks already?"

"Close to it," he said. "Taylor seems to be in better spirits."

"I don't know. That smile she gave me was the first one I'd seen since she woke up from the sedative."

"She'll get there."

I nodded. "I hope so."

We were nearly to the pier by that point, and Court pulled me off of the path, grinding us to a halt.

"I just... I know you saw Josh this weekend," he said with his hand still on my arm.

"I did," I said in confusion. "How do you know that?"

"I'm guessing that you're not following your own celebrity status right now?"

I groaned. "Oh god, what happened?"

He pulled out his phone and then passed it to me. I cringed before I even read the headline. Then, I cringed some more.

"Fuck," I groaned. "Jesus, fucking fuck."

I skimmed the article. I *hated* tabloids. I hated tabloids and paparazzi and these fake fucking journalists. The lies they spun like spiderwebs. It was just drama. Pure, unfiltered cotton-candy-spun drama. And not a lick of it was the truth.

"That is not what it looks like," I told Court.

"It looks like you were hugging."

"We... were," I said. "I told him about Taylor, and I just lost it. I started sobbing, and he consoled me."

"Okay," he said. "That seems... reasonable. I suppose."

"You know I told you not to believe everything you see in tabloids. They're all lies."

"I did tell Katherine that when she showed me the pictures. But you know... just in case."

I looked at him in confusion. "In case what?"

"You really were reconciling, English. I couldn't have that." He reached out and took my hand. "There was no way I was going to stand back and let Josh weasel his way back in. I had to come out here even though your dad told me to give you more time. There was no more time. There was just now."

"Court..."

"I didn't know if you were going to talk to him again. But it was a good enough reason to come see you and bring you home."

I swallowed. "I'm not home now?"

"Nope."

"And where is home if not LA?"

"With me."

I laughed at his utter confidence. "That's pretty presumptuous, considering how we last left off."

"I know," he said smoothly. "I know that you're probably still mad at me. That you want to throat-punch *me* for ruining everything. But I want to bring you home with me anyway."

"You think I'll just come back to New York with you?" I asked, humoring him at this point.

He laughed. "Hardly. I think you'll kick and scream the whole way."

"Well, at least you know me."

He stepped forward, cupping my face in his strong hands. He tilted my head up until I was looking into his eyes. He was so sincere. So sure of himself.

"Anna English, you can kick and scream as much as you want. You can call me names and fight me on every little thing.

I don't care about any of that," he told me. "I still want you with me because I love you."

I gasped at the words. They rang with truth. "You... do?"

"Yes, I do. And that's the real reason that I went to see Jane," he admitted. "I didn't realize that at first. I was just having... I don't know... all of these confusing feelings. I'd never felt this way before. I'd thought that I loved Jane. I'd thought that she was the one for me. I'd dated her for two years. And then you happened."

I swallowed. "Me?"

"Yes, you, Anna. You changed it all. Made me see that I hadn't loved Jane. Not really. And it wasn't until I saw her and talked to her that I realized the truth."

"And what's that?" I whispered hoarsely.

"I never even knew what love was before you."

A tear trickled down my cheek. "Court."

"I'm sorry that I lied," he said. "It was wrong and stupid. And it won't happen again. I'm a hundred percent yours, Anna. I want to be with you and only you. If you'll have me?"

I stared up into his baby-blue eyes reflecting the bright California sun. I'd been dreaming about him since I got here. Wishing that Josh were actually Court when I had seen him. Thinking about how I could go on without New York in my life. Without Court Kensington.

I'd thought just today that I needed to give my dad some more slack for the slights I'd imagined as a kid. It seemed maybe... I needed to offer Court that same slack. He'd flown all the way out here. And... he loved me.

"Anna?" he asked cautiously.

I nodded once then. "I love you, too."

"Right answer," he said, making me laugh.

He dipped down low and captured my lips against his own.

40

ENGLISH

I felt guilty for leaving Taylor behind. But my dad had already told me it was past time for me to go back to my life, and I found he was right. Taylor didn't even mind. We just promised we'd be better sisters, even from thousands of miles away.

We'd hugged until neither of us could breathe. Then, I'd done the same with Ashley and my dad before departing with Court to the airport.

Winnie had been the most put out. She'd been looking forward to opening the agency in LA and having me around all the time. But I'd promised her that the agency was still on. We would just have two offices, like we'd had the last six months. It had worked out pretty well. I had a feeling it would work out long-term, too.

Court and I stepped out of LaGuardia the next day to his car service waiting to pick us up and take us back to his apartment.

"I haven't slept since Halloween," I said, snuggling against his side as we drove through the darkened city.

"Well, I hate to break it to you, but you're not sleeping tonight either."

I tilted my head up to look at him. "Is that so?"

He smirked at me, capturing my lips again in a heart-thumping kiss. "It is."

"And why is that?"

He leaned down so that he breathed against the shell of my ear. "Because I'm going to fuck you all night."

I giggled a little deliriously, but my body pulsed in response. "If you're lucky."

His hand slipped up my inner thigh. "I am."

We barely made it back upstairs to his apartment before tearing each other's clothes off. I was tired, but I wasn't *that* tired.

I staggered back against Court's bed as he hustled out of his slacks. I scurried backward toward the pillows, and when his boxers fell to his feet, he crawled after me, pinning me to the bed.

His fingers hooked into the hem of my thong before quickly dragging it down my legs. He threw it over the side of the bed and then crushed his lips down to meet mine.

I wrapped my legs around him, and he obliged me by shifting us closer together but not quite. Not where I needed him.

I moaned deep in the back of my throat as he brushed across my clit. "Court."

He chuckled at my begging. "Tell me you love me."

I opened my eyes and gazed up at him. "I love you."

"And that you're mine."

"I'm all yours," I assured him.

Then, he smiled and slid inside of me. I tipped my head back and groaned. He wasn't gentle with me, but it wasn't exactly like before. This was... more. Somehow so much more. Our sex had been great before, and I had a feeling that intense fucking wasn't going anywhere. But right now, in this moment, I just wanted him to claim me. Take me as his own. And he did.

When we climaxed together, I cried out and then lay back, panting. He just stared down at me as if I was the most precious thing on the planet, stroking my blonde hair back against the pillow.

I fell asleep like that and woke sometime later, alone.

I groggily stood up and padded to the bathroom before going in search of Court.

He was seated in the living room with a book laid out before him. So deeply engrossed that he didn't even look up when I entered. I wrapped my arms around him from behind and kissed his neck.

"Good book?" I whispered.

He leaned back and kissed me. "Very. I thought you'd sleep all day and night."

I yawned. "I thought I would, too. But I'm a shit sleeper."

I stepped around to the other side of the couch and curled up next to him.

"Lark kept calling," he said, sliding a bookmark into his book. "I told her you were going to sleep all night. But the gang is back together. She said they'd be at Sparks if we wanted to join."

"Do you want to go?"

He shrugged. "I wouldn't mind a repeat of earlier."

I drew him in for a long kiss. "I think we're going to have many, many repeats. Let's go out."

"You're sure? You still look tired."

I huffed. "Thanks," I said sarcastically.

"Not like that."

"Yeah, I know." I waved my hand at him. "But I still think it'll be fun."

He nodded. "As long as you're coming back with me tonight."

I grinned. "Every night."

We arrived at Sparks at midnight. I didn't have much of anything at Court's house and had scrounged up a black dress that I must have left there on another occasion. But I didn't even care. It didn't matter what I wore when I was with Court and surrounded by my friends.

Lark threw her arms around me. "I thought you had gone back to LA forever."

I laughed and squeezed her tight. "Court convinced me to come back."

"To come home," he corrected.

"Well, whatever he did, I'm glad he did it," she said, releasing me. "I missed you like crazy."

"You finally aren't working insane hours."

"Still pretty crazy hours," she confessed. "But nothing like campaign hours. I'm settling back into City Hall."

Whitley nearly attacked me then. "You're back. I told Lark and Katherine not to worry."

I raised an eyebrow at Katherine. "You were worried?"

"Well, you're one of us now, aren't you?" Katherine said primly.

I bit my lip and nodded, wrapping my arms around her before she could protest. Katherine just shook her head and patted my shoulder.

"There, there," she said gently. "Someone has to manage Court Kensington. We all know that he can't do it alone."

My eyes flicked back to Court's, and he shrugged. "Not wrong."

"I think you handled the end of the campaign well enough," I admitted.

He winked at me. "I thought it'd be a disaster, but apparently, the funding has doubled for the lacrosse program almost overnight. And a few of my buddies that I played with growing up and at Harvard have offered to coach other teams."

My jaw dropped. "That's incredible."

"Yeah, I thought it was the end of my time in the program. But it turned out to be the best thing that I could do for it."

"I love that."

"So," Lark jumped in, "do you have holiday plans?"

I shook my head. "Nothing but work. You?"

"I was thinking... maybe we could all get away for a week. Go to one of my parents' resorts in the Caribbean."

"*You* would go to a St. Vincent's Resort?" I asked, flabbergasted.

Lark's relationship with her parents was shoddy at best. They'd relented on her job and Sam, but I couldn't imagine her relenting on the company.

"Okay. I might have said that I'd have time to go down there and check things out. It's a brand-new resort, and they want eyes on the ground before it officially opens. But you know... I could probably swing us all suites," she said with a laugh. "Since you know... I own part of it."

"I'm in," Court said at once. He slung an arm around my waist. "She's in, too. We need to get away."

I laughed. "All right. Christmas at a St. Vincent's Resort it is. Who else is coming?"

"Well, I've invited Penn and Natalie, but I think they're going to her parents' for Christmas. Gavin and Whitley and Robert are for sure in." Lark glanced over at Katherine, who raised her eyebrow. "Are you and Camden free? I know it's so close to your anniversary. I didn't know if you'd have plans."

Katherine looked to Camden, who had just entered the conversation.

He just stared back at her. "Do we have plans, Katherine?"

She swallowed and went pale, averting her gaze. "We could meet you after our anniversary."

Lark grinned broadly. "That'd be great!"

But I was still frowning with interest at Katherine's response. Why the hell had she gotten so pale? What was going to happen over their anniversary? Sometimes, I just *did not* get them at all.

I shook it off and decided Katherine and Camden might always remain a mystery.

"Dance with me?" I asked Court.

He pulled me close on the dance floor, and I leaned back against him. We danced and danced and danced some more. I was glad that we'd left the house. Even though I would have just as much enjoyed staying in. But I loved our friend group. It felt so real. So... personal. Like we'd entered a new phase of our friendship. No longer just the start of something, but that something had solidified.

We stepped back off of the dance floor, and I checked my phone reflexively. I'd started looking at it all the time after Taylor. And to my surprise, I'd missed a text from Winnie.

Holy shit! Look at what just came out about Margery!

I clicked the link, and my eyes widened in shock. Court read over my shoulder as it was revealed that Margery had been part of some ring that put young girls with old male directors. Video footage had been leaked of her involvement, and already, three of her highest-billed clients had left. One of them being Josh Hutch.

I gaped. "Holy fucking shit!"

Court swore, "What the fuck?"

"How could anyone even get this footage? This is insane. It's going to close the whole agency around the scandal."

Court glanced up and away, toward Camden, and then back. "He wouldn't."

"He? He who?"

He shook his head. "It was Camden."

I raised an eyebrow in question. "What was Camden?"

"He found and released the footage."

"But... how?"

"He owns one of the biggest hotel chains in the world. You have a Percy Tower in LA, right?"

I nodded slowly, realizing what he was insinuating. "But... but *why* would Camden do something like that? He hardly even knows Margery."

"He found out that Margery had me followed and then released the pictures of me and Jane."

My mouth dropped open. "Fuck! Of course she did."

"And if Camden knew that... that she'd hurt me and hurt you... he'd stop at nothing."

"But he doesn't even seem to care. He doesn't even talk to me. Actually, he's really kind of scary when I've been alone with him."

"I don't know. Camden is a man of action, not words. He protects his own. I've seen it before."

My head spun. "Wow. Should I... should I thank him?"

Court laughed. "If he wanted credit, I think he would have told us he did it."

"But this is going to solve all my problems. He made it so that she's going to have no way of coming after my business with Winnie."

"Exactly," Court said. "Victory enough."

I shook my head, deeply confused. Camden Percy was both utterly terrifying and somehow incredible. Or maybe just incredibly powerful... which maybe made him more terrifying. As long as you stayed on his good side, everything would be fine.

"Don't worry about it," Court said, rubbing away the furrow in my brow. "Go dance with your girls. Enjoy the evening."

I stood up on my tiptoes and kissed him full on the mouth. "You're the best train wreck to ever cross my path."

He laughed. "You're the best fixer I could have ever asked for."

And then we kissed, slow and passionate and needy. His hands skimmed my waist. Our hips moved together. All felt right with the world.

EPILOGUE

TEN WEEKS LATER—ENGLISH

It snowed the last day of Jane's trial.

It felt like it'd snowed every day of her trial. Every day that we'd been dragged through that holiday season as we waited on bated breath to find out the verdict. And now, we were here. At this moment.

Guilty on three charges of grand larceny. Ten years in prison. Jane was going to appeal. That much was clear. She'd spent the trial completely self-absorbed, seemingly without a care in the world. She'd hired a stylist and a hairdresser. I had no clue how she could afford it, considering she owed millions of dollars.

And the entire time, she had acted like it was a forgone conclusion that she would be released. That everything would work out for her. As it always had.

Her face fell when she was sentenced. Like it had all finally come crumbling down.

Court looked away and then slowly slipped out of the courtroom. I followed. I didn't want to see it either.

I stepped outside. Out of the courthouse and into the still-falling January snow. I'd thought it a marvel at first. Beautiful and white and cold. And now, it was mostly just an annoyance. They'd said it didn't snow that much in New York City. They'd been wrong.

"Hey," I said softly as I approached Court. The shoulders of his peacoat were already dusted with snow. I dragged gloves out of my pockets and stuffed my hands into them. "How are you doing?"

He breathed out heavily, the air fogging in front of him. "I'm glad it's over."

"She's probably going to appeal. It could drag out for another year or more."

He nodded. "I know."

"But the worst is over, I think."

"Yeah."

"Are you going to be okay?" I asked gently.

He turned to me then and brushed a snowflake off the tip of my nose. "Yeah, I am. I don't love Jane. I never loved Jane. I'm just sorry for her. For how delusional she is about everything… and how she used me in it."

"It takes a great deal of sympathy to feel that way about someone who wronged you."

He laughed and then sighed. "I just want to shake her and wake her up. Is that sympathy, too?"

"Probably," I said with a grin. "Are you ready to go back?"

He nodded and reached for my hand. "I'm ready to go home."

"Your place or mine?" I asked.

He tugged me a step closer in the snow, leaving tracks behind. "I was kind of thinking *ours*."

"Oh?" I whispered, hardly breathing.

"Move in with me."

"It's a little soon."

He brushed his nose against my own freezing one. "I'm tired of having a bachelor pad. I'm tired of sharing between our two places. I just want you with me all the time. So... move in with me, Anna."

I bit my lip and then nodded. "I could do that. Should I sell my place?"

He waved a dismissive hand. "Keep it for work. Use it as your office for E&B. Do whatever you want. But be with me."

"I like that," I admitted.

"Good. Because I'm never letting you go."

I giggled, a girlie thing that just bubbled up out of me. "And can I redecorate?"

"You can do whatever you want."

"Whatever I want?" I asked with raised eyebrows.

"Oh no, what is it that you do want, Anna English?"

I bounced on my toes with a grin. "A kitten."

He huffed. "You want a cat?"

"I was thinking like the smallest little ginger kitten that is going to melt your heart."

"You don't want a dog?"

I laughed and shook my head. "Neither of us has time for a dog. I love dogs. Don't get me wrong. But cats can kind of fend for themselves. Kind of like us. So... I think a kitten."

He shrugged and pulled me toward the car. "A kitten then."

We drove across town and pulled up in front of a shelter. I couldn't hide the giddy feeling taking over my body. I'd always wanted a cat, growing up. There had been feral ones that I fed, but they never lasted long. Not in LA. And Josh was deathly allergic. We couldn't have any pets whatsoever. This would be my first real pet.

We stepped through the doors and padded through the different cells. My heart wrenched, as I wished I could adopt them all. Big and small.

There were no ginger kittens, but a litter of calico kittens stole the show. One in particular kept scurrying all over as if she owned the place. She absolutely resisted being controlled but let me rub her belly for a full minute. And I knew she was the one.

"What should we name her?" I asked Court.

He stared down at the wild, unruly kitten I'd chosen. "Train Wreck."

I snorted. "How about Muffin?"

"Muffin? That savage thing? Looks more like a Trouble."

"All right," I said, glancing down at the cat again. "Do you want to come home with us, Trouble?"

Court just laughed. "I think she does."

We paid her fees, bought her a ton of supplies, and then took her home with us. She promptly attempted to ruin Court's penthouse, but he didn't seem to care. Trouble was too cute. And we were going to redecorate anyway.

A few hours later, I leaned back against Court. Trouble was passed out between us on a blanket. Court pressed a kiss into my forehead.

"I love you, Anna," he breathed against my hair.

"I love you, too." Then, I ran a finger down Trouble's forehead. "We love you, Trouble."

Court just laughed and drew me in for another kiss. "Today couldn't get any better."

I grinned devilishly and then climbed carefully over the kitten and into his lap. "Oh, I think it could."

The world slipped away, as it always did. Until it was just me and Court. And nothing else mattered.

THE END

ACKNOWLEDGMENTS

I absolutely adored writing *Cruel Desire*. It brought me so much joy. All the fighting and angry hate sex. I'm so glad that I got to write Court & English with all their fiery passion. *You* helped me get here. So thank you!

Also to everyone who helped make this book a reality: Rebecca Kimmerling, Rebecca Gibson, Anjee Sapp, and Lori Francis for reading early. Staci Hart for the incredible cover and helping me keep my sanity the whole way through. Danielle Sanchez for being a dear friend and taking the load off of me with PR. Devin McCain for being the best assistant there ever was especially with all the stunning graphics. Jovana Shirley for her talent with editing. I'd be lost without you! Erin Mallon & Stephen Dexter for the incredible audio narration. I love how you brought my characters to life. Katie Miller, Diana Peterfreund, Mari Mancusi, Laura Barnes, Jessica Hawkins, Kandi Steiner, BB Easton, Bethany Hagen, and many many more who helped me get through this crazy author life.

And last but not least, my own love of my life—Joel. Thanks for listening to me rant about the characters and taking care of the pups. You're the best.

Dear readers, I hope you loved Court & English as much as I did and fall in love just as hard with Katherine & Camden in *Cruel Marriage*!

ABOUT THE AUTHOR

K.A. Linde is the *USA Today* bestselling author of more than thirty novels. She has a Masters degree in political science from the University of Georgia, was the head campaign worker for the 2012 presidential campaign at the University of North Carolina at Chapel Hill, and served as the head coach of the Duke University dance team.

She loves reading fantasy novels, lounging poolside, traveling to far off destinations, baking insane desserts, and dancing in her spare time.

She currently lives in Lubbock, Texas, with her husband and two super-adorable puppies.

Visit her online:
www.kalinde.com

Or Facebook, Instagram, Twitter, & Tiktok:
@authorkalinde

For exclusive content, free books,
and giveaways every month.
www.kalinde.com/subscribe

CPSIA information can be obtained
at www.ICGtesting.com
Printed in the USA
BVHW042001100223
658130BV00022B/133